Coney Island Quickstep

CONEY ISLAND
QUICKSTEP

a novel by
George
Gipe

Thomas Y. Crowell Company

Established 1834/ New York

Designed by Joy Chu

Manufactured in the United States of America

Library of Congress Cataloging in Publication Data

Gipe, George.
Coney Island quickstep.

I.   Title.
PZ4.G517Co   [PS3557.16]   813'.5'4   76-56764
ISBN 0-690-01197-0

3   5   7   9   10   8   6   4   2

I might as well thank my good friend and associate, George Udel, for creating the best parts of this book, as he'll probably take the credit anyway.

CONTENTS

SPRING

1

"I presume you are trying to kill us, Philip"

Werble.

Werlerble.

In the semidarkness of the Idaho City Bank, Robert "Pinky" Pinkerton swiveled his head as if to search for the growling stomach that could give them all away. At the same time, he tensed his abdomen, hoping to control the noisy demon inside his own gut.

Werb.

Now the only sound inside the bank was the gentle, monotonous tick of the wall clock over the tellers' cage. With a half-smile of satisfaction, Pinky lifted his head the smallest bit to sneak a glance at the quiet street of Idaho City. Although in his mid-forties, his jaw still retained the firmness of a much younger man, and his frame, while not awesome to behold, was strong and muscular. When Pinky spoke, the piercing blue eyes added respect to his words, and the curly graying hair flanking his tanned features completed the picture of a typical western lawman who had outwitted and outwaited a hundred desperados of the 1870s and 1880s.

But now it was 1891, the era of a nervous stomach which had started vocalizing promptly on his fortieth birthday and resisted most forms of treatment. The chalky substance given him by a doctor in Helena helped occasionally, but seldom, it seemed, when he was in a crowd or needed his stomach to be silent. Like now. Even as he knelt in the corner of the bank awaiting the arrival of Bill Whalen and his gang, Pinky could feel the murmurs of discontent which usually preceded a—

Werwerlerbleerblelerblerblerblerble.

"Gawdamighty, is that you, Pinky?"

The deputy behind him asked the question in a low voice, but the quiet of the deserted bank made it seem louder, more accusing.

"Something I ate," Pinky whispered.

"Sounds like the head and tail's still alive and kicking," the deputy whispered back.

"Yeah," Pinky laughed nervously.

To himself, he said, "Damn it, control yourself!" Messing up this ambush would be a terrible blow for the Pinkerton National Detective Agency, considering the amount of time and money they had invested in setting it up. It had cost more than $600 to finally find and then bribe a gang member's brother into selling him Whalen's plan for the Idaho City Bank. A smart and deliberate crew, the Whalen gang had never walked into an ambush. Four times during the past year, they had staged a distraction in one part of town, and then when the coast was clear, quietly entered the bank, sometimes even using passkeys, cleaned it out, and were gone before anyone suspected a thing. Twice the robberies weren't discovered until the businesses opened the next day. Because all four banks were clients of the Pinkerton National Detective Agency, Pinky had sworn to stop the gang. Not to stop them was bad for business and, even more important, bad for his pride.

Now, if Pinky's informant was right, the Whalen Gang would soon be walking into a box canyon—a long corridor which Pinky and his men would close off from the front and still other deputies close from the building's rear. Once halfway down the corridor, the Whalen Gang's days would be over.

The quiet of the night was suddenly broken by a volley of shots, followed by shouting and still more shooting. A free-for-all had broken out in the saloon district and everyone on the streets was running, either for safety or to see what was happening.

As he heard the diversionary shots from the other end of town, Pinky's stomach tensed until it felt like a clenched fist below his belt, a knot of pain that would not go away. Pressing himself closer to the wall, he reached back to tap the knee of the deputy behind him, then reached up to ease his .44 a little higher in the holster. "They's comin'," the deputy whispered, his voice mixing with the sound of boots on the planking outside the bank.

Pinky slipped his head lower. He and his men were less than five feet from the entrance, shielded from direct view by a half wall leading into the corridor. They could not be seen unless, for some strange reason, one of the Whalen Gang stood on tiptoe to peer over the railing.

A key turning in the lock broke the silence, followed by a cool breeze against Pinky's cheeks. The footsteps and squeaking boards told him that at least four men were inside the bank. All that remained was for them to move twenty feet down the corridor. Then they would be trapped. Pinky waited.

Werlerblewerblewerlerblerblerblerblerblerblerblerbler-blerblerble.

"What the hell is that?"

"There's somebody in here!"

"Let's get the hell outahere!"

The deputy leaped to his feet and yelled, "Throw down your guns. It's the law; you're under arrest!" But the Whalens were nearly out the door, their rear guarded by Bill Whalen, one of the deadliest men with a six-shooter in the West, and as Pinky rose, his weapon drawn, Whalen threw out the entire contents of his revolver, a series of deafening blasts that tore into the deputy's shoulder, sending him kicking backwards against the tellers' cage. At the same time, Pinky felt a spurt of fire in his right hand and saw his .44 hit the wall ten feet behind him. "Gaddamn it," he roared, and scrambled back to pick up his weapon with his left hand. Charging for the door, he was followed by the three deputies from the rear of the bank.

It was too late. Joined by the rest of the gang, Bill Whalen was already atop a strong horse and half-hidden in a swirl of dust.

The hoofs tore into the hard ground, creating a rapid tattoo of sound as first one horse then another inched ahead of the rest. Their riders leaned forward, applying the whip generously, cheeks pressed against the glistening necks of their mounts. Occasionally a head turned sideways to glance at an adjacent rider, but for the most part the four eyes of each team remained locked on the path ahead. If the excited roar of those who watched them speed away reached their ears, it was not apparent.

Tick-tick. Tick-tick-tick.

"They're off! Pegasus is in the lead. Flying Dragon second. Fiery Serpent third."

Tick-tick. Long pause.

It was the beginning of the first race at Gravesend on Monday, May 18, 1891.

At the track, situated near Sheepshead Bay on the tip of Coney Island, New York, nearly eight thousand men and women watched the wave of horseflesh through a variety of telescopes, binoculars, and even opera glasses. A cheer went up as the gray stallion called Flying Scud flashed into the lead, for he was the favorite of the fans who had placed legal bets at the track.

"Flying Scud has taken the lead at the quarter post!"

Gravesend Race Track, the closest track to metropolitan New York City, was not the most sumptuous course in the area. But it was decidedly posh. Its grandstand, three tiers high, consisted of twenty vertical pillars of wood, painted to resemble marble, rising to a mansard roof, at the center of which was a triangular booth from which rose a majestic flagpole. At either end of the structure smaller poles carried the forty-four-starred banner, marking, as it were, the bow and stern of a great rust-colored troopship. People were everywhere one looked—against the rails of the three decks, spilling down to ground level against the curiously-out-of-place white picket fence that flanked the judges' booths at the finish line. The booths, shaded by cupolalike permanent umbrellas of bright crimson, were octagonal in shape, decorated with latticed woodwork, inhabited by eight to ten men each.

At ground level, the real work of the track was carried out. Beneath their portable canvas umbrellas, bookies and touts mingled with shillabers, bettors, and jams of tarts. Youngsters barely in their teens, barefooted, their baggy trousers held up by suspenders, raced back and forth between derbied men of all ages and shapes. The race having started, dust was everywhere, a saffron shimmer which seemed to bother no one but the genteel ladies watching the race from the comfort of their polished landaus and victorias prominently displayed at favored locations near the finish line. It was noisy, gritty, warm, but it was also the most exciting spectacle of the spring.

From the triangular booth at Gravesend—the Western Union telegraph facility—the message went out: "It's Flying Scud, still in the lead." As the words were cried out ten miles north in the poolroom of Peter DeLacy at 33 Park Row, New York City, another cheer arose from the two hundred fans who had placed illegal bets on the same race. There were no binoculars or opera glasses here, for there was nothing to see except a thin man seated next to a Western Union telegraph ticker. But what he said commanded attention and respectful silence.

Tick. Tick-tick.

Almost to a man, the crowd at DeLacy's leaned forward in expectation of the transcriber's next pronouncement.

Thomas Wynn, the man at the desk, waited one dramatic moment, then called out: "Coming up to the half . . . Flying Scud still leading, but suddenly he is off-stride . . . and here comes Water Nymph! She's really closing ground . . . she's sweeping wide . . . she passes Flying Scud! Did she go too wide? . . . Flying Scud is back in stride and challenging her . . ."

A chorus of groans and cheers mingled, then silenced as the telegraph sounds started once again.

Tick-tick-tick.

"Get moving, Scud!" a lone voice cried out, but it was quickly silenced by the twisting of necks and staring eyes. While the telegrapher was taking down the information, silence was the rule. One did not cry out in church or at Peter DeLacy's while the man at the ticker was bent over his pad.

"Flying Scud is fading badly!"

A silent groan.

"Pegasus is starting his move!"

A cheer, choked off by more telegraphic signals.

"And here comes Bygone Days! Look at him run! It's Bygone Days and Pegasus fighting for the lead as they near the three-quarters mark! Jockey Andy Ledbetter wants to force Pegasus to go wide! He's keeping Bygone Days glued there! Pegasus is going wide! Bygone Days is moving out . . . and Pegasus cuts inside and takes the rail . . . he's right up with Bygone . . . neck and neck!"

"What happened to Water Nymph?"

"Go, Pegasus!"

"Bygone Days! Move! Move!"

Thomas Wynn let the crowd have its choral interlude. He knew when the ticker started again and his lips opened, the turmoil of sound would drop to a whisper. As the clacks started again, he made a note on his pad but did not speak. Then a longer series of sounds followed, giving the horses' positions at the top of the stretch.

"Jesus Christ, Snowshoes is last," a young man at the far end of the room whispered to himself. Because he knew telegraphy, twenty-eight-year-old Waite Nicholson received the race details before the rest of the crowd, but he kept the information to himself. That would have spoiled Thomas Wynn's enjoyment at being the center of attraction. Nevertheless, Waite could not suppress a sigh as he translated the series of sounds which spelled bad news for him.

"Damn," he murmured. "If that nag loses, I'll be in the hole by seventy-five bucks."

To some of the customers at Peter DeLacy's, which attracted the better class of horseplayers, that might not have been a great deal of money, but to Waite Nicholson, it was plenty.

"It's—" Tom Wynn began, then dramatically withheld the news.

Divorced from the race by his certainty that Snowshoes had no chance to win, Waite Nicholson did not bother to translate the Western Union message. Instead, he studied the people clustered around the room. Most were standing, although a few sat in plush chairs provided for them by the establishment. Some stood in tight groups with one member clutching a single pink ticket which obviously had been purchased for all of them. Others, rather better dressed, stood by themselves in apparent nonchalance, or talked with one of the few ladies who were present.

Waite smiled. He was a people-watcher of long standing. Looking at the individual faces, he could determine in a few seconds how much the race's outcome meant to each bettor. Waite thought he could even pick out several policemen or representatives of citizen reform groups scattered about the spacious room. They seemed to be furtively studying the clientele rather than listening to Thomas Wynn. He also felt he'd spotted a reporter. Reporters generally took notes, either furtively on pads or on their shirt cuffs. They also dressed in a particularly uninspired and seedy style, Waite knew.

It was no accident that most reporters, policemen, and reformers picked DeLacy's as a good spot to observe the sinful nature of illegal betting in New York City. Compared to Eole Pearsall's or the dingy rooms of Gump Halloran or Paddy Reilly, which were located over saloons and guarded by hordes of disreputable-looking toughs, DeLacy's was as pleasant as Delmonico's restaurant. One entered through a pair of heavy mahogany doors trimmed in brass, followed a circular staircase of some ten steps—carpeted with a thick purple material, of course—into a central room fifty feet square. On all four walls of the room, floor-to-ceiling mirrors alternated with panels of solid oak on which resided portraits of former New York mayors, pugilists, and even one notorious sanitation officer, Jackson S. Schultz. His pink and cheerfully round face seemed to cast a benevolent glow over the room, as if blessing the bettors who so happily contributed up to five hundred dollars per race to the coffers of New York's most genial and famous pool seller, Peter DeLacy.

Because there were no windows, however, the DeLacy establishment was depressing, albeit prestigious. When the place had first opened, the Park Row wall of the room had been blessed with a series of high colored windows—not unlike the stained glass of New York's better churches, one wit remarked —but the blizzard of 1888 had destroyed nearly half of the glass in one horrendous shower of splinters (luckily, there were no bettors nearby at that time) and DeLacy had promptly converted the wall to brick. He attempted to add color and light with an inordinate number of gas fixtures, but the room still retained an atmosphere of gloom.

DeLacy's clientele did not seem to care, or if they did care they seemed to prefer the dark richness of the place. Only the better types came here—bankers, merchants, fugitives from Wall Street, with a smattering of younger men who were, more often than not, clerks on their way up.

Waite Nicholson was just such a young man on his way up, or at least so it seemed. At the moment, he was not exactly sure. Pressing the tip of his oxblood boot into the thick carpet next to the bar which lined the Park Row wall, he waited for Wynn's next pronouncement. His face was noncommittal. He didn't seem to care who won the race. That was his way. "Take your time," his now-departed granny had once said. "Keep your feelings off your face." Waite smiled at the remembrance of her many conferences with him. "A clear head will always rise to the top in a sea of confusion," was another of her aphorisms. "What I mean is, divide and conquer."

Waite understood. He smiled. "If only Granny could have helped me pick the horses," he mused.

She had called him "her pride and joy." Some pitied him

when his parents died, leaving him orphaned at eight, but Waite could not honestly say he experienced an emotional vacuum. Granny had filled that, lecturing him, laughing with him, and occasionally beating hell out of him just to make absolutely certain he knew who was boss. His schooling was meager, but when he grew into a lithely muscular blond with a yearning to get ahead in the world, she had encouraged him. "Why don't you take up telegraphy?" she suggested. "It's something that will be around for a while, and you can sit down doing it."

At first he had not been sure. "Telegraphy?"

"It's another language," she said, "and you don't have to fool with conjugations and all that crap." (Granny was frequently quite informal.) "Not only that, pretty soon, everybody's going to need telegraph operators."

She then glanced, he recalled, over the barren twenty acres of farmland left them after the most recent mortgage—was it the second or third?—foreclosure. "You're no farm boy," she said. "You're a city type. So my advice is to get yourself to the city and learn something. Won't be long before I'm ready to roll into eternity, so you better start looking out for yourself."

He had taken her advice, left the Wisconsin farm for the bustle of Milwaukee, where he had in fact learned the art of transmitting English via a series of dots and dashes. It had come as second nature to him. After a year with an Illinois railroad, he had come east, found a position with the Western Union Telegraph Company—not as a telegrapher but as a secretary—for the sumptuous salary of nearly five dollars a week.

And now he had bet a substantial portion of a month's wages on a horse race. Granny, he knew, would have taken the belt to him for such an insane act. But he could not seem to help himself. Like the other bettors at DeLacy's, Waite Nicholson stood silently, hoping, praying for the miracle he so sorely needed.

Tick-tick. Tick.

"It's still Pegasus and Bygone Days at the stretch, with Dan McGinty coming up fast!" Thomas Wynn intoned.

Waite's attention returned to the race. For a half-minute, lost in his own reflections, his mind had drifted from the metallic sounds. He suspected that his horse was still out of it, but suddenly the hope of every gambler filled his heart and mind. Was it possible that the nag had pulled up to a respectable position during the time he was preoccupied? Feeling the need to get closer to the action, Waite walked briskly to the leather-covered bar near Wynn's desk, put his foot on the rail, and listened.

"It's still Pegasus in the lead. Jockey Bill McNair is giving him the whip. They're into the last turn . . . Water Nymph is fading fast. Now it's Snowshoes making a real run at the leaders on the outside. . . . It may be too late. It's still Bygone Days and Pegasus, neck and neck! But here comes Snowshoes! He's a white avalanche! Look at that horse move!"

"Come on, Snowshoes!" Waite murmured hoarsely.

"It's Pegasus, Bygone Days, and Snowshoes! They're practically even as they enter the stretch! What a race! Here they come! Pegasus, Bygone Days, and Snowshoes!"

The room was deadly silent. Closing his eyes, Waite Nicholson repeated "Snowshoes" over and over to himself, actually trying to keep his brain from translating the telegraphic information. He did not want knowledge now. He wanted hope!

"Come on, Snowshoes!" Waite whispered.

"It's Snow—" Thomas Wynn cried, then corrected himself. "No! It's Pegasus! Pegasus wins! Snowshoes second, Bygone Days third, and Dan McGinty fourth."

A chorus of elation and misery engulfed the room as winning customers flocked to the payoff booth. "Next race starts in twenty-five minutes," Thomas Wynn called out, then with a brisk hitch of his trousers, strolled over to help the clerks reward the winners.

"Goddamn," Waite Nicholson groaned. "Seventy-five dollars down. That's it. If I don't get that back in the fifth race, I'll never bet again."

Tearing his ticket into fragments, he hurried out of the poolroom. It was nearly two o'clock and he knew Mr. Humstone would be furious.

Two blocks away, in the editorial offices of *The New York Times*, Rodney Roberts took a deep breath and glanced down at the fresh edition of the paper on his desk. Licking his index finger, he turned to page four and found the heavy line of type which read: POOLROOMS MUST GO. A BLOT ON OUR INTEGRITY.

Rereading his copy, he felt a glow of satisfaction at the strong, yet logical attack he had leveled at the pool sellers, those sixty off-track establishments which dealt in illegal gambling. "How many youngsters will go hungry tonight because father has tossed his last dollar into the whirlpool of sin?" he had written. "It is all very well to moralize about the sinfulness of gambling at Gravesend Race Track, but the fact remains that many working men cannot take time off to go there and lose the wages their strong backs have earned. But it is only a matter of minutes to drop in at Pearsall's or DeLacy's and bet on a race. There too they will find liquor and easy credit, which only further threatens their moral and physical well-being."

Skimming the rest of the lengthy column, Roberts decided it was a good effort. The campaign against pool sellers sold newspapers. But it also happened to be a crusade in which he freely joined. The pool sellers *were* a blot on the integrity of New York. He had been to a poolroom once, seen the looks of avarice and degradation steal over faces which reflected Christian values until the greedy hand of gambling took possession of the soul. He had heard the howls of despair, seen how quickly a man's wages could be dissipated. Backed by the *Times*'s prestige, Rodney Roberts meant to close each and every poolroom in New York.

At fifty-five, the slightly paunchy, round-faced Rodney Roberts did not look the part of a crusader. Even when formally dressed, his clothes tended to fit him like baggy socks, and his features were not strong enough to inspire fear or awe. Yet it was a fact of New York's political life that Mayor Hugh Grant owed his job to Rodney Roberts, who had promoted him as a reform candidate and sold the idea to a majority of the voters. "When Roberts hums," it was said, particularly in the rival newspapers, the *World* and *Herald*, "Hughie starts to dance."

That was not true, of course. Once in office, Grant started doing pretty much what he wanted, a fact which frequently infuriated Rodney Roberts, especially when he saw the new mayor turn his back on crooked police commissioners, a growing prostitution problem, the continued sin and poverty of the Tenderloin, and the prosperity of the pool sellers. The situation, Roberts decided, had to be reversed. Making an example of the gamblers would be a good way to start—which meant he had to speak with, or rather listen to, Aurelia Ironsides. With a sigh of resignation, he moved to the door of his office and nodded to his secretary.

A moment later, his office was inundated by a large, nearly overpowering woman. Six feet tall and two feet wide at the shoulders and hips, Mrs. Ironsides rarely walked if it were possible to charge. By frontally assaulting the offices of many public figures in New York, she had succeeded in building an image of power and influence that was synonymous with moral reform. People respected her, not because she had eliminated any of the evils attendant to life in the big city, but because she seemed capable of eliminating them with a single swipe of her massive fists. When she spoke, as she so frequently did, her voice was thunderous, a call to arms that would have put Henry the Fifth to shame. "Together," she had said once at a rally at Steinway Hall, "we can make this a city of God. A city without sin, gambling, lascivious entertainment, drinking, lewd language, dancing, or other Godlessness."

While even Rodney Roberts doubted that New Yorkers really wanted their city that way, he had to agree that Mrs. Ironsides sounded convincing. He was particularly happy to discover she was against the pool sellers, for they were his target at the moment.

"What is happening, Mr. Roberts?" she said loudly as soon as she crossed the threshold. "I walked up Park Row on my way here and saw every pool seller doing business as usual. Are we going to move against them or aren't we?"

"We are," Roberts replied evenly.

"When?"

"As soon as Captain McEvoy and his men arrive."

"But they were supposed to be ready for the raid right after the second race," Mrs. Ironsides countered. "My people were prepared to act as witnesses after the second race."

"Will they be able after the fifth?" Roberts asked, glancing at the clock on the wall of his office.

"Yes. They've been instructed to purchase a betting slip for every race until the police arrive."

"Good," Roberts said. "I'm sorry for the delay. Frankly, I think Captain McEvoy was hoping something would happen to call off the raid. He called to say his men were needed at the quarantine hospital but I repeated the commissioner's orders and he finally agreed to come. They should be here in time to get to DeLacy's by the end of the fifth race."

"Harumph," Mrs. Ironsides replied, plainly irritated at the

delay. Then her lips curled downward in a gesture of disgust. "The police in this city are insufferable," she grated. "I suppose even Captain McEvoy is being bribed by the pool sellers."

"No doubt," Roberts nodded. "But since I started my editorials and had a talk with the mayor, things have improved somewhat. At least the police commissioner is cooperating, thank heaven."

"We must root out all who are being paid off and see that they're sent to perdition," the ponderous woman said.

"One thing at a time, madam," Roberts smiled. "If we can put the gamblers out of business, we'll have made a good start."

"Yes," Mrs. Ironsides agreed. "But only a start. Too often we apply pressure and then relax. If we close the poolrooms, we must press on. My organization will back you in whatever worthy campaign you wish to pursue, and we hope you will back us."

"Of course."

Rodney Roberts could not help smiling faintly at the way Mrs. Ironsides continually avoided identifying her "organization" by its official title.

Two years before, at the mass meeting which saw the spontaneous creation of Mrs. Ironsides' "organization," someone had suggested they call themselves the Anti-Sin Society. The title was passed by acclamation and released to the newspapers. Too late, the founders realized the initials of their upstanding organization were A.S.S., a fact which was duly pointed out by every leading paper in New York except the *Times*. Trying to ease the pain of their error for them, Rodney Roberts had editorialized: "The founders of this important society should not be held up to scorn and ridicule simply because their initials happen to symbolize the very same people who are heaping the scorn on them." That had been rather a nice touch, Roberts thought at the time, and he had been rewarded by a pleasant note from Mrs. Ironsides, thanking him and adding that the executive committee planned to change the society's name in the near future to the Society Against Sin. Predictably, the new title was ignored by the public and rival newspapers and the organization continued to be known simply as ASS and its members as ASSES.

At fifteen minutes to three, the door opened and Roberts' secretary announced the arrival of Captain Terence McEvoy of the New York police and Mr. Dudley Fellows of the district attorney's office.

"Where are your men?" Roberts asked the captain.

"They're down by the loading platform, awaiting my orders," he replied.

"Very good," Roberts said. "Shall we get started?"

"Well, that's just it, Mr. Roberts. Mr. Fellows here is from the D.A.'s office and he says we can't pull the raid, that it ain't legal," Captain McEvoy said as his features took on a happy glow.

Mrs. Ironsides rose to her full height. "Not legal," she bellowed. "Flapdoodle! I've never heard of such a thing. Why, of course the raid is legal. This is just another example of our corrupt police department shirking its duty!"

"Please," the young, sallow-faced man with a thin mustache interrupted. "I'm afraid there has been a misunderstanding." Then, looking at the captain, he continued: "Captain McEvoy has presented my case a bit too strongly. I did not say the raid was illegal. But as the district attorney's authorized deputy, I felt it best to make certain you were aware of the manner in which the pool sellers are now operating." With that, he reached into his pocket, unfolded a piece of paper, and presented it to Mrs. Ironsides.

"As commission agents," she read, "I ask you to send for

me to the Brooklyn Jockey Club blank dollars to be placed there on the blank race on the blank horse at track quotations, if such can there be obtained. I now pay ten cents, your charge for executing this commission. Signature, countersigned by Thomas F. Wynn, 33 Park Row." With an expression of disgust, Mrs. Ironsides passed the slip of paper to Rodney Roberts.

"Of course we know of this ruse," she said imperiously. "It's ludicrous. The idea that the pool sellers aren't accepting bets themselves but are only acting as agents of the track is so patently false that—"

"Yes, it's probably a ruse," nodded the man named Fellows. "The problem is, it hasn't been tested in court yet. Therefore, a raid may be premature. Even worse, it may be a great deal of trouble for nothing and have the insidious effect of encouraging the pool sellers if the raid should be declared illegal. That is what I told Captain McEvoy. I wanted to make certain you knew how the pool sellers are operating before you proceeded with the raid."

"Mrs. Ironsides' witnesses have been instructed to place bets without signing these bogus commission slips," Rodney Roberts said. "We know they make everyone sign these for the first race of the day. But later, especially before the fifth race, which happens to be the Long Island Handicap, we can be sure they'll never take the trouble."

"Indeed," Mrs. Ironsides roared. "Right after the race, two members of my organization will be at DeLacy's. They will have their betting slips and will be prepared to testify that they placed bets without signing the commission forms. Then we'll have them, regardless of whether the commission ruse is legal or not. Isn't that so, Mr. Fellows?"

"Yes," the thin man replied, "you would certainly have a case then."

"Are you sure?" asked Captain McEvoy. "I mean, I don't want my fellas bustin' in a place and then lookin' like a bunch of chumps."

"Don't worry," Mrs. Ironsides smiled. "When this is over, everyone in New York will have a completely different view of both you and your men, Captain."

Captain McEvoy smiled, saluted, started for the door, and then slowed his brisk pace to a shuffle. He had begun to wonder exactly what the old harridan meant by that.

Philip Dwyer, ex-butcher, former co-owner of Dwyer Brothers Meat Company, which boasted of "the fastest meat delivery wagons in New York," and now president of Gravesend Race Track and the Brooklyn Jockey Club, still enjoyed maneuvering his double-harness carriage through the congested streets of the city. There was, after all, a knack to it. One didn't have to follow the sluggish flow of commercial traffic. A quick spurt here, a turn and burst of speed, a moment of hesitation followed by a decisive move were all weapons enabling him to move from one point to another with astonishing speed. As he did so on this beautiful Monday morning in May, Dwyer's sixty-year-old physique took on ramrod strength. Sitting upright, over-dressed in the latest style, his black, drooping mustache bending slightly in the breeze created by his own speed, he seemed content.

On his immediate right sat his liveried driver, Rochemont, who was trying to hold onto the seat as inconspicuously as possible, so as not to imply criticism of his employer. Behind him sat his wife and daughter. His wife Sophie, a dough-faced woman whose continued efforts to hold her chin up and thereby reduce the visibility of the fat below it made her assume a belligerence that was somewhat uncharacteristic. Not that she was a pleasant woman. Even though Mrs. Dwyer said most of the correct and elegant things, many people sensed a crudity beneath the surface that betrayed her Five Points birth and confinement to the Irish ghettos of New York for twenty years before economic rescue by Philip. At the moment, however, her chin did not jut forth. Leaning back against the velveteen interior of the carriage, she visibly shook for some minutes as the vehicle moved quickly through traffic, then said in a high, petulant tone: "I presume you are trying to kill us, Philip."

"No, I ain't," her husband replied. "I'm just trying to save some time getting to my meeting with Humstone."

Sophie Dwyer tried to remain calm, but as the carriage suddenly bounced high over a loose cobblestone, she lost her composure and shrieked, "Philip, if you don't let Rochemont drive this carriage I'll scream!" The threat apparently did not particularly bother Philip Dwyer, for he did not slow the horses' pace. Instead, with a quick flip of the reins and a guttural sound from the side of his mouth, he induced the team to clamber around a produce cart, missing it by a matter of inches. Satisfied with his feat, he smiled and said, "Are we going too fast for you, Mary?"

His daughter, seated to the right of her mother, did not hear the question at first. For the past minute or two, she had been watching the movements of a young blond man, who had been running alongside their carriage with astonishing speed. Dodging draymen and pedestrians, occasionally darting into the street when approaching a particularly crowded section of sidewalk, his long legs carried him forward with clockwork precision. Mary wondered if he had a message for her father, except that he kept his eyes generally straight ahead and at one point when her father encountered a rare impassable obstruction, the young man actually moved ahead of them. They soon caught up with him, however, then passed him again. As they did so, Mary glanced at the man, who returned the gaze without breaking stride. For a moment, his eyes penetrated deep into hers, then, still running at top speed, he reached one hand up to doff his derby and smiled broadly.

It was his undoing. At the very moment his attention was taken from the path before him, a drayman rolled a beer keg between two carts and started back for another keg. A split second later, Waite Nicholson felt his right knee strike an object, then spun head over heels in a perfect somersault, landing on his back in the middle of the sidewalk.

Mary let out a short, involuntary shriek, her hand rising to her mouth and her head turning to make sure the young man was all right. When he quickly brushed himself off, stood shaking himself for a moment like a wet dog, then started running again, she felt better. It was at that moment that she heard her father say something, but exactly what, she was not sure.

"What did you say, Father?"

As she leaned forward to acknowledge his question, her dark hair moved across her cheeks, accentuating the black eyes and well-formed mouth. Philip Dwyer was continually amazed at how beautiful his daughter had turned out. He only hoped her mind, now partially confused by young and radical ideas, would grow to the same maturity.

"I said, are we driving too fast for you?"

"Why are you asking my vote?" she replied sweetly. "You said yourself a woman's place is in the home and not the voting place."

Philip Dwyer cursed under his breath and gave the reins another angry flip. The horses moved forward even quicker, accompanied by heavy theatrical sighs from the heaving breast of Mrs. Dwyer. "Please, Philip," she finally said in a fairly even voice. "I beg of you, stop the carriage! Make us walk but don't kill us!"

Without comment, Philip Dwyer increased the tension on the reins until the team slowed appreciably. He then handed the reins to the poker-faced Rochemont. "Drive carefully," he said.

As the team slowed for a clogged intersection, the Dwyers heard a sharp burst of applause and yelling. High above the sound of general voices was a single howl of pleasure. "Twenty to one! I did it! Twenty to one!" This was followed by a series of happy curses that burned the ears of Mrs. Dwyer. A second later, they saw the speaker, his hands grasping a mass of dollars, emerge from Paddy Reilly's poolroom next to the Victoria Tavern. His boiled-beef-and-cabbage complexion streaked with tears of happiness, the man walked in tight circles around the sidewalk, stopping passersby and showing them the money.

"That's disgusting," Mrs. Dwyer murmured finally, turning her eyes from the man.

"Just because he won some money?" her husband asked.

"No," replied Mrs. Dwyer. "Because he thinks it is better to earn money that way than by honest work. And for every drunken fool like him, there are fifty miserable souls inside that vile poolroom. I honestly wish you'd do something about it, Philip."

"What do you mean, do something?" Dwyer almost shouted. "I'm against gambling. I don't drag people into my tracks, and I certainly don't shove them in places such as that. Leave me out of your sermons."

"Nevertheless," his wife persisted, "you let Western Union sell them the information right from the track. Without that information, those dens of sin would be forced to close. And yet you aid and abet them. It's disgusting."

"Disgusting, is it?" Dwyer shot back. "Well, I'll have you know Western Union pays a thousand dollars a day for the use of that ticker. Think about that while you're buying your expensive clothes at Madame Zingar-zulu or whatever her name is.''

"Zingarelli," Mrs. Dwyer said. "As for the money, Philip, all I can say is—what shall it profit a man to gain the whole world and yet lose his soul? The degradation with which you're involved is not worth a thousand dollars a day! It's not worth two thousand or even three thousand dollars!''

Before Dwyer could respond, the barouche came to a halt. They were at Madame Zingarelli's. With a motion of his hand, Dwyer indicated to Rochemont that he should stay with the women, then grasped the reins in hands which still shook with pent-up anger.

He stared ahead angrily until a quick glance from the corner of his eye told him everyone was safely on the sidewalk and traffic was clear. Then he gave the horses a slap and moved forward. As he drove off, he heard Sophie's voice, high and whining. "Don't forget, Philip, it's not worth it. You tell your friend Humstone that.''

"Go drown your head," Dwyer muttered softly, his retort safely lost in the sound of New York traffic.

Sophie, he had decided, was intolerable. She wanted desperately to be accepted by the better elements of society, which included boresome matrons, supercilious half-wits who fancied themselves clever, and loathsome reformers along the lines of Aurelia Ironsides, the most formidable object since the armored cruiser. Philip Dwyer hated all of them, yet he knew they were necessary. Born into a family of butchers, Dwyer secretly hated the smell of the abbatoir. The aroma of money and the New York Legislature was much more to his liking, and the support of New York's monied classes could be the difference between a wealthy racetrack operator and a wealthy and respected servant of the people.

Even daughter Mary was becoming more than a bit annoying

with her mania for equality of the sexes. The two of them argued frequently, and it infuriated him that Mary usually made him twist his words and logic until he hardly knew what he himself believed. She would be far better off, he reasoned, when she found a level-headed young man and settled down.

Angry at the ingratitude of both his female charges, he was still steaming with suppressed indignation as he stormed into the office of W. C. Humstone, president of the H. C. Ditmas Company, Western Union's most profitable subsidiary. The secretary's desk and chair greeted him with stony silence.

"Where the hell is everybody?" Dwyer called out.

A few seconds later, the door to the inner office opened and W. C. Humstone himself stuck his head out. He glanced quizzically about the empty room, shook his head, and exhaled wearily. "I'm sorry, Mr. Dwyer," he said. "My secretary must have stepped out. Sometimes he takes his lunch a bit late. Come in, won't you?"

With a grunt, Philip Dwyer followed the Western Union executive into his office. As he stepped through the threshold, he quite suddenly made a decision. That was the way he often arrived at conclusions—impulsively, without much attention to logic or experience. It was, in fact, the way he and brother Michael had transferred their talents from the butcher business to proprietorship of the Brooklyn Jockey Club and Gravesend Race Track. "I like the looks of that horse," Philip had said to his brother one day in 1874. "If the A.S.P.C.A. says he is diseased, they're wrong. I'm willing to bet a hundred dollars he could win a race or two at Saratoga Springs."

Philip Dwyer had been right. Now he felt another surge of intuition. Sophie, for all her irritating moralizing, was right, too. The degradation of selling souls to hell was not worth a thousand dollars a day. It was worth much more than that! And fortunately, the purpose of his meeting with Humstone was to sign a new contract between the Ditmas Company and his Brooklyn Jockey Club for the fall racing season. At each meet a formal agreement was made which allowed Western Union, via the Ditmas Company, to retain its telegraphy station at Gravesend Race Track and transmit racing information. In the past, the signing had been an automatic thing, but this time, thanks to his dear Sophie, Dwyer vowed it would be a different matter.

"How is your family?" Humstone smiled, gesturing to the plush chair opposite his desk.

"All right," Dwyer muttered, accepting the seat as his mind tried to work out exactly what he was going to say.

"Would you care for a smoke?" Humstone asked, offering Dwyer a cigar from a richly engraved humidor.

Dwyer nodded, sucked the end of the dark green cigar, lit it, and spoke through the first heavy maze of smoke. "W. C.," he said firmly, "I'm not going to renew the contract."

Humstone tried not to react, even affected a bit of nonchalance by lighting a smoke for himself, but he showed his preoccupation by holding the match an inch away from the cigar's end as he himself became lost in thought. "Well, Phil," he murmured finally, shaking the match just as it started to burn his fingers. "Is there something wrong with it? It's exactly like the last six we've signed except for the dates."

"That's it," Dwyer responded. "Everything's the same. But there's one change that's going to have to be made. You know where it says, 'for the consideration of one thousand dollars each day.' Well, that's what's going to have to be changed. A thousand just isn't enough."

"Well, er . . . ." Humstone asked, taking a strong pull on his cigar before realizing he had not yet lit it, "what would be enough?"

The exact price of degradation had not yet occurred to Philip

Dwyer. What had Sophie said? One thousand wasn't enough. Not two thousand. Not even three thousand. A basically unimaginative man, Dwyer then made his decision. "Four thousand dollars," he said. "Four thousand dollars will be enough."

Humstone managed a sickly smile. "Four thousand dollars, Phil," he repeated. "That certainly is enough for just about anything. But we're not looking to buy your track. Just use a little room. So let's be serious, all right?"

"Damn it, Humstone, I am serious," Dwyer shot back, leaning forward in the chair and pointing his smoking cigar at the man behind the desk. "You know I'm always serious when I talk business." The growing redness of his neck indicated that the famous Dwyer temper was not far from being ignited.

A man of some temper himself, W. C. Humstone made a strong effort to control himself by stamping out his still-unlit cigar. Lean and silver-haired with a small mouth and angular Roman nose, Humstone did not project the fierce image of many successful businessmen, but he was not used to being challenged with so little warning. Moreover, he did not like ultimatums, especially when they were directed at him. As he pushed the frayed end of his cigar around the ashtray, a dozen quick, angry responses flashed through his mind. They went unsaid. Instead, he replied evenly, "I'm serious when I talk business, too, Mr. Dwyer. And, seriously, four thousand dollars a day is out of the question."

"Well, that's it then," Dwyer said. "You can take your wire out this summer and forget about covering my fall meet."

"Damn it, Dwyer, you're being unreasonable! We've had our little differences in the past and always been able to iron them out. If you'd wanted a little bit more money, I'm sure we could have managed it. But you can't just storm in here and demand four times the rate. That's like sticking a gun in my ribs."

"Are you calling me a common thief?"

"No," Humstone replied hotly. "I'm saying you've killed pigs with more delicacy than you've shown to me today."

"Well, maybe they deserved it more than you," Dwyer shouted.

Determined not to be drawn into a violent argument, Humstone decided to change the subject. "How is your beautiful wife Sophie?" he asked in as even a voice as he could muster.

Philip Dwyer didn't understand the conversational flip-flop. Hadn't they been discussing pigs? Was this Humstone's obtuse way of insulting his wife?

"Why did you bring her up?" Dwyer shot back.

The brief, deadly pause that followed was interrupted by a light rap on the inner office door.

"Yes?" Humstone called out.

Waite Nicholson entered, carrying a handful of papers and envelopes. When he saw Dwyer, he smiled and said to Humstone, "I'm sorry, sir. I didn't realize you were busy. I was just bringing in these letters for you to sign."

He turned to leave, but Humstone motioned him back, relieved at the interruption, which he hoped would give him the opportunity to think. "Come in and meet Mr. Dwyer, president of Gravesend Race Track and the Brooklyn Jockey Club and one of our best business associates. Philip, this is my new secretary, Waite Nicholson, a very bright young man."

"How do you do, Mr. Dwyer," Waite said. "Mr. Humstone has spoken very highly of you. I'm honored to meet you."

Dwyer grunted.

Another pause followed. Ordinarily gregarious, Waite was not anxious to speak, lest he reveal how out of breath he was as a result of running all the way from DeLacy's.

As Waite put the letters on Humstone's desk, his superior returned his attention to Dwyer. "Now then," he said. "What were we talking about? Oh, yes, your wife Sophie. How is she?''

"She's worse than Mary, with her high-society friends. Would you believe she's involved with that idiot Ironsides woman and her ASSES?''

"Well, you know how those reformers are. They come and go. She'll get over it soon.''

"Maybe,'' Dwyer muttered. "But there could be trouble brewing. When she got home last night, she was just bustin' to tell me about something they're planning. Didn't take but half a mind to figure out there's goin' to be a raid on DeLacy's. If I'd lifted my eyebrows, she'd have probably told me everything, including date and time.''

Humstone, having noticed that Waite had shuffled and reshuffled the mail several times, said, "Would you bring the Gravesend file box and excuse us for a few minutes, please?'' His tone was pleasant enough, but emphatic.

"Yessir,'' Waite said.

He left. As was his habit when men of wealth and power spoke, however, he had not missed a word. Nor did he intend to.

After getting the file, he once more left the office and closed the door, but his ear was not more than an inch from it.

As soon as the young man was gone, Humstone turned his best smile on Dwyer. "Phil,'' he said placatingly, "we've been friends for years—''

"Three,'' Dwyer said.

"Well, at any rate,'' Humstone continued, "I think we've got a fine relationship. Now I'm perfectly willing to consider a possible increase, especially if we can do it under the table so the rest of the tracks don't know about it. But you just can't come in here and demand four thousand. It's not . . . well, it's just not businesslike.''

"I don't care," Dwyer retorted. "It's a nasty business. Those reformers are talking about raids, and are already stirring up trouble with the newspapers. Suppose the *Times* starts to give me a hard time?"

"We're well protected," Humstone soothed. "After all, pool sellers are on good terms with the police. And, of course, so is Western Union."

The debate was becoming too much for Dwyer. He characteristically returned to his earlier resolve. "Say what you will, it's still four thousand."

"But you've agreed to a contract," Humstone snapped, snatching up the file from the desk. "And it gives us an option on the fall meet even if you don't sign a new contract."

"That only gives you the right to have a telegraph station at Gravesend Park," Dwyer replied. "It doesn't guarantee you the right to send information from that station."

"What do you mean by that?"

"I mean, I can cut your wire if it pleases me."

"But, that's ridiculous," Humstone stammered. "It's implied in this contract that the station be functional. That means the wire must be kept intact and our operators allowed to transmit whatever information they desire."

"My lawyers will see about that," Dwyer replied, jumping up and heading for the door.

"Now just a minute, Phil," Humstone said beseechingly. "I think we're both losing our heads again. There's no need to drag our lawyers into it. Take a day or two to reconsider, and give me some time to do the same. All right?"

"Sure, but the price will still be four thousand dollars a day. You keep that in mind," Dwyer said.

Two seconds later, he was out of the office and on his way back to Madame Zingarelli's.

Humstone shook his head, glanced out the window, and

continued to wonder just what had gone wrong. It was unthinkable that Western Union should pay Dwyer four thousand dollars a day for the right to send telegraphic information on the races from Gravesend Park to subscribing pool sellers. Not that the money wasn't available. The problem was Monmouth, Guttenberg, Morris Park, and dozens of other racetracks in the vicinity. The standard figure paid by the Ditmas Company was a thousand per day. That figure had been established by the Western Union Telegraph Company's board of directors. Raising it for one track owner could start an insidious chain reaction of greed that would wreak havoc with Western Union-Ditmas' net profit of 65 percent. No, it would not do to raise Dwyer's allowance, certainly not by four hundred percent. To himself, Humstone debated which arguments to use against the wily and temperamental Dwyer. For a moment, he considered telling him that the profit earned by selling pool information went for worthy projects, such as the creation of better telegraphic facilities for small towns.

Finally, he shrugged, went to the door, and motioned to Waite.

"Yessir?" Waite asked deferentially. "Is there—"

"Trouble? Yes. I want you to go to DeLacy's and tell him it's important that we have a meeting about four o'clock. I'm going to stop by the main office first."

"Very good, sir," Waite said, smiling. Now he wouldn't have to think of an excuse to free himself for the fifth race.

The man who was known as the King of the Pool Sellers of New York City looked and dressed more like a bank president. In fact, his father had been one, but choosing not to follow him, Peter DeLacy had started a highly successful insurance business of his own. A clean-shaven nonsmoker with glistening black hair, DeLacy's nonchalance was not studied or affected. He was a relaxed man, at peace with himself, but at the same time he knew exactly what was happening around him. The slight smile and crinkling around the eyes which accompanied it, both suggesting merriment, were genuine. So too were his powers of assimilation and observation. For twenty years he had disarmed the careless as an investigator for his large eastern fire and theft insurance company. Those who were slipshod judges of character frequently mistook his genial disposition for weakness—to their dismay. He was, in fact, a wise and cynical man, but he was more amused by his own cynicism than embittered by it. And although basically an introvert, he enjoyed watching others enjoy themselves. Thus, shortly after his wife died, he sold his insurance business and did what he had always teased her about—took over the operation of a first-class saloon and restaurant which he had acquired in an investment package years earlier. It was this same Sans Souci Restaurant which eventually became DeLacy's poolroom.

By May of 1891, the establishment at 33 Park Row was only one of three DeLacy poolrooms. And though many of his society friends and acquaintances claimed to be scandalized by his new profession, he was too wealthy to be insulted or ostracized. The situation amused him, as did his elevation to King of the Pool Sellers, an unofficial title which he had never sought. Rather, he had gradually drifted to the top, mostly on the basis of his shrewdness, ability to bring warring parties together, and innate honesty. Of course, many New Yorkers scoffed at the very idea that a pool seller could be "honest." Even Peter DeLacy's daughter Dottie felt this way. A fiery redhead of twenty, Dottie was constantly at genial odds with her father and even belonged to Mrs. Ironsides' Anti-Sin Society, a fact which *The New York Times* seldom failed to mention when convening a meeting. But Peter DeLacy did not complain or talk of filial "ingratitude." He knew that if he wanted to remove Dottie from the influence of the ASSES, all he had to do was drop a line about receiving secret information from her. But for the time being, the situation amused him and he saw no reason to end it.

"Your life is your own, Dottie, my dear," he said now, leaning back to place his feet on his desktop. "You can do whatever you please. But I wish you'd leave this old fellow alone. I'm not really that bad, you know."

"I know," Dottie smiled. "You have one sin and that's all."

"I eat too much," Delacy said, patting his midsection.

"You encourage gambling," Dottie corrected.

"Darling daughter, the man who manufactures carriage wheels encourages traffic accidents. The man who makes shotguns encourages killing. The man who produces bottles and glasses encourages drunkenness, because I don't know a single drunkard who got that way by using his cupped hands. I don't drag people in here. All I do is provide a service which they're free to use or not use."

"But it's an illegal service," Dottie persisted.

"The Ives Law is illegal," DeLacy retorted. "Why should betting be legal at the track and illegal outside? That's like saying you can sin all you want, so long as you do it in church. As a matter of fact, I think part of my reason for going into the pool selling business was to shock my hypocritical, church-going friends. What they've never understood is what's good for one should be good for all. When the bluenoses shut the windows at Gravesend and Monmouth and other tracks, I'll operate an ordinary quiet restaurant. Not before."

Dottie looked at the clock on the wall. It was nearly three-thirty. The night before she had been informed about the raid on Peter DeLacy's at the ASS meeting and sworn to secrecy. "Very well," she had said. "But I'd like to get my father out of there. I don't want him arrested like a common criminal."

The three members of the ASS executive committee with whom she spoke gave grudging assent. "But you must not make him the least bit suspicious," one of them warned.

"Don't worry," Dottie promised. "He hasn't taken me out for a long time. I'll jolly him into escorting me someplace, and he won't be suspicious."

And so Dottie DeLacy, Anti-Sin Society member and daughter of New York's poolroom king, suddenly realized she had to act quickly to remove her father from the premises. "I want you to take me to Mercadante's, Daddy," she said, somewhat abruptly.

"Fine," he replied, absently.

"Now," she smiled.

"Why?"

"Because I'm hungry."

DeLacy looked at his daughter blankly for a moment, then nodded. "That's a good reason," he said. "I'm a bit empty myself."

Peter DeLacy glanced at the clock. Three-forty. There really wasn't much for him to do until six, when the poolroom closed and the day's receipts were totaled. "Wait just a minute," he said. "I'll get my coat."

He was in the process of adjusting his tie before the mirror when a light rap sounded on the door.

Roger Mellon, his manager, entered. When he saw Dottie, he smiled, slightly embarrassed, and said, "Oh, sorry, Mr. D. I thought you was alone."

"That's all right, Roger," DeLacy said. "What do you want?"

"Fella out here, I think he's Mr. Humstone's deputy administrator or something like that. He says Humstone's coming here to see you at four o'clock."

"Did he say why?"

"No, he didn't say, just that it was important and that he hoped you'd be here."

Peter DeLacy shrugged, looked at Dottie. "I'm afraid I'll have to wait for him," he said. "We could have something sent up here from the kitchen."

Dottie tried to think of a reason that would override the importance of Humstone's visit, but gave it up after a few seconds.

Noting a sheaf of papers in Mellon's hand, Peter DeLacy said, "Is there anything else?"

"Yeah, I brought this list of fellas who owe money," Mellon replied. "Thought you might want to look it over."

"Well, since I have to wait for Humstone, I might as well," DeLacy said.

He took the sheets and ran his well-manicured finger down the list. "Scratch Evans," he said. "Two hundred is far too much. It's all right to carry McCutcheon but only till he reaches a hundred. That shoe company he works for is going to go out of business before too long, mark my words. Who's Nicholson?"

"Nicholson," Mellon repeated. "Oh, yeah. He's the one who's Humstone's deputy."

"Is that why we carried him to seventy-five?"

"Yeah, Mr. D., and I got the impression he's important. That right?"

"Never heard of him. Tell him seventy-five is enough. But do it politely and do it yourself. Don't have Deke or Murph talk to him. And send him to me if he loses any more."

"O.K., boss."

After Mellon left, Peter DeLacy continued to scan the sheets in front of him, occasionally making a light pencil mark alongside one of the names. Then, he looked up at his daughter and said with a shake of his head, "This is one part of the business I really do hate. When fellows get behind and owe more than they can afford to pay, I almost feel like running myself into the station house.''

Dottie smiled weakly in reply and glanced at the clock. She wondered if her father had prophetic powers.

It was ten minutes of four. Ten minutes to post time of the Long Island Handicap.

"All right, men," said Captain McEvoy. "You know what we gotta do. You six go in that van and me and the rest will go in the second. Keep your heads down and don't move till you're told and everything'll go fine.''

The squad of policemen looked slightly incongruous on the loading platform of *The New York Times*, but they were well shielded from public view by the two delivery vans which had been drawn up to the entrance. On each was the emblem of the newspaper in large-face German gothic script, beneath which was the line, "Price Two Cents.'' As Captain McEvoy waved his arm, the first six officers clambered into one of the vans and pulled the heavy curtain of brown canvas across the back.

As the others prepared to board the second van, the imposing figure of Aurelia Ironsides emerged on the loading platform from the freight office. "Good," she said, nodding at the transportation provided for the men. "At last we're getting a little strategy and action around here."

Giving a hitch to her skirt, she thrust a massive boot on the rear step of the second wagon and prepared to climb aboard.

"Begging your pardon, ma'am," Captain McEvoy said nervously. "This could be dangerous. Not a place for ladies, if you don't mind my saying so.''

"I do mind," Aurelia replied. "If I'm not along, you might wind up at Sunken Meadow instead of DeLacy's.''

"Oh, no worry about that, ma'am. We know where we're going."

"Good. We'll all go together."

Placing her bulk atop a stack of newspapers, Aurelia Ironsides pursed her lips and looked around her. Then, in an authoritative tone that made Captain McEvoy start, she said, "Well, come on, let's go. It's four o'clock. They're off!"

2

"My witnesses have been kidnapped!"

"What did you say, Bob?"

"Nothing," Pinky said, pressing his open palm lightly against his stomach in an attempt to assuage its growling discontent. Unlike everyone else, including Mr. Beadle who had written a dime novel about the exploits of Pinky Pinkerton, William Pinkerton referred to his younger brother as "Bob."

"I'll be with you in a second," William said, scratching some figures on the papers before him. Without looking up, he continued, "That stomach still giving you trouble, huh?"

"It talks back occasionally," Pinky replied.

The Denver office of the Pinkerton National Detective Agency was functional and spacious. A huge portrait of the brothers' late father, Allan, took up nearly half of one wall to William's right. To the left was a series of much smaller prints of thugs and thieves—not, as one might expect, of western lineage, but city men. One of brother William's first official run-ins had been with the notorious Gophers and Hudson Dusters gangs of New York's Hell's Kitchen. The leader of the Gophers, who made their headquarters in saloons on Battle Row, Thirty-ninth Street, between Tenth and Eleventh avenues, was known as "Mallet" Murphy. The uncrowned king of New York gangdom until William Pinkerton came along, Murphy boasted that the mallet was his scepter. Now he was gone, along with many other departed thugs with colorful sobriquets such as "Goo Goo" Knox, "One Lung" Curran, "Stumpy" Malarkey, and "Happy Jack" Mulraney, but as memories of William Pinkerton's youth, they had earned a hallowed spot in his heart as well as his office.

"You're a lucky fellow, Bob," William Pinkerton said finally, shoving the papers to the side of his desktop.

"How do you figure that?"

"You're going to take over our New York office."

"Why?"

William smiled slightly. Considerably paunchier than his brother, his round face had the consistency of old leather, but it was not unpleasant. Now he spoke slowly, diplomatically, choosing his words with care. "I'm afraid that after what Bill Whalen did to your hand," he said, "you're going to be out of action for a while, at least as far as using a gun's concerned."

"I only lost half a finger," Pinky replied. "Damn thing kept getting in my way, anyhow. Besides, you know as well as I do that we don't do much head-to-head shooting anymore."

Werble. Werlerble.

A deadly silence settled over the office.

"That's the real reason, isn't it?" Pinky asked. "You're still mad 'cause I spooked the Whalens just when we had them."

William shifted in his chair. "Well, Bob," he murmured. "It's not that I'm mad. It's just that between your stomach and that hand, I think it'd be better if you took over in New York. Look, the office is still new and with Benson retiring and Jackson not being half as smart as you, you're what's needed there. Not a gun, but a head. Intelligence. Patience. You've got those things." He leaned forward. "Listen, I'd give anything to be in your boots."

"Then why don't you go and I'll stay here?" Pinky retorted.

"Because I got a wife and five kids in school and you're still single, that's why."

"What can I say?"

A long pause.

Werblelerblelerblelerbllerbllerble.

"Anything but that," William Pinkerton replied.

For one of the few times in his life, Waite Nicholson hesitated. He had a great feeling about Laughing Water, the spirited filly he had seen at Gravesend less than a fortnight ago. Except for a bad start, she might have lapped the field, and now odds were being posted at 6 to 1. Twenty dollars placed on her nose would not only wipe out the seventy-five dollars Waite was in debt but add a little profit. The problem was that powerful stallion, Rex, with odds of just 3 to 1. He was the definite favorite, and reasonably so, for he had won his last three outings and was considered almost unbeatable.

Waite looked down at his money as the line ahead of him decreased. Laughing Water or Rex? Wipe out his debts or at least attain respectability? It was a difficult decision, made only seconds before he faced Thomas Wynn, the thin-faced announcer and banker. Waite wanted no part of scant respectability. If he could not go all the way, he wasn't particularly interested.

"Twenty on Laughing Water," he said. "To win."

Wynn marked a pink ticket and handed it to Waite. For the first race, there had been twin commission slips to fill out, but now, with the poolroom jammed with customers eager to bet on the outcome of the Long Island Handicap, Wynn and Mellon, the manager, had gone back to the old quick method.

"Next," Wynn said.

Waite pocketed his slip and drifted over to the bar. "No matter what happens," he said to himself, "this is it. I'm not going to ruin myself gambling."

He knew he would stick to his decision. Not because he was particularly moral or strong-willed. But he did hate losing. When he was a youngster, he had tried for a while to fight it out with the other boys. After losing what he thought a sufficient number of battles, he made a conscious decision to avoid further combat. His fortunes had improved after that, as had his easily bruised complexion. As his grandmother had said, "A clear head rises to the top in a sea of confusion." A young man engaged in physical combat, he had learned, seldom had a "clear head." So too with the gambler. He is too involved with the outcome of a single event—which he cannot control—to take advantage of other events.

"Therefore," he said in summation to himself, "Laughing Water will be my final horse racing bet. If I win, I'll pay off my debts. If I lose, I'll just have to find some other way to raise the money to pay them."

He ordered a beer and watched the customers break up into groups awaiting the beginning of the race. Having made his decision, a strange calmness came over him. In five minutes, he would know exactly what his financial condition was and could begin working to improve it. Although his position as Humstone's secretary was neither prestigious nor high paying, Waite wanted to keep it. If, as Philip Dwyer had hinted, there was trouble brewing, he wanted to be around in order to profit from it. "If there's to be a sea of confusion," he said, parroting Granny, "I want to be the coolest head."

"They're at the post," Thomas Wynn cried out, and silence promptly descended over the room.

Tick. Tick-tick.

"They're off!"

"It's Othmar jumping out to a big lead, then Laughing Water and Monopolist," Wynn called.

"Well, at least she got a decent start this time," Waite thought.

"At the quarter pole, it's Othmar by three, Laughing Water, Monopolist, Exotic, and the rest in a bunch."

Leaning with his back to the bar, his elbows hooked over the edge, Waite surveyed the crowd. For some reason his gaze was drawn to a short, thick-lipped man in his thirties and a hook-nosed older man standing on the edge of the main group. While others stood on tiptoe for the illogical purpose of getting a better look at Wynn, these two kept flicking their eyes toward the door.

"At the half it's still Othmar running strong with Laughing Water a length and a half behind. Now Regina's making her bid, but her stablemate, the big stallion Rex, is still back with the bunch."

The eyes of the two men met. Waite noticed the younger one move his hand to his vest pocket and raise just a sliver of pink, an action which caused Hook Nose to nod and, with exaggerated nonchalance, pull a ticket from his side pocket and look at it.

"At the three-quarter pole," Thomas Wynn called, his voice taking on a slight bit of urgency, "Othmar and Laughing Water are even. Regina third. Monopolist fourth. The rest in a group but here comes Rex starting to pull away from them."

"Come on, Rex!" the young man shouted.

There was something about the way he said it that struck a false chord in Waite Nicholson's mind. He had seen and heard others get carried away at various poolrooms. They knew it was against the rites of the crowd to cry out, but often they simply could not help themselves. This man, Waite knew immediately, could help himself. The slightly naughty smile on his face indicated he was playing a part, rather like a young boy saying his first curse words in front of his contemporaries. Instead of being torn from his soul, the cry for Rex's victory seemed planned and contrived.

No sooner were the words out of the young man than Hook Nose looked down at his pink ticket and cried out, "Come on, Nomad!"

"Come on, Rex!"

"Go, Nomad!"

Heads turned to glare at the two men. They had been tolerated at first because their exhortations had not interfered with Thomas Wynn's ability to decipher the message coming over the wire, but this was too much!

Abashed by the sudden attention, the two men fell silent. After the crowd turned away from them, Waite noted them exchange quick, embarrassed grins.

"Now we're into the stretch. It's Othmar and Laughing Water, with Rex three lengths behind and closing fast. Regina fading. Nomad fifth, then Monopolist and Exotic. It's the three of them! Othmar trying to hold on! Laughing Water running with that jaunty stride! Rex coming on strong!"

Waite noticed Hook Nose glance toward the door. Another man, leaning casually against the jamb where he had a clear view of the street, nodded very slightly. Though his immediate financial future was tied up in Laughing Water's still strong showing, Waite sensed that even more important things for him were afoot. He therefore gave his full attention to the three men.

"It's Laughing Water and Rex now running stride for stride. Laughing Water and Rex, with Rex edging out in front! They're heading for the finish line!"

Wynn's words were hardly noticed by the two men, who edged slightly away from the group of interested customers. More than ever convinced they were plotters of some sort, Waite added up the evidence in his mind. Both acted like new bettors, unaware of the basic rules of poolrooms; Hook Nose had had to consult his betting slip before calling out the name of his horse; and here was Thick Lips, with a near-winning ticket on Rex edging not toward the banker's cage, but toward a third man stationed at the door. Suddenly, Waite was absolutely certain Philip Dwyer's remark about the possibility of an ASS raid was more than mere conjecture.

"It's Rex by a neck! They're almost at the line! Laughing Water is making a last bid! It's no use! It's Rex. The winner is Rex! Second, Laughing Water, then Nomad, Monopolist, Othmar, Exotic, and Regina."

As the crowd erupted into an explosion of mixed joy and misery, Waite saw the two men take a step toward the rear of the poolroom. He made a quick decision, thrust himself away from the bar and walked briskly toward them. Touching the thick-lipped fellow on the arm, Waite said in a brisk, conspiratorial tone: "No, not yet. You've got a winning ticket. Cash it and we'll really have the goods on them."

Thick Lips looked confused, but he stopped in his tracks. When Hook Nose seemed about to protest, Waite said quickly to him, "You go, too, so you can testify you saw him paid off."

Taking both men by the arm, he gave them a gentle push toward the cashier's cage along with a final bit of advice. "When you cash the ticket," he said, "make sure you keep half of it for evidence. I'll take care of things out front until you're ready."

Though obviously bewildered, the two men were overwhelmed by Waite's composed assurance. After exchanging puzzled glances, they hurried to get in line at the cashier's cage. Walking as fast as he could without breaking into a run, Waite moved to the door, touched the third man on the sleeve, and murmured out of the corner of his mouth. "They're cashing the winning tickets. Don't do anything until you get my signal."

Without waiting for a reply, he looked both ways, then strode off to the left down a corridor marked "Private." Once in the corridor, he broke into a run. Taking the steps of the narrow stairway leading to Peter DeLacy's office four at a time, he reached the top, burst through the door and shouted, "You're going to be raided!"

Mellon shot to his feet. "Damn!" he spat.

Dottie DeLacy's eyes widened as her hand flew toward her mouth to suppress a shriek. Only Peter DeLacy remained calm.

After taking a split second to note the extreme good looks of the thin but quite pinchable young lady standing next to Peter DeLacy, Waite's eyes moved to those of the pool-selling king. "I'm Nicholson from Mr. Humstone's office, sir," he said, "and I think you're about to be raided."

"What makes you say that?" DeLacy asked, standing and leading Waite toward the door.

"There are three fellows who are acting suspicious, sir," Waite explained. "One of them was starting to signal outside. I made them think I was one of them and I've stalled them for a few minutes. But as soon as they cash their ticket, you're to be raided, I'm sure."

"Get Deke, Murph, and Willie and meet us downstairs," DeLacy said. Mellon raced out of the room. "Dottie, you wait here. Young man, come with me."

"But, Daddy, what about our lunch?" cried out a desperate Dottie.

It was too late; the men were already out the door.

At the bottom of the stairs, DeLacy and Waite found Mellon and three tough-looking men. DeLacy, showing no signs of panic, said, "Nicholson, you point out the men with the betting slips. Rog, get them out the back way, make sure you get the slips back, then drop them off in the Bowery. But no rough stuff, if you can avoid it." Turning back to Waite he said smilingly, "After that, we'll signal the police and watch the fun."

Waite led them to the banker's cage just as Thick Lips was turning away, cash in one hand, a torn pink ticket in the other. Hook Nose was still at his side, but as he saw the group of burly men bearing down on him, his eyes registered panic and he bolted for the front door.

Waite's boot shot out, tripping Hook Nose, whose head banged against the brass rail below the bar with a musically flat tone. "There's one," he said, giving Deke a light shove in Hook Nose's direction. "And here's the other."

With that, he moved toward Thick Lips, followed by the other toughs. Dropping both his money and ticket, Thick Lips let out a little yelp of pain, even before his sleeve and arm were grabbed by Murph's great paws. At the same time, Willie hooked his other arm and the two men whisked the frightened fellow out of the room like a leaf caught by a sudden wind. Stooping down, Waite retrieved the slip and cash and handed them to Mellon. Deke grabbed Hook Nose by his ankles and started to pull. Hook Nose, in desperation, reached out to grab something that would halt his splintery progress, but all he managed to get was a spittoon, which overturned and spilled its contents across his chest and neck. Sputtering and cursing, he disappeared through the rear door behind Deke.

It all happened so rapidly, the crowd barely had time to react. During the entire brief episode, the third man's gaze had been riveted outside, up the street and toward his left. No sooner had the two confederates been rattled offstage, however, than he returned his attention to the poolroom. Unable to spot his confederates, he looked confused until he caught sight of Waite. With his eyebrows, he asked what to do.

Waite gave him a solemn nod. At that, the third man leaned out the door and waved his hand in a quick circular motion.

Less than a block away, men clambered out of *The New York Times* vans in organized confusion. Four raced up the alleyway bordering Peter DeLacy's poolroom, two stopping at the side entrance, the others continuing around the back. Another line of officers, clubs drawn, lumbered up to the front of the poolroom. And from a store entrance directly across the street, a pair of *Times* reporters who "just happened to be on hand" darted through the Park Row traffic to appear at the scene. One of them, preoccupied with finding the nub of a pencil he carried in his watch pocket, was suddenly struck by a large hurtling object, thrown to the sidewalk fifteen feet away, and did not regain consciousness until the next day.

Although Aurelia Ironsides felt a slight twinge of pain in her left shoulder as she struck the man, she did not break stride in her determination to be first into DeLacy's poolroom. To a man, the police officers had shown no respect for her sex. When the signal was given, they leaped to their feet and rushed past her. Hampered by the full skirt, she had descended from the *Times* van only with great difficulty, by which time the squad of men was halfway down the block. Following in their wake, Aurelia ran with great leaping strides, one hand clutched to her ample bosom, the other holding her large flowery hat in position. As the hand at her chest was also grasping a heavy leather handbag which flapped back and forth with every stride, she seemed to resemble a runaway Percheron which had suddenly gone berserk at feeding time. But the noise created by her advance, plus her imposing size, scattered ordinary pedestrians like bits of paper in a storm—except for the *Times* man who, with a single long moan, lifted his head as if to rise, then lapsed into the stupefied position of a defeated prizefighter.

His compatriot, five feet to his left, had barely time to witness the collision, realize that the huge mass of crinoline was rustling furiously in his direction, and make a decision which way to leap. That decision was to hurl himself to his left just as the perfumed avalanche thundered by. Feeling himself losing balance, the man's left hand shot out, striking the back of a man in a checkered suit, catapulting him violently sideways.

W. C. Humstone was not usually so concerned about his own problems that he failed to notice what was going on around him. Philip Dwyer's ultimatum had left him stunned, however, so that he was constructing imaginary proposals and counter-proposals in his head as he crossed the intersection next to Peter DeLacy's poolroom. One part of his brain heard the noise and confusion, but another negated it with the knowledge that poolrooms were frequently uproarious places. He wondered instead what DeLacy, the strong-willed and generally quiet man, would say to Dwyer's demands.

Stepping up on the sidewalk, he suddenly saw a flash of black and white.

"Ooof!" said Humstone, as the man in the checkered suit slammed into his midsection. Whirling backwards and sideways, his arms flailing, the Western Union executive suddenly felt his right hand smash into an object that was simultaneously hard and squishy. He then felt a hard poke into his midsection.

"Help!" he cried out, slipping to the sidewalk.

Rough hands hoisted him to his feet. An angry police officer with a bleeding lip put his face two inches from Humstone's. "Trying to get away, eh, mate?" he challenged. "Well, just try taking another swing at me." He raised the club menacingly above Humstone's head.

The front of DeLacy's was jammed with people coming and going. Just inside the door, Mrs. Ironsides had taken over. "There's no use your trying to escape," she announced in a penetrating baritone. "This place is surrounded. Everyone stay calm and no one will get hurt."

"Now just a damn minute!" Captain McEvoy interrupted, suddenly appearing at the side of the large woman. "If you'll pardon me, ma'am, I'm in charge of this here raid. I'll make the announcements."

Momentarily taken aback, Mrs. Ironsides peered down at the red-faced captain and took a step backwards. Moving ahead of her and holding his hands above his head, Captain McEvoy looked around at the anxious faces, then said, "Everybody just be calm, see? This here poolroom is surrounded so there's no use trying to escape. Just be quiet and nobody'll get hurt."

"What's the trouble, officer?" Peter DeLacy asked, gently pushing his way to the front of the crowd.

Waite Nicholson, sitting comfortably on the edge of Peter DeLacy's desk, heard the confusion downstairs but could not make out any specific words. After seeing that Deke, Murph, and Willie had gained the safety of the rear alley with their cargo of "drunks," he had come back into the poolroom. Then, realizing he might be singled out by the third confederate, he walked calmly upstairs to DeLacy's office. The attractive redhead was still there, he was pleased to notice.

"How do you do," he smiled, when the woman turned to face him with a disapproving expression. "My name is Nicholson. Waite Nicholson."

The woman nodded.

"I'm with Western Union," Waite said. "The Ditmas Company, to be exact. Mr. DeLacy is one of our best customers. Fine man, Mr. DeLacy. A fine gentleman."

"Yes, so I understand," Dottie said.

"Have you . . . known . . . him long?"

"More than twenty years. I'm his daughter, Dottie."

Waite smiled broadly. "Oh. Pleased to meet you." He put out his hand and she laid hers in it briefly.

"Do you make a practice of reporting on all of the police activities?" Dottie asked.

"Just when they are raiding our best customer," Waite replied. "But you don't seem happy that I warned your father they were coming. I should think you'd be delighted."

"If you hadn't come," Dottie said evenly, "he would be up here in relative safety instead of down there where he can be arrested."

"Oh, there's no chance of that," Waite smiled.

"Then why are you hiding up here?"

Waite shrugged, not sure that he liked this young woman's quickness. Of course, he could have explained and justified his situation, but he didn't feel like taking the time. Instead, remembering her plaintive cry as they had left the office only moments before, he put on his most engaging smile and said, "Miss DeLacy, could I interest you in having a late lunch with me?"

"No, thank you," she smiled back.

"Any particular reason?"

"I don't eat," she said.

"This here establishment is under arrest," Captain McEvoy was saying.

"The owners of this establishment," Mrs. Ironsides corrected. "You can't arrest a building."

"What's the charge?" Peter DeLacy asked.

"Violation of the Ives Law," McEvoy responded.

Peter DeLacy scratched his chin. "Well, it seems to me, Captain—correct me if I'm wrong—that the Ives Law prohibits anyone from accepting bets on horse races—unless they are at the track or acting as commission agent for the track."

"That's right."

"Well, if that's the case, I think you'll find that we've been operating within the law." With that, Peter DeLacy withdrew one of the commission slips from his pocket and handed it to the captain. "You see, all we do is act as agents for Gravesend Park and various other race courses."

"Flapdoodle!" Mrs. Ironsides interjected. "That's nothing but a blind. And we have proof."

"What proof?" DeLacy smiled.

"Complaining witnesses," Mrs. Ironsides said, her eyes searching the room. "Tilden!" the large woman cried out. "Street! Tilden! Street! Come here! Now is the time."

No one moved.

Peter DeLacy turned to face the crowd. "Perhaps I can help," he smiled at Mrs. Ironsides. "Did anyone here make a wager on a horse without signing a commission form?"

A chorus of "No, no, no . . ." greeted his question.

"Something's fishy here," said Captain McEvoy, scratching his head. "Everybody says—"

"Oh, shut up, you idiot!" Mrs. Ironsides snapped. Then, turning to the third man, she asked, "Bumbry, what's happened to them?"

The man formerly stationed at the door scratched his head. "I don't know, ma'am," he mumbled.

"Who gave you the signal?"

"Oh, the other fella."

"What other fellow?"

Bumbry looked around the room. "That's what I was wondering. I don't see him now," he murmured.

"You fool," Mrs. Ironsides fulminated. "There was no other fellow."

"There must have been. He gave me the signal and told me to wait a couple more minutes."

"I've got the other man!" a voice called.

All eyes turned to a tall police officer dabbing at his mouth with a bloody handkerchief. With his other hand, he held W. C. Humstone firmly by the scruff of his collar. "He's in league with them, all right. Hit me in the mouth while trying to escape."

"I did no such thing," Humstone replied, rubbing his stomach which was still sore from where he'd been poked by the officer's billy stick.

"Then how come I'm bleedin' and you got a bloody fist, mate?"

"It was an accident. I was pushed, damn it!"

"Is this the man who gave you the bogus signal?" Mrs. Ironsides asked, turning to Bumbry.

"No, ma'am, he's much too old. The other was young."

Humstone scowled as giggles arose from the crowd. "Captain," he said, glaring at McEvoy. "I'm W. C. Humstone, president of the Ditmas Company. I demand that you either charge me with assault or release me."

"And if you think you have a case against me, I'd like to be formally charged also," said DeLacy. "If you can't do that, I'd appreciate it if you'd let us get on with the next race."

"Arrest them, you idiot, arrest them all!" shrieked Aurelia Ironsides.

Beleaguered from all sides, a look of utter misery stole over McEvoy's face. "I'm sorry, ma'am," he said to Aurelia, "but unless your witnesses show up—"

"Search the place!" Mrs. Ironsides demanded. "They must be holding them captive."

McEvoy shook his head and asked his officers who were gathering about him, "Did any of you see anyone leave?"

"No," came the reply, almost in unison.

Standing on tiptoes, McEvoy then looked over the heads of the crowd in the direction of an officer who had just come in through the back door. "How about you, Gaffney?" he called out. "Did anybody go out that door?"

The officer walked forward. "Nobody, sir," he said, "just some toughs carrying out a couple of drunks."

"Drunk?" Mrs. Ironsides thundered. "How do you know they were drunk?"

"Well, if you'll pardon me for saying so, ma'am, I smelled drunks before, and they was the drunkest-smelling drunks I ever smelled."

The crowd laughed appreciatively.

"My witnesses have been kidnapped," Mrs. Ironsides charged. "It's obvious they were prepared for us." She turned to glare at Peter DeLacy. "You've won this time, Mr. DeLacy," she warned. "But we intend to drive you and your kind out of business and put you all in jail. Mark my words on that. I shall return."

Pivoting quickly, she flung her arms in wide, sweeping arcs, clearing the way for her exit.

"What about this one, Chief?" Humstone's captor asked.

"Well, what about him?" McEvoy snapped. "Don't you know that's Mr. Humstone of Western Union?"

"But he still hit me in the mouth, Captain."

"Forget it," McEvoy replied irritably. "It was an accident, just like he said."

"Didn't feel like no accident to me," the officer persisted.

"Damn it," McEvoy said. "Let him go."

Considerably cowed, the officer released Humstone.

"New recruits give me a pain in the arse," McEvoy murmured. "They think that badge gives them the right to run in whomever they please."

"Well, I'm sorry for what happened," Peter DeLacy said. "I'd like to offer you and your men a drink for your trouble, but I know you're on duty."

Licking his lips, McEvoy nodded sadly. Turning to his men, he said, "Outside, boys, outside."

As they were leaving, DeLacy gave a knowing glance to Mellon and said, "Well, good-bye, Captain. You and your men are to be commended for your fine work." Then, patting McEvoy on the back, he took the still flustered Humstone by the arm. "Let's step over to the bar and get you a drink to settle your nerves."

"How many of you are there?" Mellon asked McEvoy, reaching in his pocket and withdrawing a roll of bills.

McEvoy hesitated a moment, then said quickly: "Twenty. Twenty-one, countin' meself."

"That's quite a gang," Mellon said, smiling slightly.

"Well, you got a big place here," McEvoy replied.

Mellon counted out one hundred and twenty-five dollars and handed them to the captain. "Give each of the boys five dollars from us and tell them to buy themselves a couple of drinks as soon as they're off-duty," he said. "And keep the rest for yourself."

McEvoy took the money furtively. "That's real kind of you, Roger," he said.

"Think nothing of it, Captain," he replied. "We've always taken good care of our police friends, as you well know."

A minute later, as the twelve officers reported back to *The New York Times* vans, Captain McEvoy made a quick head count, pulled some money from his pocket and announced: "The management wants you all to have a couple drinks on the way home tonight."

With that, he handed his men a dollar each, hopped into the van, and smiled at the thought of a job well done.

When he heard the footsteps on the stairs, Waite removed himself from the edge of Peter DeLacy's desk.

The door opened and DeLacy entered, followed by W. C. Humstone and Roger Mellon. "Disgusting business," Humstone was saying. "That's what gambling does. Here I am, a perfectly upstanding businessman, assaulted by an officer during a gambling raid. It's a taint, I tell you. No one's free from it, once it starts."

"I didn't know you were so much against gambling," Peter DeLacy said.

"Oh, I am," Humstone replied, still rubbing his stomach. "Personally, I never gamble. I disapprove of it, one hundred percent, from a moral standpoint. From a business standpoint, I am afraid it is something that will always be with us. Therefore I see no contradiction in the work we do at the Ditmas Company. After all, if we did not provide the gambling information to those seeking it, I am sure the vacuum would be filled by disreputable persons, thereby encouraging further corruption. In a way, I look upon the Ditmas Company as a buffer to the spread of gambling's evils."

"You're a very articulate man, Mr. Humstone," DeLacy said, his eyes twinkling slightly. "I've never heard it expressed quite that way."

Humstone smiled, bowed to Dottie DeLacy, who had stepped away from the window.

"This is my daughter, Dorothy," DeLacy said. "Mr. W. C. Humstone of Western Union's Ditmas Company."

"Charmed," Humstone smiled. Then, his eye catching Waite, he said, "I presume you've met my secretary, Mr. Nicholson."

Waite attempted a smile. The word "secretary" seemed to reverberate about the room. True, he had not actually described the nature of his position with the Ditmas Company, but in order to rise above the fifty-dollar debt plateau, he had implied rather graphically to Mellon that the relationship between himself and Humstone was considerably closer than boss and secretary. Now he felt naked, trapped not only by his low position but by the sudden knowledge that he was even deeper in arrears as a result of Laughing Water's drying up in the homestretch. He had known, of course, that Humstone was against gambling, morally if not vocationally, but he had not expected to be trapped in the same room with him under these conditions. One word concerning his inflating his importance or the slightest remark about his gambling certainly would be enough to cost him his job. Wincing inwardly, Waite saw the frown crease Roger Mellon's brow as he said, "But—"

Waite froze, dreading Mellon's next words.

"See how the sixth-race receipts are going, will you, Rog?" DeLacy quickly interrupted. "They may be jammed up at the cage."

Still staring at Waite, Mellon slowly nodded. "Sure," he said.

As he left, Waite felt the pain in his chest subside as respiration continued once again.

"I'm sorry you dropped by just as the unpleasantness was happening," DeLacy said.

"Well, unpleasant as that was," Humstone grimaced, "I'm afraid I have even more unpleasant news."

The brief silence during which Humstone's gaze moved quickly toward Dottie and back to her father was full of meaning.

"Pardon me," Dottie said. "I have some shopping to do. I'll let you talk business."

She gave her father a little kiss on the cheek and started for the door. Waite stepped forward to open it. "Would you allow me to see you outside, Miss DeLacy?" he said.

"Please don't," she said. "I'm sure you're needed here, Mr. Nicholson."

She smiled and left.

As soon as the door was closed behind her, Humstone got right to the point by describing Dwyer's outburst. When he paused, Peter DeLacy asked: "Do you think Dwyer was serious about cutting the line?"

"I think he was at the moment, but I am sure he'll get over it."

"What about the money part?" DeLacy said. "Will he get over that?"

"I don't believe so," Humstone replied. "He just didn't seem inclined to negotiate."

Peter DeLacy scratched his chin. "I wonder what got into him? Well, I don't guess it matters. The important thing is that you do something to placate him for now. You know we can't operate without that information. Even if you have to offer him more money—"

"I'm against that," Humstone said firmly. "It could start a nasty precedent."

"Well, then, what do you propose doing?"

Humstone didn't answer. Both his mind and expression were blank. Waite, who sat quietly in a corner, was meticulously taking in every detail.

"Why don't you just send him a very friendly note for now?" DeLacy said. "Tell him we're willing to negotiate whenever he sees fit, but suggest that it would be better if we wait until the meet's over. That way you can keep him from getting upset and doing something crazy while the track's open. After that, we'll have all summer to work out details for the fall meet."

"Very well," Humstone nodded. Then his eyes widened. "Say, you don't think Dwyer had anything to do with this raid, do you? He said he'd heard something about a raid."

"I doubt it," DeLacy shrugged. "What would have been in it for him if they had closed the poolrooms?"

"I don't know. It just seems strange, his acting so queer on the day this happened." Humstone winced at the sudden pain in his stomach. "And speaking of the raid," he said acidly, "I thought you had police protection."

"Well, we do," DeLacy said. "But this is a democracy. The do-gooders have to have their day once in a while, too."

"I would hate to think this would be a common occurrence," Humstone murmured.

"I don't think we have to worry about that."

Humstone put on his hat and started for the door. "Come, Nicholson," he said. "We'll have to compose a nice letter to Dwyer. Then, I'd like you to deliver it to him personally—but not until tomorrow, when he's cooled off."

"Oh, Mr. Nicholson," DeLacy called suddenly, as he and Humstone stepped into the hallway.

"Yessir?"

"Could I have a word with you?"

Waite walked back in the room. Humstone continued down the stairs. Casting a nervous glance at the departing figure, Waite said, "I'm sorry about running up a gambling bill, Mr. DeLacy. It won't happen again, I promise. As a matter of fact—"

"That's all right," DeLacy interrupted, placing a hand on the young man's arm. "That was pretty clever work, picking out those plants and stalling them for us."

"Thank you, sir."

"So you forget about the bill, all right? You don't owe us a cent."

Waite nodded. "Thank you. I'd also like to thank you for not mentioning my gambling in front of Mr. Humstone. And I'm sorry I exaggerated my position to Mr. Mellon."

"Well," Peter DeLacy said. "We all tend to do that, I suppose. And sometimes we're entitled. You're a bright young man. Not a very lucky gambler, but you certainly seem to know how to get from one place to another and show yourself in the best possible light. That's bright. Real bright."

"Thank you, sir."

"Nicholson!" Humstone's voice interrupted.

"Coming, sir!" Waite called.

With a little wave and a smile, he started after Humstone.

Peter DeLacy walked slowly back to his desk, tapped his fingers rhythmically on it for a moment. Then slowly, reflectively, he said to himself, "Yes sir. Real bright."

3

"I wouldn't be surprised if that son-of-a-bitch could knit me a sweater, too"

As the Chicago-Rock Island-and-Pacific train rattled through Davenport and across the Mississippi into northern Illinois, Pinky Pinkerton hunched deeper into his seat and thought dark thoughts. Passing herds of grazing cattle, he wondered if he too were being put out to pasture, never to engage in battle again. Not a combative man, he had to admit he liked the mental exercise of law enforcement as much, if not more, than the thrill of the physical chase. He would miss that. If work in New York involved nothing more than protecting little old ladies' jewels and scouting adulterers, he would surely go mad. "Don't even think about it," he said to himself.

The wounded hand was much improved, which was more than he could say for his stomach. He had gone to another doctor, who prescribed something known as Moxon's Effervescing Magnesia Aperient, to be taken six times a day. It hadn't worked. Neither had Scheffer's Saccharated Pepsin; nor Austin's Iris Versicolor and Extract of Gentian. "Hell," he said finally, "I hate the stuff, but I'll just start drinking a lot of milk."

That had wrought no miracle, but had muffled the werbling to a certain extent. Pinky tried to find encouragement in that. But he could not shake off a feeling of malaise as the train neared Chicago and the farms grew closer together. There was no reason for him to be depressed by Chicago, he reasoned, except for the fact that he had been born there at the time his father was founding the Pinkerton National Detective Agency. Because it represented youth-now-fled and the ambiguous glory of being a Pinkerton, loved by half the population and hated by the other half, Pinky guessed he preferred other places to Chicago.

He was even more depressed a few minutes later when the conductor, who had stared at him closely several times during the trip across northern Illinois, finally pointed a finger at him. "Say," he said with a grin, "didn't you used to be Pinky Pinkerton, the lawman?"

"My son," Pinky lied.

"You got the same features," the conductor said. "Tell him I read the book about him and really liked it."

"Sure will," Pinky nodded.

"How's he doin' these days?"

Pinky thought for a moment. "Pretty bad. Had both eyelids shot off by Bill Whalen. Now he can't sleep worth a damn."

The conductor clucked sympathetically, then shrugged. "Chicago comin' up," he called out.

Waite Nicholson decided to walk at least part of the way to Philip Dwyer's. He was in no particular hurry; Humstone's directions were to deliver the letter personally sometime "that morning" and it was only a bit after nine o'clock. Also, Waite enjoyed watching people, trying to make quick judgments as to what they did or what they were like. He even enjoyed studying architecture, believing it a key to those who lived within each set of walls.

The Western Union telegraph office, for example, if its building was any indication, was a company without a great deal of false modesty. Or taste. For the main office at Dey Street and Broadway was a hideous mixture of mansion and church. The bottom six storeys were more or less conventional, but from that point upward, the building turned into a disorganized mass of sharp triangular outcroppings, gradually melding into a central tower, on which, facing north and south, was emblazoned the name of the company.

Although it was after the traditional reporting time for work, there were still a great number of persons on the street. Derbied men dressed in dark gray or brown suits moved quickly across the broad triangular intersection opposite St. Paul's Chapel and Churchyard. At the north end of the open area was one of New York's largest employers, the Post Office, a great five-storeyed pile of columns topped by a strange series of rounded roofs. To the west was the Astor House, stark and rectangular, whatever charm it may have once had now marred by the atrocious series of fire escapes across its front.

Waite strolled for a mile or so, then hopped aboard a horsecar for the ride up Fifth Avenue. From this point northward, the derbies gradually changed to tall silk hats, the shop girls walking briskly and talking loudly gave way to elegant ladies in long skirts, leg-of-mutton sleeves and fashionably plumed bonnets. Here was an entirely different world from Lower Broadway south of Park Row. People worked down there. People with money lived up here.

As the people changed their appearance, so did the buildings.

North of Canal Street appeared the first true mansions occupied by families of wealth, although not necessarily good taste. The Astor mansions, at Thirty-third and Fifth Avenue, for example, were nothing more than a pair of granite piles. The Stewart Mansion, on the other hand, resembled an iced and decorated four-layer cake. It seemed a friendly, as well as an opulent, place in which to live.

The home of Philip Dwyer, at Fifty-third Street, was considerably more modest. It was, like its neighbors, brownstone, but the portico was of genuine marble. Waite paused a moment at the entrance, straightened his lapels, and pulled back the solid brass knocker. His trio of knocks was strong and decisive, for during the trip from Lower Broadway, he had decided what course of action he would take. Granny, he had concluded, was right. In a sea of confusion, the smart and aggressive man rises. If possible, he would try to sow the seeds of conflict. He had no desire to move into his own Stewart Mansion when he was Philip Dwyer's age. If he could not make it by the time he was thirty, the hell with it. Therefore, he had decided to create a rift between the pool sellers, Western Union, and Dwyer. When the rift developed, he would find a way to take advantage of the situation. For the moment, he would project an image of polite but deadly earnestness. That would impress Dwyer, as it had already impressed DeLacy.

A moment later, when the servant girl showed him into the parlor and he met Sophie Dwyer and pretty Mary, his prim facade nearly cracked. Under normal circumstances, he would have enjoyed a good laugh with Mary about their mild flirtation and his downfall. But with Mrs. Dwyer hovering in the background, Waite passed over the incident with as much blandness as he could muster. "I have a letter from Mr. Humstone of Western Union," he said simply. "If possible, Mr. Humstone would like to know Mr. Dwyer's response."

Sophie Dwyer smiled, sent the servant girl for her husband, and beckoned Waite into a nearby chair. "Are you from New York?" she asked, hoping to generate some conversation.

"No ma'am," Waite replied. "I'm from Wisconsin."

"Oh, out West," Sophie smiled. "That's near Chicago, isn't it? We visited the stockyards there once. Philip started out in the meat business, you know."

"Yes," Waite smiled back. "In the short time I've been here, I've heard from many sources how Mr. Dwyer had the fastest meat delivery service in the city."

"It had to be fast," Mary straight-faced. "It was only minutes from going bad."

"Mary! That's not true!" Sophie countered.

"I'm aware that your daughter is joking," Waite said with a smile that he hoped would appear indulgent. Actually, he avoided laughing uproariously at the young woman's remark only through a great deal of self-discipline. Most children did not poke fun at their parents so openly. Waite found Mary Dwyer refreshing as well as attractive, but he didn't wish to encourage rebellion on her part. At least not yet.

Mary, on the other hand, was not so enthusiastic about Waite Nicholson. At first, she found him quite attractive, even thought she saw a flash of sensitivity in his eyes. But as he talked so vapidly, so much like a professional politician, it became increasingly difficult for her to believe he was the same young fellow audacious enough to flirt while dodging sidewalk traffic.

Her father entered just as the conversation dragged to a halt. Relieved, Sophie introduced Waite as "a charming young man from Western Union but don't let him turn your head, Philip."

"Thank you, we've met," Dwyer replied. His face was expressionless as he accepted the letter from Humstone and read it to himself. The room was filled with silence, broken only

when Mary suddenly said, "Daddy, your lips are moving."
Waite looked away barely in time. Damn her, he thought,
she'll make me laugh yet and break out of character. But he
managed to maintain a relatively passive expression until Philip
Dwyer, not dignifying his daughter's jab, finished reading the
note.

"I find this very interesting," he said. A slight smile told
Waite that Humstone's conciliatory tone had impressed the
track owner. "Tell Mr. Humstone that I'll have to think this
over."

Waite did not like the sound of that, but he forced a smile to
his lips. "Thank you, sir," he said, nodding and starting for the
door.

After two paces, as planned, he turned to face Dwyer once
again. "Sir," he said, "would you mind if I said something to
you?"

Dwyer looked at him over his spectacles. "Go ahead," he
replied.

"Well," Waite began, smiling tightly. "I don't wish to seem
disloyal to my employer. I firmly believe that when you work
for someone, you owe them your loyalty. But when it comes to
moral issues, I also believe one has to take a stand consistent
with one's own upbringing. That's why I feel obliged to speak
out against both you and my employer, Mr. Humstone."

"Speak out against me?" Dwyer challenged.

"Yes, sir," Waite replied. "I know of the arrangement
between the track and Western Union, obviously. And it is my
opinion that Mr. Humstone is wrong to exploit the weaknesses
of those who are inclined to gamble, and it is wrong of you to
allow him to do so."

"Bravo!" chortled Sophie Dwyer.

"Of course, I am no businessman," Waite continued. "I'll
probably never make anything of myself because of my naiveté,

but it seems to me that a man of your proven mercantile powers could find many ways to compensate for any amount of lost revenue. Perhaps lesser men need to prey on helpless gamblers, but I don't see why you do."

"I've never preyed on helpless people," Dwyer said. "My brother Mike signed that original contract with the Ditmas Company."

"Philip!" Sophie Dwyer interrupted. "That's not true. You both signed that contract together."

"Well, he signed it first," Dwyer shot back.

"Only because M comes before P," Sophie replied.

"Please," Waite said. "I had no intention of provoking a family disagreement. It's just that I felt I had to speak out. Perhaps you will see fit to report what I've said to Mr. Humstone and have me fired, sir. But I honestly believe that to compromise now is to compromise with the lives of men, women, and children who cannot speak for themselves. I think that a man of your strong character should rise above compromise."

"What would you have me do?" Dwyer asked, with more than a trace of sarcasm. "Cut the wire?"

"Sir, it is not my place to tell you," Waite smiled. "But if I were you, I would."

"Oh, Philip, I'd be so proud of you if you did," murmured Sophie.

"Well," Dwyer muttered. "I'll think about it."

Sophie was breathless. "Mr. Nicholson," she said. "Would you care to accompany me to a meeting this morning? The Anti-Sin Society has been called together for an important discussion. I'm sure your presence will be appreciated."

Waite hesitated. He was sure his presence would *not* be appreciated by the three men who had been foiled by him. On the other hand, it could be an excellent opportunity to find out what the ASSES were brewing.

"It won't matter that I work for the Ditmas Company?" he asked, widening his eyes. "You see, I happened to be in the poolroom with Mr. Humstone during the raid. The men who were ejected probably saw me. They might even think—"

"Oh, don't worry about them," Mrs. Dwyer replied. "They won't even be there. This will be just the executive committee."

"Well, then I would be honored to accompany you."

"I'll get my hat," Mrs. Dwyer said, scampering off.

Philip Dwyer cleared his throat. "You may tell Humstone that I've read his 'sincere' letter," he said. "And for the time being I will do nothing. As for you, there's no need to worry. I realize the chance you took, and I appreciate it. As to the wire . . . well, I'm going to have to think about that a while. Good day."

Shaking hands, he placed a black derby on his head and left.

After a brief pause, Mary Dwyer smiled. "Well," she said, "it seems to me that you should resign, Mr. Nicholson. Being around all that sin must make life unbearable for you."

Waite did not answer. In fact, he could not think of a reasonable reply.

"Would you care to come with us, Mary?" Mrs. Dwyer said, returning to the room.

"No, thank you, Mother," Mary replied. "While you were out, Mr. Nicholson gave me an excellent tip on the final race at Gravesend and I've got to find a poolroom right away."

As they walked, Waite only half-heard the sing-song trivialities of Sophie Dwyer. Instead, he found himself reflecting on the peculiar negative reactions he had received from the latest pair of new women to enter his life. Dottie DeLacy seemed to disapprove of him because he favored the gambling interests; Mary Dwyer disapproved of him because he opposed them.

Then, even as he mused, he heard the name of Dottie DeLacy mentioned.

"Pardon me," Waite said. "I didn't catch what you just said, Mrs. Dwyer."

"I asked if you know Miss DeLacy. The pool seller's daughter."

"Oh," Waite murmured. "I saw her the one time I accompanied Mr. Humstone to DeLacy's place."

"She's a member of our society, too," Mrs. Dwyer said.

"Oh?"

The single syllable masked an ocean of confusion that washed over Waite's mind. Dottie DeLacy, a member of ASS! She had seen and heard him warn her father of the raid. What would Waite do if she was at the meeting?

"That is, she used to be a member until yesterday," Sophie added, solving his dilemma.

"What happened then?" Waite asked, trying not to sound overly interested.

"It had to do with our raid being foiled," Mrs. Dwyer said. "Somehow Peter DeLacy was forewarned. Only she could have told him. She was informed last night that she would no longer be welcome at the society."

Waite's spasm of guilt for causing Dottie's downfall was overpowered by an even greater spasm of relief that he was still in the clear.

The meeting produced even more information than Waite dreamed possible. After an opening prayer and tirade by Mrs. Ironsides, the rotund reformer announced that a second raid was planned the next day. "And this time we won't fail," Aurelia added. "To make certain of that, we've taken the precaution of enlisting police cooperation in order to obtain evidence. As you know, Misters Tilden and Street did not handle themselves as professionally as they might have last week. Tomorrow, the incriminating ticket will be purchased by an undercover member of the police force. In order to explain the mechanics of the raid, I should like to introduce Mr. Dudley Fellows of the district attorney's office. Mr. Fellows . . ."

The thin-faced man with a pencil mustache stepped forward and spoke briefly to the group. As he did so, Waite Nicholson, the people-watcher, observed him carefully. There was a certain characteristic of the eyes and downturned mouth that intrigued him. He recalled the line from Shakespeare about men with lean and hungry looks. "I have a feeling," Waite said to himself, "that it would be possible to do business with this fellow Fellows."

After the meeting, tea and Viennese delights were served. Mrs. Dwyer introduced Waite to all the ladies, never failing to add, "Oh, if only my daughter Mary could fall under the influence of such a nice, Christian fellow!"

Most of them responded to the general effect that they would fall under his influence, Christian or non-Christian, any time Waite saw fit. It was during the middle of one such conversation that Waite noticed Mr. Fellows working his way toward the door. "Excuse me," he said at that point. "I'd like to have a word with Mr. Fellows. He made such a nice presentation and I'd like to compliment him before he leaves."

His conversation with the sallow lawyer lasted nearly a half hour. It began with a series of generalities on both sides, proceeded to theoretical specifics, then practical considerations. When the two men finally shook hands and Fellows departed for his office, Waite returned to the scattered membership of the Anti-Sin Society with a smile of confidence.

"The Clover Stakes is about to begin. We're just seconds away."

"They're off! Standard is off to a great start. He's followed by Moderator, La Traviata, and Dry Monopole. Civil Service is fifth, then Drizzle, Judge Morrow, and Uncle Bob."

Long pause, then more telegraphic noise.

The crowd leaned forward in expectation of Thomas Wynn's next pronouncement, but he decided to let them wait a few moments longer.

The fact was, he enjoyed the attention. For a major part of his youth, Thomas Wynn, now forty-seven years old, had wanted to become an actor. He had even considered running away with Barnum's circus one fateful summer when it passed through his small Ohio town. But the moment of decision passed and Thomas Wynn settled down to the life of an ordinary, unobtrusive citizen. After serving ten years as a railroad ticket agent for the Toledo and Ohio Central, he learned telegraphy, married, and moved to New York when he learned of an opening with the new H. C. Ditmas Company. In 1888, he began working out of Gravesend Race Track, ticking off information pertaining to weights, odds, and the progress of the races to the poolrooms in New York. After a while, however, he yearned to be on the other end of the wire, especially after he visited Peter DeLacy's place on Park Row, and observed Sam Fisher, the race caller, in action. "Look at that," Thomas Wynn remarked to a friend who had accompanied him. "That man has respect. No minister in church ever had a better audience, no actor on the stage delivered his lines before such a receptive audience. It's like a great dramatic performance. I'd give anything to be able to do that."

"Why not ask DeLacy?" the friend suggested. "I understand he's a reasonable man."

Wynn took his advice. Although there were no immediate openings, DeLacy created an alternate's position for him. Then, in 1890, when Fisher left, Wynn became the fulltime race caller. He soon developed a technique all his own to make a race more exciting. By hoarding information until the last moment, by supplying details that didn't exist, and by making every stretch run seem like a do-or-die, neck-and-neck finish, he kept his audience entranced and feeling they had gotten their money's worth even when their horses lost.

Not everyone liked this flamboyant style. Among the race callers at Jimmy Adams's or Paddy Reilly's or any of the sixty pool selling establishments of New York City, opinion was divided as to how a race should be announced. Some callers gave nothing more than the basic facts transmitted from the telegrapher at the track. Others emulated Thomas Wynn, but at best they were pale imitations. True connoisseurs of the best Park Row poolrooms generally praised the thin, prematurely white-haired Thomas Wynn as the best in his business.

"Coming up to the quarter pole," he cried, "Standard's got a length on La Traviata. Moderator and Dry Monopole are holding steady, Civil Service, blocked in, will have to go wide if he wants to run. Judge Morrow, Drizzle, and Uncle Bob are bringing up the rear."

Fifty feet away, near the entrance of DeLacy's poolroom, a barely perceptible series of nods passed between four men, the last of whom lit a cigar and blew a massive smoke ring.

Upstairs, in the office of Peter DeLacy, Waite Nicholson leaned back in the soft leather chair and puffed on the thin Havana given him just moments before by the King of Pool Sellers himself.

He had brought a report written by a confused W. C. Humstone on the widening gulf between Western Union and Philip Dwyer. While DeLacy was reading it, Waite recalled the process of evolution that had led him to his present position. At first, he had regarded the upcoming raid as an excellent opportunity to ingratiate himself with DeLacy, but he had discarded that strategy after only a few minutes. The inspiration had taken place while he sat next to Mrs. Dwyer at the ASS meeting.

Why not allow the raid to take place? he mused. This would put the pool sellers in jeopardy. A member, or members, of the gambling community would be placed on trial. The pool sellers would immediately panic, begin to search desperately for someone—anyone—who could get them out of the legal tangle. Someone who had made a deal with an important member of the opposition—Mr. Dudley Fellows, for example—would be hailed as a savior. That savior, Waite Nicholson decided, would be himself.

And if worse came to worst, he further mused, if the situation became outright war . . . well, he could deal with that, too.

The next morning, after his discussion with Fellows, he had taken the Prospect Park and Coney Island Railroad's early car to Gravesend Race Track. Pad in hand, he had circled the course, jotting notes to himself, measuring distances. After that was finished, he returned to the Western Union Telegraph Office, waited patiently until he was alone, and then began meticulously picking out a letter on one of the company's newfangled typewriting machines. It was hard work, but if all went well . . .

Sounds of confusion and strife coming from the main room suddenly interrupted his reverie. This was followed by a triple buzz on the line leading from the poolroom to DeLacy's desk.

"Must be trouble," DeLacy said, leaping from his chair and starting out of the office.

Waite followed, not too closely. When they arrived downstairs, four plainclothesmen were clutching Thomas Wynn and showing their badges to Roger Mellon, the manager.

"This man is under arrest," one of them said. "We have a witness who'll testify that he made an illegal bet on the last race."

Thomas Wynn turned a plaintive face toward DeLacy. The Clover Stakes had been another of those popular races with a large amount of betting. While working at the cage, Wynn had obviously sold a quick ticket to the detective rather than making him fill out the commission form.

"What's his bail? I'll pay it now," DeLacy said.

"You can't do that. Only the judge can set bail."

"But Tom here is my only telegrapher. My alternate's sick today."

The detective shrugged. "Come on, Mac."

They led Wynn out.

"What are we gonna do, boss?" Mellon asked DeLacy. "Wembley's sick."

Waite, of course, was ready for this.

"Mr. Mellon," he said. "I'm a telegrapher. I could call the last two races for you. Certainly not as well as Mr. Wynn, but at least you'll be able to finish the day."

"Sure," Mellon said. "It would be a great favor if you could help us out."

DeLacy looked at Waite closely. "You really are a bright boy, aren't you?" he said softly.

"Jack-of-all-trades, master of none," Waite replied modestly.

"Come on, let's get you started," Mellon said.

"One thing, if you don't mind," Waite replied. "If there's some way you could arrange a screen between me and the bettors so they wouldn't know who was calling the race. I'm not sure what Mr. Humstone would say—"

"Certainly," DeLacy nodded, motioning to Deke, Murph, and Willie. "Deke, you and Willie fix up something. And Murph, you go tell my lawyer to get Tom out as soon as they set bail."

The trio scattered as DeLacy, Mellon, and Nicholson strolled back to the center of the poolroom. "Next race in fifteen minutes, folks," Mellon announced calmly. "Our agents are standing by to place your bets with Gravesend Park."

Two hours later, as he sat in Peter DeLacy's office, Waite sipped a beer and decided he had not done such a bad job. With the exception of a horse named Orageuse, which he continually mispronounced, and a long wait between the beginning of the stretch and final announcement of the winner, Waite's race-calling career had gone off quite well. DeLacy had complimented him with a pat on the back before checking the final receipts and going to the station house himself. "Stick around if you want," he had called over his shoulder. "I'll be back as soon as I see why it's taking so long to get Tom out." He obviously expected to get the charge dismissed within a few hours, but Waite knew differently. The Anti-Sin Society and *The New York Times* meant to use Tom Wynn as an example. And to judge by Peter DeLacy's uncharacteristic dark scowl, the proceedings had started off in fiery fashion. "That bloated cow," he muttered when he returned to his office with Wynn and Mellon. "The whole bunch of them are hypocrites."

Waite looked at the crestfallen Wynn. "It was my fault," he said. "I just didn't recognize those cops."

"Forget it," DeLacy said. "Those sanctimonious, psalm-singing, holier-than-thou, witch-burning professional saints." He looked at Waite. "Five thousand dollars bail," he said. "Can you imagine that? For a man who takes a dollar bet."

"You mean Mr. Wynn has to stand trial?" Waite asked ingenuously.

"That's right," said Mellon. "Tomorrow afternoon, three o'clock, The Tombs. Court Number Three. That's the big one where they try murderers."

"Court Number Three," Waite repeated. "That would be

Judge Carter." When Mellon nodded, Waite thought for a moment, then said. "And is the prosecutor named Fellows?"

"That's right. You a lawyer, too?" Mellon asked.

"Well, no," Waite replied. "But I have a fair working knowledge of the New York courts. I think I know a way to get to the judge and prosecutor."

His eyes widening in amazement, DeLacy looked at Waite coldly. "Something like that could be really bad trouble if it wasn't handled right," he said.

"Yessir," Waite nodded, looking DeLacy straight in the eye. "But I'm sure I can handle it and handle it right. In fact, I can guarantee it."

"In that case, you're on."

"Funds will be available?"

"Of course, whatever you'll need," DeLacy replied emphatically.

Draining his beer, Waite picked up the other pair of mugs and strode for the door. "I'll drop these off at the kitchen on my way out," he said. "And I'll report to you tomorrow by two o'clock as soon as I make the arrangements; and, Mr. DeLacy, thank you for your trust in me."

With a little wave, he opened the door and left.

DeLacy smiled. He stood there for a minute, listening to the sound of Waite's rapid footsteps bouncing down the staircase. Then, as the silence of an otherwise hectic day and evening engulfed him, he shook his head. "Christ," he said softly, "I wouldn't be surprised if that son-of-a-bitch could knit me a sweater, too."

"This man is so excellent he even impersonates dogs"

The Lower Broadway office of the Pinkerton National Detective Agency was situated on a side street, partly to hold down overhead and partly so that prospective clients would be less likely to be recognized.

Some fastidious persons might have been repelled at the Duane and Rose Street office, even though it was less than half a mile northeast of the grand intersection of Park Row and Broadway. It was certainly not plush; next door was Paul Sach's Restaurant, a hole-in-the-wall which competed with a larger saloon diagonally across the intersection. Situated below ground level, the saloon's entranceway was a modest triangular wedge, the roof supported by a single wooden post on the sidewalk. Four steps down led to the inevitable pair of swinging doors and the cool darkness—no doubt symbolic—of the interior.

The five-storey building in which the saloon was located was obviously the star of the block. It belonged to Alfred Van Beuren and Henry Munson, who specialized in general advertising, designing bill posters, and "rock and fence painting." Accordingly, as if to demonstrate the proprietors' skills, the building was decorated with elaborate art work. On one corner, for instance, a gigantic woman had been painted, her feet even with the second-floor windows, her bonneted head with the fifth. She was wildly out of proportion, the dainty feet giving way to a skirt (and presumably, a pair of legs) fully two storeys high. Under her right arm, she carried a batch of posters. In her left hand was a sign that read simply: "40 Rose Street." Although she was at least thirty feet tall, the lady's waist was extremely small—only about six inches across.

On the westernmost edge of the building was yet another four-storey-high sign. It advertised an Empire Theatre production of "Billy the Kid" by "Rotan Tomatus." At the lower edge of his poster, the designer had cleverly painted some goats, who were in the process of eating the bottom sections of the announcement.

Pinky was not repelled by the garish scenery. In fact, he rather enjoyed it, although there was not a great deal of leisure time during his first few days there. He usually began at dawn, studying the files and familiarizing himself with his staff, permanent, part time, and emergency. In the event of a major case, he was happy to note, he was authorized to use more than a hundred men of varying experience. Generally speaking, however, the permanent staff consisted of less than a dozen employees, including Russell Glock, who functioned somewhere between deputy and secretary.

Glock reported at 8:30 and the two men spent a genial half-hour discussing life and crime in the big city. "I think you'll find New York less of a challenge than the West," Glock concluded. "Unfortunately, you'll probably have so much paperwork that you won't even be able to work cases yourself."

That was what Pinky dreaded. "Isn't there anything exciting happening here?" he asked.

"Oh, yes," Glock replied. "The soupspoon murderer is still at large, but we can't tackle that unless we're asked, of course."

"The murderer kills with a soupspoon?" Pinky asked, a frown of interest creasing his forehead.

"No, he leaves them in his victims' mouths. Most curious."

"Maybe it's just a restaurant with very bad food," Pinky said.

His first days behind a desk had been every bit as boring as he had expected. For every client, he made a sincere effort to be enthusiastic and helpful, but in each case his mind rebelled by championing the viewpoint diametrically opposed to the customer's. While the prissy man droned on about his wife's infidelity, for example, Pinky found himself in perfect agreement with any woman who would desert such a fool; when the factory chief ranted about the menace of unions, Pinky developed good basic arguments to counter everything he said.

The "countess" whose show dog had been maliciously clipped by a rival owner was even worse. She spoke for fifteen minutes on how wonderful dogs were and how she had been betrayed by someone envious of the Prince of Wurtemberg's great success at international shows. Feeling his stomach beginning to churn, Pinky decided to pass up the case and call it a morning. "I'm sorry, Countess," he said finally. "We're not equipped to handle dog cases."

"But what am I to do?"

Pinky pulled a card from the file. "Here's the name and address of another detective agency," he said. "This man is so excellent he even impersonates dogs."

"Oh, thank you."

Werlerble.

The countess turned back to him. "I beg your pardon. Did you say something?"

"Yes. Werlerble."

"Of course," she smiled vacuously, sweeping out of the office in a swirl of imitation pearls.

Sophie Dwyer was nagging him again, and Philip didn't like it. She was shrill, persistent, and even worse, accurate. He had allowed the days to slip by. The spring meet at Gravesend Race Track would end in a few days. "You promised to do something in the name of virtue," Sophie concluded, "but you've done nothing. Evil will triumph, thanks to you. Why, even the corrupt police have made an arrest."

"One arrest," Philip scoffed. "Sixty poolrooms and they make one arrest."

"Nevertheless, that man Wynn will be made an example," Sophie replied, tying the strings of her bonnet firmly beneath her chin. "Are you coming with me?"

"Where?"

"To court. His trial is today."

"Well, no," Philip muttered. "I'll find out what happens soon enough."

"You don't care what happens to him. You want him to get off."

"Well, make up your mind," Philip snapped.

Sophie exhaled wearily and started out the front door. A moment later she returned, and thrust a letter at her husband. "This just came by messenger," she said. She then threw back her shoulders haughtily and departed.

Waite arrived at The Tombs early—to meet Dudley Fellows and assure himself that all was well. Low and massive, The Tombs, so aptly named, was a granite version of an ancient Egyptian mausoleum. Four huge ugly columns made up the entrance way, six steps above the street. For a third of their height, starting from the bottom, they were solid, then abruptly the single cylinder became eight smaller cylinders, all stuck together like a package of breadsticks.

The more conventional Criminal Law Court was connected to The Tombs by a double-fronted Romanesque bridge over Franklin Street. Broad sidewalks of concrete flanked both buildings where small groups of people had collected—lawyers and bail bondsmen and fearful-faced persons who looked like defendants, talking nervously, consulting small sheets of paper, occasionally glancing at the Centre Street horsecars as if awaiting someone of great importance.

In a way, Waite felt he himself was on trial, for what happened inside the building was vitally important to him, vastly more important than to Dudley Fellows, who casually strolled up a few minutes late. "Is everything all set?" Waite asked.

"Yes. I'll be direct-examining Sykes—the cop who made the bet—and I'll make several, shall we say, oversights. If your lawyer keeps his mouth shut, the judge can't help but rule in your favor."

"What about the judge," Waite said. "Is he—"

"Yes," Fellows smiled. "Believe me, you haven't a thing to worry about. I'll take the money now."

Waite hesitated. "I have only half," he said. "I get the rest the minute Wynn gets off and you'll get it five minutes later."

"How do you know the pool sellers won't back out?" Fellows asked, his eyes narrowing.

"Because DeLacy is a straight shooter."

"All right. I'll meet you next to the statue of Demosthenes as soon as everybody clears out."

"Right," Waite said. Straightening his tie, he slipped into the courtroom just as the clerk intoned, "New York versus Wynn," and started to read the charge.

The letter was typewritten and contained no signature or name, but when Philip Dwyer saw the phrase "admirer of you" in the first line, he read it with care.

"Dear Sir," the letter went. "We have never met, but I have long been an admirer of you, both as a retail meat dealer and sports entrepreneur. It is presumptuous of me to write you perhaps, but because we have dined together, so to speak, I honestly feel there is a bond of friendship between us. Sir, while I was in a tavern the day before yesterday looking for a friend, the conversation between two men turned on your relationship with their employer, the Ditmas Company. One of them stated flatly that you would never dare sever relationships with them by cutting their telegraph line from your track because you were too greedy to give up the money they paid you. The other fellow agreed with him and added that even if you weren't, 'Old Humstone has him wrapped around his little finger!'

"After a while they were joined by some pool sellers who allowed as how you lacked both the courage and moral stamina to strike at the pool sellers, as well as Mr. Humstone. When I spoke up and told these stupefied persons that you were the most admirable of men, they laughed at me and would have afflicted me with physical violence had it not been for the intervention of my friend. Since that incident, I have given much thought to the days when the name Dwyer stood not only for fine meat but meat that was delivered quickly, fairly, honestly, and for a reasonable price. I cannot conceive of your being in any way under the control of those disgusting vice dealers, and therefore thought it necessary to inform you that although many people think that the Ditmas Company and the pool sellers have you on a set of strings, there are others of us who still admire you. Sincerely written in the knowledge that those who deride you will soon praise you—a secret admirer."

Philip Dwyer stood up, his face slowly trying on various shades of red, starting with pink and settling for crimson. "Rochemont!" he shouted, when he had finally composed himself sufficiently to talk. "Prepare the carriage. I'm going to the track."

The trial of New York versus Thomas Wynn began with the prosecution's summoning of police detective Algernon Sykes, the man who had purchased a betting ticket from DeLacy's poolroom.

"Don't worry," Thaddeus Thacker whispered to Thomas Wynn as they watched the swearing in. "I know this chap and he's a born liar. I'll back him in a corner and beat the stuffings out of him."

"Just get me off," Wynn replied mildly. "Forget the stuffings."

Peter DeLacy had not been enthusiastic about Thacker's ability as a trial lawyer, but a rapid decision had been necessary because the regular attorney of the Pool Sellers' Association was abroad. Somewhat reluctantly, DeLacy allowed himself to be seduced by the general knowledge that Thacker was assertive, if nothing else. Besides, Waite had assured him that Wynn would need no special defense. What he did not know was that Thacker had a penchant for grandiloquence, that ten years before, he had suggested defending Guiteau, the assassin of President Garfield, on the grounds of self-defense. To Thacker, every opposing lawyer and witness was an enemy, part of a larger plot to destroy himself, America, the world. Thus every word that dropped from their lips he regarded with the utmost suspicion. "Don't worry," he said now to DeLacy. "I'll do everything in my power, which is considerable, to save your good name."

"Forget me," DeLacy replied. "I'm not on trial. Concentrate on my employee, Tom Wynn."

"That's a very short-sighted attitude," Thacker said firmly. "One must not forget what their ultimate objective is. You."

Twenty feet away, prosecutor Dudley Fellows talked quietly with Sykes during the brief pause. "Now don't forget," he said. "Just say yes to every question, no matter how ridiculous it seems. That's all you have to do. Just say yes."

"Yessir," Sykes replied. "But what do I say when the other fella starts asking me things?"

"Unless he's an utter fool," Fellows replied, "he won't say a word. So you don't have to worry about that."

"You may begin your examination, Mr. Fellows," the judge said, gaveling the courtroom into silence.

"Thank you, Your Honor. I intend to call just one witness. We will prove that this witness purchased a betting ticket on May 26 from Mr. Thomas Wynn, in direct violation of the Ives Law, which prohibits off-track betting."

"Proceed."

Sykes was duly sworn in.

"Now, Officer Sykes," Fellows began. "Did you enter the poolroom of Peter DeLacy on May 26 of this year?"

"Yessir."

"And did you purchase a betting ticket?"

"Yessir."

"And was that ticket on the horse Army Lass?"

Sykes frowned, then said, "Yes . . . sir."

Thomas Wynn put his hand over his mouth, as if struck by a massive coughing fit. "What's the matter?" Thacker whispered. "Is something the matter?"

"Not at all," Wynn replied, smiling. "Army Lass died last year."

Thacker immediately bounded to his feet. "Objection, Your Honor!" he intoned.

"On what grounds?"

"On the grounds that the horse just named is deceased."

"Objection overruled," the judge replied. "Irrelevant."

Thacker sat down. "What the hell did you object for?" Wynn said.

"Well, they're lying," Thacker muttered. "We can't let them get away with that. One unchallenged lie leads to another, until it's possible to build a case constructed entirely of fabrications."

"Sounds to me like they're just digging their own grave," Wynn said.

"You think that because you lack my experience," Thacker countered. "These men are crafty devils and will stop at nothing. You wait and see."

Prosecutor Fellows stepped to a box on the table and withdrew a pink ticket from it. "Is this the ticket you purchased?" he asked, holding it in the air fully twenty feet from Sykes.

Sykes squinted for a moment, then said, "Yessir."

Fellows started to hand the slip to the bailiff, then quickly withdrew it with an embarrassed smile. "Begging your pardon, Your Honor," he said. "This is not the piece of evidence I wanted to offer. I don't know how it could have happened, but this is a hat check from Tony Pastor's restaurant. If it please the court, I wish to offer this piece of evidence instead." With that, he took a second pink ticket from the box.

"Proceed," the judge said.

Holding up the second slip, Fellows asked, "Is this the ticket you purchased, Mr. Sykes?"

"Yessir."

"We wish to offer this as evidence."

Thacker was on his feet once again. "Objection, Your Honor!"

"On what grounds?"

"On the grounds that it's impossible for the witness to have read a word on either of those slips at the distance they were held."

"Objection overruled."

"What are you doing?" Wynn hissed, tugging at Thacker's coat. "I don't care if he identifies that door as the betting slip. The more mistakes they make, the better—"

"I am your attorney," Thacker interrupted coldly. "And I shall handle this case."

But he sat down. Fellows then stepped close to Sykes and asked, "Mr. Sykes, is the man from whom you purchased the betting ticket in this courtroom now?"

Looking directly at Thomas Wynn, Sykes replied, "Yessir."

Fellows slowly pointed his finger towards Peter DeLacy. "Is that the man who sold you the ticket?"

Still continuing to look at Wynn, Sykes said, "Yessir."

The crowd exploded with laughter and confused murmurs.

"I object," Thacker interrupted. "Prosecution is leading the witness in the most flagrant manner."

"Objection overruled," the judge said scornfully. "I caution the spectators to quiet down or I will clear the court."

"The prosecution rests," Fellows said.

"Does the defense wish to cross-examine?" the judge asked. His voice carried the plain implication that Thacker would have to be insane to do so.

"Yes, Your Honor, I certainly do!" Thacker replied in ringing tones.

Thomas Wynn grabbed his sleeve. "What for?" he demanded. "The lunatic just testified he bought a hat check on a dead horse from Mr. DeLacy and not me. I'm free. My Aunt Molly could get me off. All we have to do is keep our mouths shut."

"But can't you see the deeper implications of this, Mr. Wynn?" Thacker murmured. "They're after all of you. The dead horse was used deliberately to implicate you for fraud. If a horse is dead, there's no possibility of his winning the race. That's fraud, to sell someone a share of a product such as that. It's a crime carrying a more severe penalty than pool selling. And by not identifying you as the seller of the ticket, they strike at your employer, Mr. DeLacy, the real person they're after. Can't you understand that, man? They don't want you. They want DeLacy! It's a dastardly plot."

"But they can't get him unless they arrest him first," Wynn replied hotly. "They can't arrest one man and then convict another man in court. Even I know that."

"I intend to destroy this tissue of lies," Thacker said. Raising his bulk with grim determination, he strode to the witness box. "Mr. Sykes," he began. "That is your name, isn't it?"

"Objection!" Fellows interrupted. "Counsel is badgering the witness."

"Objection sustained," the judge said.

"I was merely trying to—" Thacker began.

"Defense will proceed with cross-examination or be held in contempt of court," the judge countered.

Reddening, Thacker returned his gaze to Sykes. "Mr. Sykes," he said, "what did you say was the name of the horse you placed a bet on?"

Sykes opened his mouth, hesitated.

"Objection, Your Honor," Fellows interrupted again. "That question has already been asked and answered."

"Objection sustained."

"But, Your Honor," Thacker fulminated. "I'm merely trying to establish the fact that—"

"If you have any relevant questions, Mr. Thacker, you may continue," the judge said.

"Mr. Sykes," Thacker said wearily. "You testified that the man who sold you the betting slip is in this courtroom."

"Yessir."

"Could you point him out to me, please?"

"Just a moment," interrupted the judge, his head turning toward Fellows, who half-stood at his table. "Does the prosecution wish to object on the grounds that defense counsel is leading the witness?"

"Oh, yes, Your Honor," Fellows said.

"Very well. Objection sustained."

"How could I be leading him, Your Honor?" Thacker demanded. "All I asked was if he could point out the man who sold him the ticket."

"You led him with your eyes, Mr. Thacker," the judge replied coldly. "The court could see that you very deliberately glanced at someone other than the man previously identified by the witness. We will not allow such flagrant violations of the rules of fair judicial procedure to occur in this court."

"Good Lord," Thacker muttered.

The judge sat bolt upright. "Nor will we allow blasphemy. If you wish to continue the cross-examination, Mr. Thacker, you may. But the court does wish to know what possible point you are trying to establish."

"I am trying to prove . . ." Thacker replied, moving away from Sykes toward the middle of the courtroom, "I am trying to prove . . . that . . . I don't remember, exactly."

"Are you trying to prove that this witness is lying?"

"Yes, I think so."

"You think so!"

The rotund lawyer seemed to stiffen. "Yes, Your Honor. What I am trying to do is prove that that man over there—Mr. Peter DeLacy—is innocent of selling betting slips. The guilty man is right there!"

With that, Thacker pointed his finger at Thomas Wynn.

"But that is the man you're defending," the judge said.

"Yessir. But to win this case I have to—"

"Yes?"

"To lose it . . ."

"Objection, Your Honor," Fellows said. "Unless defense counsel has some witnesses to prove his client is guilty, I move that this entire cross-examination be stricken from the record."

"Sustained."

A look of desperation came over Thacker's sweating face. "Witnesses? Very well," he said finally. "I wish to summon to the witness stand . . . Mr. Thomas Wynn."

"For what purpose?"

"To prove that he was the man, not Mr. DeLacy, who sold the betting slips."

"You wish to summon your own client in order that he shall testify against himself?"

"I do."

Thomas Wynn's eyes moved quickly from the judge to Thacker to Fellows to Peter DeLacy.

"Your Honor," said Fellows. "In the name of justice, I move that Mr. Wynn not be forced to testify."

"Sustained. I am now ready to issue a verdict."

"But, Your Honor—" Thacker protested.

"Defense counsel will return to his seat during the rendition," the judge warned. He waited until silence had settled over the room, then said, "Mr. Fellows, you have presented a very strong case against the illegal gambling forces of this fine city we're all so very proud to live in. You are to be congratulated for an incisive and direct style and also for the manner in which you defended the rule of equal justice for all. This court also wishes to applaud your decision not to burden it with a long list of repetitive witnesses during the presentation of your case. In short, your methods, compared to those of the defense, are most admirable. That is why it upsets me to have to rule against you in this case. The fact is, the evidence presented simply does not prove beyond the shadow of a doubt that Thomas Wynn sold illegal betting slips. I therefore rule, not guilty. Defendant is dismissed.''

Reporters rushed for the doors as the courtroom filled with the sound of angry and cheering voices. Only Thaddeus Thacker stood still, his eyes lifted toward the ceiling, hands clenching and unclenching. "Shocking," he mumbled over and over. "The most shocking miscarriage of justice I've ever seen."

"Disgusting," Aurelia Ironsides cried from the back of the room. "An outrage! This trial has been a mockery from beginning to end!"

A chorus of sad heads wagged in agreement. Here and there could be heard a faint clucking, a weary exhalation of breath.

Waite Nicholson stood to one side of the room, his face carefully masked of all emotion. A short distance away, Dottie DeLacy studied him, wondering just whose side he was on. The trial over, the participants and audience separated into two groups. Near the front of the court stood the exultant forces of her father, laughing and congratulating themselves and talking in animated tones. To the rear stood the Anti-Sin Society members, glum, angry, their voices gratingly muted.

A moment later, as she was preparing to leave, Dottie saw an excited man enter the courtroom from the back door. From his dress, appearance, and the ever-present pad and pencil, he was obviously a reporter. All eyes went to him as he stopped near the rearmost bench, breathed deeply once, and then shouted for all to hear: "The line's been cut! Dwyer has just cut the telegraph line from Gravesend!"

The two groups of contrasting persons quickly changed attitudes. Cheers erupted from the mouths that were downcast only moments before; groans emanated from those who had barely finished congratulatory sentences.

"Praise the Lord!" Aurelia Ironsides declared in a strong baritone voice. "He works in strange ways sometimes!"

Waite Nicholson was silent, but he could barely suppress a feeling of exaltation that was growing within him. "It worked! Damned if it didn't!" he thought.

At Peter DeLacy's poolroom, all was confusion. Alternate announcer Howard Wembley's voice ended on a shrill note as he cried out, "They're in the stretch!"

A chorus of satiric remarks followed.

"They've been in the stretch for five minutes!"

"Why don't we all walk down to Gravesend and catch the end of this race?"

"Somebody better hang lanterns on them nags so they don't fall in the dark."

"This is what happens when you got ten horses and only twenty-six legs."

Roger Mellon, hearing the howls of derision, raced from Peter DeLacy's office to where Howard Wembley sat in disgusted silence. "What's the matter?" he said.

"Line's dead," Wembley replied. "Nothin's comin'."

"Well, we got to do something," Mellon said, licking his lips nervously. "I'll call Ditmas on the telephone and find out what's happening. You stall the customers a while. Tell them there's been an interruption."

"Good Lord, they know that already," Wembley muttered. As Mellon scooted off, Howard Wembley tried to think of something, but finally decided to stick to the truth. "Ladies and gentlemen, I'm sorry to say that we are having some trouble with the telegraph line," he called out. "As soon as it's repaired, or as soon as we can get verified information on the finish, we'll announce it. Until then, please be patient. There will be no betting on the next race until the trouble is over."

The reaction of the bettors, who had seen the line go dead once or twice before, was scornful, but generally good-natured. Some of the more realistic ones, realizing that they were in for a long wait, drifted over to the bar and had themselves a drink.

"Please, sir," the Ditmas Company telegrapher pleaded. "Let me at least send them the names of the winners."

It had been ten minutes since Michael Chance and his partner had been interrupted near the climax of the fifth race at Gravesend. As the horses came up to the halfway mark, Chance had become aware of several figures entering the small transmission room high in the grandstand. With one hand on the telescope mounted on the windowsill and the other on the key, Chance, a new man, was making his first "solo" mission. The purpose was to observe the race and simultaneously send back reports to the pool sellers.

While immersed in his own virtuosity, Michael Chance felt a sudden surge of wind catch the papers on his desk, scattering them. Without removing his eye from the telescope, he said angrily, "Shut the door, you damn fool."

The "damn fool" was none other than Philip Dwyer, followed by a pair of uniformed track policemen. "Do you know who you're talking to, boy?" Dwyer asked, his face reddening.

"No," Chance said truthfully. "And until this race is over, I don't care."

Philip Dwyer had fully intended to halt the transmission of data after the eighth and final race of the day, but now he was furious. "Well, I care," he snapped. "This race is over now!" With that, he reached his hand to the power switch near the side of the door and threw it into the "off" position.

Michael Chance bounded from his seat like a man possessed. "You . . . you can't do that!" he rasped, his wide eyes staring angrily at Dwyer.

"I am Philip Dwyer, I own this track, and I just did it. Now pick up your things, both of you, and get out of here."

At that moment, the telephone connected to the Ditmas Company office in New York rang. Chance picked it up and shouted "Help!"

"What's happened?" the voice of W. C. Humstone demanded. "Is that you, Chance? Have you lost your mind?"

"No, Mr. Humstone! Dwyer has!" Chance yelled, just as the two track policemen grabbed him. The phone clattered to the floor.

Picking it up, the second telegrapher shouted, "He cut the power!" With that a guard wrestled him to the side of the room and once again the telephone hit the floor with an unceremonious clunk.

Back in New York, Humstone shook his head, which still reverberated with the sound of screaming voices and shock waves. His mouth open, he looked at the mouthpiece in his own hand, but no words issued forth.

Finally, he heard Dwyer's voice say coldly, "Yes, I cut the power, Humstone. Nobody can call me a damn fool and get away with it."

"Philip, who called you that? I'll fire him right away," Humstone asked.

"You did, you idiot!" Dwyer shouted triumphantly.

"Me? I said no such thing."

"Yes, you did. Your man was only repeating what you've been saying all around town behind my back."

"Is that what you heard?" Humstone asked in a high voice.

"Why, that's an outrageous lie and I can prove it. I don't think you're a damn fool, Phil. Or any kind of fool. Why, I have respect—"

"Never mind all that," Dwyer shot back. "I was going to cut the line anyway. Not right this minute, but soon."

"Listen, Phil, this is all some kind of horrible mistake," Humstone said beseechingly. "Let us finish this race and then we can straighten this out."

"Are the horses still in the stretch?" Dwyer asked, looking at Chance.

Chance nodded. "Since four o'clock."

"Good," Dwyer smiled. "That's where we'll leave them. They can bury them in the stretch. Now we'll see who the damn fool is!"

"Please, Phil," Humstone moaned. "We got sixty pool-rooms waiting for the result. You can't do this to me. This is bad business."

"I don't care," Dwyer muttered. "You and all the rest have been playing me for a fool, pretending to be nice by sending letters all filled with pleasant words. Only thing you were trying to do was hold me up, keep me from cutting this line so you could get through the spring meet. Well, I ain't allowing it to happen anymore. This office is closed. From now on, if you want to do your dirty work, you'll have to do it from the station in town." He slammed down the receiver.

Giving the policemen orders to see the two telegraphers off the track, then to guard the transmission switch with their lives, Philip Dwyer stalked back to his carriage.

In his office sat a crestfallen Humstone, his fists clenched angrily but no words coming from him. "Think, think," he thought.

At 5:12 P.M., slightly more than an hour after the ending of the fifth race at Gravesend, a cheer went up at Peter DeLacy's poolroom. "The winner is Flattery," Howard Wembley called out. "Tarantella second, Cousin Jeems third, Winter Breeze fourth." The information had been received only after the ousted Ditmas Company telegraphers made their way to the town of Gravesend and used the station there.

The poolroom was nearly deserted a half hour later when the group of sad-faced men representing the other pool sellers assembled in Peter DeLacy's office. Already there, besides DeLacy himself, were W. C. Humstone, Thomas Wynn, Roger Mellon, and Waite Nicholson, who had arrived after paying off Fellows and the judge.

"Do you have any idea why Dwyer did such a thing?" DeLacy asked, looking at Humstone.

"He said we've been calling him a damn fool," Humstone replied. "I don't know where he got that idea. Of course, he is a damn fool, but I haven't said anything about it. Anyway, he's furious."

"What about tomorrow? Do you think he'll cool off by then?"

"Frankly, no."

"Not even if we offer more money?"

"No. He's a real hothead."

"Well, there's still three days left on this meet," DeLacy said. "We don't want to lose them." He looked at the floor as he paced. "Where's the nearest telegraph station to the track?" he asked. "In the town of Gravesend?"

"Yes."

"I guess that's too far away."

When the silence and cigar smoke became quite heavy in the room, Waite Nicholson decided it was time to speak. "Oh, Mr. DeLacy," he said, then glanced sideways at Mr. Humstone. "If I may offer a suggestion . . ."

"Certainly," DeLacy said. Humstone nodded grudgingly.

"Well, it seems to me you can beat Dwyer by using imagination and organization," Waite said. "There's a large abandoned hotel called Sleight's, right across from the track. It has a cupola in the top with a good view of the finish line. If you could run a telegraph line from that hotel into the Gravesend station, you could get the information back almost as quickly as if you had a station right in the park. It would take some doing, but I'm sure it can be managed."

"How would we get information that they post on the boards—scratches, weights, jockeys?" DeLacy asked.

"By a system of runners and signals, sir," Waite replied.

"It would take days to figure out a workable system," Humstone scoffed.

Smiling ever so apologetically at his superior, Waite said, "Not necessarily. You see, ever since Dwyer was in our office, threatening to cut the wire, I've been thinking." With that, he pulled a piece of paper from his watch pocket and added: "If you could supply six men for observation from different points, twelve for runners, and another half a dozen to guard certain areas, I think we'd have no trouble at all. I've also jotted down a list of other things."

"Really," Humstone interrupted. "What sort of nonsense is this? I think it would be more practical if I called on Dwyer once again."

"But you said yourself it's no use," DeLacy said. "And we don't want to lose the rest of this meet. You can call on Dwyer if you think it'll do any good. But in the meantime, we have a contract with you. That means you'd better start making other arrangements to get us the information. Can your men run a line from that old hotel to your regular station in the town of Gravesend by tomorrow at noon?''

"Yes," Humstone nodded. "We could do that."

"Of course," DeLacy added, "we have to get permission to use the hotel. Who owns that old place, anyway?''

Waite pulled another slip of paper from his pocket. "This is the name of the fellow," he said, with another slight smile. "I've already taken the liberty of speaking with him . . . in a discreet way, of course . . . and I think we can rent the place for about a hundred dollars a day."

"Fine," DeLacy said. "Now we need somebody to run this operation. How about young Nicholson here?''

"Me?" Waite said, his eyes wide.

"Him?" Humstone echoed.

"Certainly. He seems to be very resourceful, and I have a lot of confidence in him."

Waite looked modestly at the floor. "Thank you, Mr. DeLacy," he said finally. "I'll be most happy to try and help out, if Mr. Humstone will allow me."

"All right," responded the bewildered Humstone. "You can consider this your vacation."

"Vacation?" said Peter DeLacy, with a twinkle in his eye. "Why, this young man deserves extra pay for something like this. As a matter of fact, an assignment like this calls for somebody in a more responsible position than a secretary."

"Well, I . . . er . . ." Humstone stammered.

"After all, we're going to be trusting this man with a lot of money and personnel," DeLacy said. "That calls for a step up, in my judgment."

"What would you suggest?" asked the beleaguered Humstone.

"The Special Projects Officer position is open, sir," offered the ever-helpful Waite.

"But that calls for five times your salary," Humstone puffed. "That's unheard of." But when he turned to Peter DeLacy for sympathy, he was met by a stern gaze that somehow, silently, accused him of avarice, lack of imagination, and assorted minor character deficiencies.

"These are unheard of times," DeLacy said simply.

"All right, all right," Humstone muttered. Looking at Waite, he said, "The job is yours. I'll clear it at the main office and see that you get all the support you need."

"Thank you. Thank you both very much, gentlemen," said Waite. "I'll try not to betray your confidence in me."

He nodded at them and walked briskly from the room, his eyes scanning the lists he had made.

"That boy's like a genie from Aladdin's lamp," Roger Mellon said, with a shake of his head. "From what you say, all you have to do is think about something and he's already got the answer . . ."

"Almost like he planned it that way," DeLacy said.

5

"This is Dwyer... we've broken their code!"

As Pinky sat with his feet propped on his desk, his eye caught the *Times*'s editorial: "We are confident now that the pool sellers are finished," it said. "Deprived of the telegraphic dispatches, they will discover it is not a simple matter to 'call' a race ten or fifteen miles away. Mr. Philip Dwyer has acted wisely and boldly. Severing the telegraph line to the pool sellers marks the end of their influence on New York gambling."

Pinky had never visited Gravesend Race Track. Yet, even as he read the last lines of the editorial, he began to shake his head. A quick montage of schemes and counterschemes raced through his mind as he put himself first in the place of the gambler in need of information, then back in his own position of law enforcement. A slow smile spread across his rugged features. "No sir," he said aloud finally. "There isn't any way you can stop them just by cutting that wire. No sir."

High in the cupola of Sleight's hotel, Michael Chance peered through the telescope. It was midmorning and the Western Union technicians were still working on the line connecting the town of Gravesend station with their new headquarters. They had run some of the line during the night, but it had been slow going and they would have to hurry to have it operational by race time.

Chance swung the telescope gently sideways, then panned it along the entire distance of the track. Theirs was a near-perfect position. Except for a section of backstretch and a small segment of the board which posted odds, weights, and scratches, it was possible to see all of the information necessary to "call" a good race.

The new headquarters could hardly be called plush. Once a well-known inn, Sleight's hotel was now a rickety three-storey pile of rotting lumber covered by peeling paint. To reach the slightly askew cupola, one had to climb a circular staircase no more than two feet wide, with steps that either slanted sideways or downhill. During the night and early morning, more than one workman not watching his feet carefully had slipped and plunged head over heels back to the third floor, cursing loudly every bump of the way. Nevertheless, the important fact was that the view from Sleight's was perfectly suited to the plan of Michael Chance's new boss—Waite Nicholson.

Through the telescope, Chance watched Philip Dwyer examine the fighting condition of his track policemen. The leader was Bill Boozey, a red-faced colorful figure well known in Brooklyn and New York as a former athlete and perennial charlatan. Once a long-distance pedestrian who took part in six-day events at Madison Square Garden and Central Park Garden, Boozey claimed he had jumped off the Brooklyn Bridge six months before Steve Brodie and Larry Donovan. Witnesses to the historic event were few, however, and shortly afterwards, Boozey formally announced his resignation from athletics in favor of becoming a track guard at Norris Park, then Gravesend. During the five-year interval, his weight zoomed, full cheeks became jowls, his thick neck was gradually enveloped by ridges of soft flesh around his collar. One moment volatile, the next pliant, Boozey was unsuited to the role of policeman. Chance was certain Waite Nicholson would have no trouble outwitting the likes of him.

On this beautiful day in May, Gravesend Race Track was in perfect condition. The infield was a green sea of heavy grass, crisscrossed by the tracks of numerous landaus and coaches parked haphazardly near the finish line. The dirt-and-cinder track, almost gray in color, had been made smooth by a team of rug boys, who even now created a swirl of dust as for the last time they circled the track near the stretch, their voices high and taunting as they raced for the finish line. One tall and gangly youth, baggy brown pants sagging almost to his hips, a red cap turned sideways on his head, led the pack, his rug flopping wildly behind him. As he loped ahead of the others, a low roar arose from the crowd, then broke into applause when the youth reached the imaginary line connecting the judges' booths. Grinning impishly, he doffed his cap, bent low, and drew a great half circle in front of him. By this time, the other boys had neared the line and one took the opportunity to push the winner from behind just as he was in midbow. The bow turned into a nosedive, then a chase. The crowd loved it. A few minutes later, when the heavy rugs had been cleared from the track, Gravesend seemed ready to have its portrait painted. By the end of the third race, the pounding horses would have churned the smooth surface into a rutty mess.

A normal young man, Chance focused the long marine telescope on one intriguing tallyho filled with a half-dozen attractive women. Each of the women had on a fancy shirtwaist with ruffled front reaching from a tight gathering at the neck to her waist and puffed sleeves tapering all the way to the wrists. Their upswept hair was topped by wide hats decorated with flowers and the bottoms of their skirts could be seen through the slots in the side of the four-in-hand coach. Like tourists on a rare outing, the women laughed, pointed, held on to their bonnets, and occasionally waved to someone. Their coach was greeted with averted heads whenever it neared a group of older, more "respectable" ladies. "Such a nice batch of soiled doves," Chance murmured. "I wonder what club they're from." Their presence, along with the heavy crowd, convinced him that today was indeed a special day at Gravesend.

From his perch, Chance could see excursion trains pulling into the modest station at Gravesend, a typical country town with dirt streets, swarms of chickens and goats, and no buildings worth mentioning. Waite himself arrived just before noon, accompanied by a half dozen toughs who carried boxes of equipment.

As one o'clock approached, Philip Dwyer paced his office of the Brooklyn Jockey Club, which was located below the grandstand of the track. At noon, he had ordered his men to physically cut all communication leading from the track except telephone lines to the newspapers and the one in his office.

"That ought to stop them," he thought, as he listened to the muffled rumble from the grandstand above him indicating good attendance. Drawn by news of the wire-cutting, many more persons than usual attended the thirteenth day of the fifteen-day meet. By 12:30, it was difficult to maneuver between the crowds of meandering men and women and even the track pool sellers, cool beneath their upraised umbrellas, began to complain. "Hey, Boozey," one of them called to the head of the track police. "How are people gonna place bets if everybody's jam-packed. We need a little organization."

"Sorry, mate," Boozey replied. "I got enough to worry about."

The first race went off at precisely one o'clock. Moments before, a barely suppressed howl of delight in Sleight's cupola had greeted the first transmission between the hotel and pool sellers' relay station set up at DeLacy's. Seated at the desk, Waite thought for a moment, smiled, then touched the keys.

At DeLacy's, Thomas Wynn smiled as he heard the happy clacking noise, made a notation, then read aloud: "The message is," he said, "what hath Dwyer wrought?"

A burst of laughter was followed by information on starting horses and the usual placing of bets.

"They're off," Waite shouted in the cupola as the horses broke from their starting positions. "It's Nelly Bly in the lead, then India Rubber, then Madstone."

Seated at the telegraph next to Waite, Michael Chance relayed the news to DeLacy's and the other pool sellers. Because it had to go through the Western Union station in the town of Gravesend, a delay of a minute or two was built into the system, but that was negligible. The crowd in DeLacy's, also larger than usual, applauded each transmission as if the news were being sent by trans-Atlantic cable.

"Old Dwyer must be chewin' his fist right up to his elbow," someone called out.

"We got 'em licked!" another added.

In the cupola, Waite Nicholson was less confident. Because the finish line was to their right and at a somewhat extreme angle, a close race might be hard to call.

Fortunately, Nelly Bly made a runaway of it, breaking across the finish line four lengths ahead of Madstone. By midafternoon, four races had been run and called with an amazing degree of accuracy. Rodney Roberts, at *The New York Times*, called Dwyer by telephone. "Philip," he said angrily, "this is terrible. My men at DeLacy's report only a few minutes' delay in those races. They've got quarter-post positions, just about everything. It's like they're in a private box at the track."

"Don't worry," Dwyer retorted. "I'll find out what's going on."

After hanging up, he turned to Bill Boozey. "What the hell's going on out there? Roberts says their information sounds like they got an observation booth someplace."

"I'll go look," Boozey muttered.

He was back after the fifth race. "Sleight's hotel," he said simply. "One of me boys saw a glint of light over there, so I sent Tony over. He said some toughs was guarding the back door and there was a telegraph wire coming out."

"We got enough men to kick them out of there?" Dwyer asked.

"No, Chief. We'd need an army."

"All right then. We'll fix them another way." Dwyer bounded to his feet. "Down in the cellar, there's an old tarpaulin that we used for covering the special guests' section. Have some of your men drag that up along with some big nails and a half dozen of those sixteen-foot poles."

"Yessir," Bill Boozey replied. He strode off smartly, wondering what the devil Dwyer wanted with a tarpaulin on a day as beautiful as this one.

Waite nodded slowly as he saw the six track policemen walk out next to the rail in front of the grandstand, place themselves at regular intervals, and each swing a long pole skyward. "They're going to block off the finish line," he said to Michael Chance, glad that he had spent the morning hastily rehearsing additional runners and signalers.

Now, as the sound of nails being driven into the wood echoed across the long, flat plain between the track and Sleight's hotel, Waite consulted a list and said: "Have Dougherty, Wilson, Schani, Perkins, Hildebrandt, and Blakesly go in and do as instructed." As an assistant stumbled downstairs with the message, Waite checked the six names off the list, then returned his attention to what was going on at the track. "Tell Wynn to pace himself so we have a minute or two to spare at the finish," he said to Chance. "We may need that time to go through another system."

At the track, following the sixth race, a large percentage of the nine thousand sightseers and bettors watched in puzzlement as six poles were nailed into place along the rail between the racing surface and grandstand. "What's that for?" some of them asked.

The track police did their best to avoid answering the question. Soon all twenty of them were involved, either trying to clear a path for the huge piece of canvas, help balance it, or assist the man on the ladder, who was driving nails into the tarpaulin and upraised poles as fast as he could.

In the meantime, the crowd slowly began to realize that their choice finish line positions were no longer choice, unless one happened to be a connoisseur of mildewed canvas. "Hey, what's going on here?" one man demanded, grabbing Bill Boozey by the arm.

Boozey pivoted to shake him off and in so doing bumped two of the ladder holders. The ladder skittered sideways as the man doing the nailing dropped everything to hold the top of the pole for dear life. A shower of nails, along with the metal can and hammer, spilled over the crowd below. As the police crew moved to avoid the falling objects, they let go of the canvas, which proceeded to run out its full length of nearly a hundred feet. Bugs, dead and alive, green mold, and rancid-smelling clumps of an unidentified brown substance fell over the audience. A horrified chorus went up from the ladies who suddenly found their choicest spring dresses adorned with a dead moth or an oozing chunk of oily dirt.

"This is outrageous!" a man cried out, thrusting his chin close to Boozey's.

"Tell it to the boss," Boozey replied, pointing to Dwyer.

"What are you going to do about this?" an irate woman demanded, thrusting her mossy bosom at Dwyer.

"I shall buy you a new one, madam," Dwyer replied shortly. "Send me a bill. Now if you will be so kind, we're trying to fight evil."

Despite the difficulties, three of the spans had been nailed into place by the end of the next-to-last race. "We're cut off from the finish line," Waite said evenly, trying to pick out his men inside the track through the spyglass. "We're going to have to rely on signals or runners to find out the order of finish."

"Wynn wants to know if there are any scratches for the last race," Chance said.

"I can't tell yet," Waite replied. "I haven't picked out Sahlman."

A minute later, however, he caught sight of his scratch man. He was standing slightly to the right of his predesignated position near the entrance to the paddock. Every minute or so, he performed a series of movements which might have seemed strange to Boozey's policemen had any been near him. First, he scratched his head very obviously, then put his left arm in a "one-o'clock" position, following it with his right arm straight out from his waist in the "nine-o'clock" position.

"Numbers one and nine have been scratched. That should be Headlight and Black Watch."

Chance relayed the information back to DeLacy's. A moment later, the horses broke from their starting positions and

Boozey's men stopped their hammering to watch the race. Blocked from seeing the finish, a substantial part of the crowd spilled out onto the track in an attempt to gain the infield before the end of the race. "Hey, you can't go on the track while the horses are on it!" Boozey cried out in vain.

"Try and stop me," one burly man said, shoving the police chief back into the tarpaulin.

His example spurred a small stampede of patrons across the track, then more and more. Seemingly oblivious to the horses' progress, dozens of men and women were still on the track as the horses reached the three-quarter mark and thundered toward the stretch.

"It's Hoodlum and Lavinia Belle neck and neck," Thomas Wynn called to anxious bettors at DeLacy's poolroom. "Now Blitzen is making a bid . . ."

"She's fallen! Look!"

One of Boozey's men pointed to a woman who had tripped and was lying in the dust between the judges' booths.

"Get her out of there!" Bill Boozey shrieked.

Even before Boozey spoke, another of his men leaped over the rail and raced to the woman's side. He grasped her by the arm, but she refused to budge, she was in such a state of shock.

"It's Lavinia Belle, Blitzen, and Hoodlum neck and neck and neck," Thomas Wynn cried in his best dramatic fashion. "The rest of the field is twenty lengths behind. It's—"

Unable to move the woman, the officer made a desperate choice. Withdrawing the revolver from his holster, he fired it above the heads of the three horses, which were coming directly at them. Once, twice, three times . . .

Terrified, Lavinia Belle was the first to rear. Then, with twin whinnies of high-pitched hysteria, Hoodlum and Blitzen shook off their jockeys and plunged back toward the rest of the field.

"It's—" Thomas Wynn cried, waiting for the keys to clack out the order of the dramatic finish.

When the rest of the field saw the three lead horses suddenly coming at them, panic spread. Two horses jumped the fence leading to the infield. Two leaped the opposite rail, scattering patrons lounging about the refreshment counters and restrooms. Only one horse which had been far behind continued loping in the direction of the finish line. By the time the lonesome horse and rider reached the line, the stricken woman had been removed to a point of safety.

"What's the number of that horse?" Waite called out, throwing his spyglass to his eye, searching desperately for a signaler inside the track.

"It's—" Thomas Wynn repeated. "The winner is—"

The clacking of keys caused him to exhale with great relief. When he finally spoke, his voice was so low, several bettors to the rear asked him to repeat the transmission.

"It's . . . Uncle Remus," Thomas Wynn said, his eyes slightly glazed. "Uncle Remus?" he repeated. "It can't be! Unless he was the only horse to finish."

Thus ended the first day at Gravesend without the Western Union wire at the track. Everyone, Philip Dwyer included, knew it had been a victory for the pool sellers.

"Goddamn them," Dwyer mumbled. "Well, that was today. Tomorrow will be different."

With the track near empty, Dwyer and Boozey took comfort in seeing that their finish-line screen was completed. Dwyer also made sure Boozey's men had roped off the section behind it to prevent patrons from crossing the track the next day.

When the work was completed, Bill Boozey exhaled mightily and said: "Now we can concentrate on finding out how they been signaling and stop them."

"You'd better," Dwyer muttered thickly.

In the cupola, Waite sighed. With the canvas running its full length, virtually all of the finish line and area leading up to it was blocked. He reviewed the situation in his mind. "We pick them up at the quarter post," he said, "and lose them at the half. The three quarters are good up to the stretch. Then we have to start guessing."

Day number two of the battle was as bright and clear as the first. With the finish line blocked from view, the track police, augmented by another dozen New York cops who wanted to earn some extra money on their day off, were able to keep their eyes on suspicious characters, and one of the first to go was scratch man Bruce Sahlman. During the interval between the third and fourth races, Sahlman had noticed the cop staring at him as he scratched his head for the fifth or sixth time, then stuck his arms out at points symbolizing time positions. Eventually the officer returned his gaze and held it. Sahlman realized it was terribly difficult to execute the movements while hostile eyes were on him, but he was determined to continue for as long as he could.

After a few moments, the officer strolled over to him and asked, "What are you doin'?"

"Lookin' at my watch," Sahlman replied, holding his arm at the eleven o'clock position.

"Ain't that kind of far away?" the officer said.

"I'm farsighted," Sahlman mumbled, sticking his left hand down at five o'clock.

"What you doin' with that hand?"

"Examinin' my fingernails, what do you think?" Sahlman replied.

"Well, you better come with me. You look suspicious."

With that, he grabbed the smaller man's arm and started to lead him out of the park.

"Looks like we've lost Sahlman," Waite murmured. "When he gets here, have him switch with Zachary as a runner. And don't let him forget to change jackets."

His assistant nodded.

The Gravesend crowd broke into cheers several minutes later as the fifth race neared its dramatic conclusion. Amid the frenetic movement of the infield, one man stood quietly, his hands folded perfectly still across his chest. At the conclusion of the race, he very deliberately placed the right hand on top of the left, raising and lowering it at irregular intervals.

A half-mile away, Chance recorded the code via telescope. "The winner is number six, St. Florian, then number four, Vivid . . . then . . ."

"There's one of them!" Bill Boozey yelled. With that, he swung his arm in a wide arc and three of his cohorts burst in the direction of the telegraph-code simulator. Like a man going down on a sinking ship, the man continued to transmit his message until he disappeared in a mass of arms and legs.

"I didn't get the last horse," Chance said. "Poor Harry."

"That means we'll have to wait for the runners," Waite said.

The long delay between winning entries was not appreciated at DeLacy's, but the grumbling subsided five minutes later when the complete order of finish was announced.

For the rest of the day, it was cat-and-mouse. Occasionally, Bill Boozey's men caught sight of a suspicious character and were able to run him down, but they seemed to be everywhere. "The trouble is," the perspiring Boozey said as they congregated in Dwyer's office after the final race, "we can't stop all them inside the track while they got so many runners goin' in and out at the same time."

"I agree," Dwyer said. "If they have runners who can leave

at any time, the worst that can happen to them is a five- or ten-minute delay. Starting tomorrow, the track gets locked after the first race. From that point on, everybody has to stay until the end."

"Right."

"Wrong," Pinky said, tossing the newspaper into a nearby trash basket.

The *Times*, with a large proportion of wishful-thinking, claimed the pool sellers were on the ropes, that chaos had resulted as a result of long delays in announcing results. It was only a matter of time, they said, before Mr. Dwyer won a complete and morally sanctioned victory over the forces of illegal betting.

"Wrong," Pinky repeated. "The boys at the track are going to have to do a lot better than that."

He stood up. There was work to do, an alleged adulteress to follow. But somehow that didn't appeal to him at the moment. "I think maybe I'll take the afternoon off," he said. "Maybe go down to Gravesend and bet on a horse or two."

Waite frowned as he saw the metal gate being swung into position. He had hoped Dwyer would not resort to this. Faced with the new dilemma, he nodded to a runner in the corner of the small room. "All right, give the signal. The track is locked. That means everybody inside has to start doing what we rehearsed so we can get the information. We'll start using all systems until they take them away from us. This is the last day. Let's hope we have enough for eight races."

"Right you are," the runner replied. With that, he clambered out the small window of the cupola, unfurled a huge red pennant, and swung it back and forth several times over his head. A cheer went up from the Gravesend crowd.

"I guess this means war, men," Bill Boozey said to his crew as they clamped the last gate lock into position.

Anticipating the lock-in, Waite had sent in a score of men and women whose sole duty was to stir up the anger of the crowd. When the gates banged shut, these workers swung quickly into action. "Hey, what's going on here?" they shouted, nudging other persons. "Do you see that? We're being locked in. Do they think we're convicts or something? This is a free country! Open those gates!"

Before long, nearly a hundred persons had collected at the main gate, screaming and harassing the guards, pressing against the fence.

"Hey, get away from there!" the guards shouted, pulling their clubs and brandishing them in the air.

"You can't lock us in here. Open that gate!"

At the end of the second race, the size of the crowd dramatically increased. "Watch out for runners," Bill Boozey cautioned his men. "Remember, nobody gets out."

"I want my mommy!" a child suddenly cried.

"We don't know where your mommy is, now go away!" Boozey replied.

"She's out there!" the child shrieked, pointing to a woman outside the track.

"Sorry, young fella."

The child broke into a terrifying wail that attracted even more people. "Sounds like they're beatin' the kid," one of Waite's men said provocatively.

"Mommy! Mommy!"

The heart-rending cry continued for nearly five minutes until Bill Boozey could stand it no longer. "Let the goddamn kid out,'' he whispered to one of his subordinates. "That noise is drivin' me crazy.''

The officer opened the gate far enough to allow the child out. With a smile of triumph, the boy promptly raced right past the woman who was supposed to be his mother and handed a scrap of paper to a man outside the track.

"The little bastard," Bill Boozey muttered. "He had the names of the winnin' horses!''

With an angry motion, he gave the gate a violent swing, striking a heavily bustled woman amidships and sending her thrashing to the ground. A man tripped over her boot and fell on top of her. The woman struck back with her parasol, flailing the helpless man about the head and shoulders. Even greater numbers of people pressed in to get a view of what was going on. "Nobody gets out!" Bill Boozey shouted. "Nobody gets out!''

The gate was pushed shut and locked. As the lock clicked shut, laughter broke out in the front ranks, then spread to the rest of the crowd that could see what had happened. In closing, the lower bar of the gate had swung shut on the man and woman, trapping them with their feet inside the park and the remainder of them outside. The lady's boots, kicking fiercely, pointed toward the sky; those of the man pointed downward.

"I now pronounce you man and wife," someone said in an embarrassingly audible voice.

"Get me out of here!" the woman screamed. "I'm going to sue you people for every cent you've got!''

"Unlock the goddamn gate!" Bill Boozey hissed.

Dwyer came charging through the crowd. "What's going on?'' he demanded.

"We're just trying to keep the runners inside," Boozey explained. "Like you said.''

"Like that?" Dwyer said angrily. "You're an idiot, Boozey. Unlock this gate immediately.''

"I can't find the key. I gave it to Jacobson."

"You did not," countered a thin-faced fellow. "You didn't give me no key, Bill Boozey."

"I'm going to sue!" the woman shrieked.

"Get this gate open, Boozey," Dwyer ordered, "if you have to pry it open!"

"I'll get a crowbar," Bill said, hurriedly pushing his way through the crowd.

By the time the gate was opened and the incident smoothed over, the third race was about to begin. During the chaotic hour, Dwyer had nearly forgotten the purpose behind his locking the gates, but he was reminded by the *Times* reporter. "They got the second race results all right," he said. "Six minutes delay, sir."

"Boozey, they're getting more than just the finish. Now you find out how they're getting the information and put a stop to it!" Dwyer thundered.

"Yessir."

As soon as Dwyer walked away, Boozey gathered his men around him. "This is it, boys," he said. "We got to arrest everybody who looks even a little suspicious, get me? Now I got me own eye on some fellas with striped canes. I'll take care of them. You take care of the rest."

Boozey's men fanned out and proceeded to take care of a large number of customers. Some were Waite's men, the majority of whom were flashing obvious signals that really didn't mean anything. Also included was a millionaire from Albany with a nervous tic, a man with a perspiration problem who kept mopping his face with a handkerchief, and two small girls improvising a game of hopscotch while their mother went for refreshments.

Bill Boozey had spotted the striped cane men during the first race and had determined to watch them carefully. That resolve had been postponed by the fiasco at the fence, but now he returned to his mission. He wasn't sure how the scheme worked, but the striped canes made him nervous.

The *modus operandi* of the Cane Gang, as they called themselves, was simple, devious, and effective. Each member of Waite's crew had a striped cane and a certain spot inside the park. The spot stood for each horse position—first, second, third, fourth, et cetera, at the finish. The man standing on each spot held his cane in such a way as to indicate a predetermined post position. Thus, the cane on the ground against the right side indicated number one, on the ground against the left side number two, on the right arm in the air number three, on the left arm in the air number four, and so forth. The beauty of the scheme was that no one man has to stand in the same general area for any length of time. Instead, the Cane Gang members meandered around between races, only taking their positions at the last moment.

As the horses broke from their starting positions for the third race, Boozey saw one of the Cane Gang members wander over toward the rail, then start back to a point right at the intersection of the grandstand and refreshment booth. Although he wasn't exactly sure, it occurred to Boozey that during the first race, he had seen another striped cane carrier at the same spot.

As the horses neared the finish line, Boozey strolled over to the tall man and took him by the elbow. "Come along with me, fella," he ordered.

"What for?" the man demanded. "What's the charge?"

"Carryin' a striped cane," Boozey replied.

"They're coming down the stretch now," Thomas Wynn called. "It's Merry Monarch, Rambler second, then Frontenac . . . but here comes Charley Post on the outside . . . Arnica, too. . . . This is going to be a close one. . . . There are five horses coming right down to the line. . . . Here they come. . . . It's . . . Charley Post first. . . . What a stretch run! . . . Frontenac third . . . Merry Monarch fourth . . ."

A puzzled pause settled over the poolroom. Finally somebody asked, "What about second?"

"What?" said Thomas Wynn.

"You didn't say which horse came in second."

"Yeah. I'll check that."

He sent a message back to the cupola.

A long pause followed.

"What can I tell them?" Michael Chance asked. "We can't say our second-place horse was arrested."

Waite thought for a moment. "Just tell them there will be a short delay on the second spot. We'll have to wait for the back-up information from our ball men." Nodding to the man with the flags, he said, "Give the ball signal."

Climbing out the window, the man waved a blue flag violently back and forth.

Less than a minute later, a dozen bright blue balls sailed over various parts of the park fence, landing on the roadway outside. "What the hell's that?" Bill Boozey yelled and, with a dozen of his men in tow, he unlocked the side wall gate and went racing off in the direction of the nearest ball.

Boozey picked it up and noticed a rough seam dividing it in half. When the two hollow hemispheres were pried apart, a note tucked inside floated to the ground. On it was written "Charley Post, Arnica, Frontenac, Merry Monarch."

"Damn," Boozey muttered. Turning to his nearest man, he asked, "Did any of these get into their hands?"

"I think so, sir. Up at the north end."

"All right," Boozey said. "They won't get away with that again. Lem, you take ten men and start patrolin' the road as soon as the next race ends. I don't want to see even one of them balls caught by them Ditmas Company boys."

The fourth race at Gravesend was almost totally ignored by much of the crowd at the park, particularly those with seats at the rear of the grandstand, for the toughs were back even before the horses started running. Standing just out of reach of Boozey's park police, they taunted the patrolmen and occasionally made feints toward the wall. Then, shortly after the race ended, a dozen persons inside the park tossed more blue balls over the fence.

"Get 'em, men!" Bill Boozey shouted. "Get them balls!"

Racing toward the floating objects, the young men outside the park tried to ward off police billy clubs with one hand and grab a ball with the other. There were several collisions involving not only cops and toughs but several pedestrians.

One resourceful guard, seeing he would not be able to catch the ball that was sailing over his head, leaped up and wielding his club like a baseball bat, swung it in a hard overhand chop. Connecting solidly, he smiled as the ball sailed back over the fence into the park.

"Home run!" the crowd cheered.

Bill Boozey stood in the midst of the collapsed and reeling bodies and made a quick survey. "We did it, men!" he exulted. "We got their balls, every damn one!"

It was true, but Waite Nicholson was not perturbed. "Well, that's one for their side," he said. "I guess we'll go with the Jackson Racers from now on."

Fred Jackson was captain of the Columbia football squad, and his racers were nine other young athletes, each dressed in Columbia sweaters but with a different-colored cap or derby. Scorning the shade of the grandstand's overhanging roof, the team gathered at the south side of the track, halfway down the homestretch, ostensibly to get a better view of the race.

As the race began, shrewd observers noted that the Columbia boys leaned against the railing in a very steady position, then milled around after the horses broke. A few moments later, as the horses rounded the first turn, the men would return to the railing, but in different positions. Like flies shooed away from a piece of food, they eventually broke up several more times but always returned to the rail. During the stretch run, four or five of them would walk quickly in the same direction as the horses, their arms waving as if rooting their favorites home. As they did this, they often drew abreast of each other, pulled ahead, or fell back, all very casually, of course.

As information continued to flow to the pool sellers, despite numerous arrests, Philip Dwyer raged. "They're making a fool out of me, Boozey, and I won't stand for it. You find out what's going on here or you're fired!"

"Yessir," Bill Boozey said as confidently as he could. Privately, though, he just could not fathom it, for no one seemed to be making signals.

During the next race, Boozey descended from the grandstand to the area next to the rail. There, he listened to the crowd, hoping for a clue. Recently, he had struggled through a novel about a new British detective named Holmes who claimed that "you see and hear but do not observe." Boozey looked and listened fiercely, as if by force of will he could discover what was happening. But the crowd seemed interested only in the race.

"Go, Hellgate!" one bettor cried.

"Go, white cap!" another returned.

"Run, Annie Queen!"

"Get a move on, black derby!"

"Go, blue hat!"

Bill Boozey was puzzled about one thing. Signaling to one of his men with a program, he asked, "Is there a horse named

white cap or blue hat or black derby in this race? Seems to me
there's an awful lot of headgear."

"No sir," replied the man, looking at the program. "What
do you make of it, Chief?"

Bill Boozey frowned. "I ain't got the faintest notion," he
said.

Moments after the end of the race, an anonymous note was
handed to Philip Dwyer. It read: "If you spent fifteen minutes
in the grandstand listening to your patrons instead of looking for
obvious signals, you would find that a lot of people are betting
on the positions of the Columbia boys along the rail. Maybe
some of them don't know why they're betting on them, but you
should."

Dwyer's face glowed with triumph. "Yes, of course, that's
it." He murmured.

Two minutes later, when he told Bill Boozey the solution to
the mystery, the fat man's face broke into a huge grin. "Sure,"
he said. "That's just what I was thinkin' about them fellas.
Let's go bust 'em up."

"No," Dwyer smiled. "Not so fast."

"You mean you don't want us to bust 'em up?" Boozey
mumbled.

"No. We'll join them," Dwyer replied.

When the telephone at *The New York Times* rang, it was picked
up by editor Rodney Roberts himself. "Hello," he said. "This
is Roberts."

"This is Dwyer," said the voice at the other end. "We've
broken their code!"

"Finally? Good, I'll start writing the story myself."

"No. Here's an even better story. We're going to use their code to make the worst horse in the race win."

"How can you do that?"

"Never mind the particulars. I don't have much time to talk. They have men along the rail standing for different horses. What we're going to do is substitute one of our men for theirs at the last minute."

"I get it. The pool sellers will then pay off on the wrong horse."

"Right. On Snowball at 200 to 1."

"Excellent!"

"Now wait. Don't hang up. Here's something else. I want you to arrange to make a thousand-dollar bet on Snowball for me. I'll have a messenger drop the money off at your office and you have some of your men spread it out at a bunch of the pool sellers, but put the biggest chunk at DeLacy's, say two hundred."

"Phil, I wouldn't advise that. If people found out you made a killing on—"

"No, this isn't for me. The winnings will be donated to charity, maybe even to ASS. It's to make sure the pool sellers lose a bundle."

"I see. Yes, that's an excellent idea. We'll get an extra out right away!"

During the seventh race, Bill Boozey's men had prepared carefully. Watching from the vantage point of the former Ditmas Company telegraph office, they made notes of the movements of Jackson's Racers and broke the code. Green cap, they discovered, stood for the number one post position, red derby was number two, and so on down the line. After checking and rechecking, they knew that black derby would represent the number seven post position in the last race. And the seventh horse in the last race was Snowball, a 200-to-1 shot.

"O.K., men," Bill Boozey said, following Dwyer's instructions to the letter. "Everybody goes out separately and remember, don't make a move until the stretch."

Ten minutes later, as the horses broke from the starting line, a dozen of Boozey's men, dressed in civilian clothes, meandered in the direction of the backstretch. One, an athletically built and youthful appearing fellow named Harvey Kittering, wore a Columbia sweater under his coat and carried a black derby in his hand.

"They're off," Thomas Wynn shouted back at DeLacy's. "It's Authority first, then Billings Boy, followed by Puritan . . ."

There was evident relief in his tone. After this last big race, he thought happily, there would be no more calls from Gravesend until fall. There had been a modicum of pleasure in outwitting Dwyer and his park police, to be sure, but Wynn had to admit that he preferred the old days, without the long delays and worry about mistakes. ". . . and Snowball bringing up the rear," he concluded.

Bill Boozey gestured to Kittering. "You just stand around in back of me and Jacobson, see? And when they get in the stretch, be ready to leap in that fella's place when we pull him out. Chances are he'll be on the end of the line so they won't notice him so much. Now you'll start edging up as they go down the stretch. Don't make your move too quick." As he talked, Boozey accentuated his words with quick, jerky movements, almost like a trainer instructing a jockey. "Then, at the last second," he added, "you'll swoop in front, the rest of me boys will move in to break up the group, and the pool sellers will think they got the winners just in the nick of time."

"It's Marmaduke battling for the lead, along with Puritan

and Billings Boy . . ." Thomas Wynn called out. "The rest of the field is far behind . . . Snowball last."

The Jackson Racers casually separated themselves into two groups. To the north side of the track, along the rail, stood Fred Jackson, wearing a green cap as Puritan, Paul Stedman, wearing a red derby as Marmaduke, and Evan Whyte, his blue cap standing for Billings Boy. To their left, standing and talking, was the second group of young men, with black-derbied Stephen Shreve to the far left as Snowball.

"They seem to be a lot of other people down there," Chance, peering through his telescope, murmured to himself in the cupola. "But they're not in the way, so I guess it's all right."

"It's Marmaduke . . . Billings Boy . . . and Puritan as they enter the stretch," Thomas Wynn intoned. "It's going to be a good three-horse finish. . . . The rest of the field is out of it. In fourth is Hourglass, fifth is Williamsport . . . then Authority . . . Montana Maid . . . and Snowball . . ."

The Gravesend crowd began to jump and cheer as the horses pounded down the stretch and the trio of young men in the red derby, blue and green caps pushed each other good-naturedly along the grandstand railing.

Stephen Shreve had just taken a slow step forward when he felt hands close around his mouth and throat. He had no time to issue the slightest cry of warning. In a second, Boozey's man, Harvey Kittering, coat off and derby on, had replaced him along the rail. It had been done so quickly and efficiently that the other members of the Jackson Racers saw and suspected nothing.

"Go, Kittering!" Boozey cried out. "Start your move now."

During the race, Michael Chance seldom took his telescope away from the Jackson Racers, but on this occasion, he temporarily had lost sight of the entire group as several spectators surged forward. He soon had the team back in view, however, and what he saw was truly amazing. Jostling first one, then another team member aside was . . . Chance consulted his notes . . . Snowball . . . black derby? . . . He checked again . . . That was correct . . . "Snowball is making a great stretch run!" he cried out.

At DeLacy's, Thomas Wynn repeated the information to a chorus of cheers. Whenever a nag left the starting line at 200 to 1, there would always be some suckers who put money on his nose. This last race of the meet was no exception. In fact, there had been a last-minute run on Snowball which Wynn figured was a result of all the big losers taking a last shot at breaking even. "Good money after bad," Wynn had said before the race. But now he was worried. Snowball? It was impossible!

The wire ticked out more information.

Automatically, Wynn translated the signal and found himself saying in a voice slightly high-pitched with incredulity, "Snowball is first as they near the finish line!" In all his years of calling races, he had truly never experienced such an unbelievable occurrence. "Good Lord, Snowball," he thought, a shiver running down his spine. "This could wipe us out."

As Harvey Kittering shoved Fred Jackson aside, the young Columbia team captain reacted quickly. "Hey, you're not supposed—you're not Steve . . ." With a lurch, he grabbed Kittering and tried to spin him around.

"It's Snowball and Puritan," Waite shouted, suddenly confused. "They're fighting . . . Jesus! They disappeared!"

"What do you mean, disappeared?" Michael Chance asked.

"They've run out of sight down in front of the grandstand," Waite said. "Hold on!"

Although the actual race of horses was well over, the crowd was still cheering. When Harvey Kittering started to make his move, the cheering swelled to a crescendo. When he and the other three leaders began struggling for first place, howls of delight washed over the park. When Kittering broke away toward the grandstand, followed by the others, then by a group of men in plainclothes and finally by what seemed to be the remainder of the entire uniformed park police crew, Gravesend seemed about to explode with cheers and laughter.

"Get 'em, boys," Bill Boozey wheezed. "Knock down the rest so Harvey can—so Harvey can—"

They knew what he meant. Soon every guard in the park joined in the chase.

The crowd roared its delight.

"Go, black derby!"

"Nab him, green cap!"

As they ran, Fred Jackson called instructions over his shoulder. "Listen, I'm first, then Paul, then Ev . . . the rest of you hold this faker until we can get back to the finish line!" He had grabbed Harvey Kittering by the shoulders, spun him around with one hand, and knocked the black derby from his head with the other.

"There will be a short wait," Thomas Wynn reported to the assemblage at DeLacy's. "The final result should be coming down any minute now."

As Harvey Kittering reached down to pick up the derby, two members of the Columbia team sailed into him, knocking him ten feet away. Rolling over and over, he saw four uniformed guards reach for the young men. "Don't worry about them!" Kittering shouted. "Get them three!" He pointed to the three men who represented the first horses across the line.

"This way," Fred Jackson cried, starting to run back toward the finish line to where they could be observed by their compatriots in the cupola. Their lithe legs churning, the trio of young men quickly evaded the guards in their immediate vicinity and sprinted toward the south end of the track. In their path stood Bill Boozey and a half-dozen men, their arms hanging low, their bodies balanced on tiptoe in anticipation of the coming collision. Sensing the moment of impact, the Gravesend crowd shouted like fans at the Yale-Columbia football game. "Touchdown! Block them! Go, team!"

One hand pushing his cap lower on his forehead so it would not be lost, the other urging his comrades on, Fred Jackson ran directly toward Bill Boozey. As the two men approached each other, Jackson made a quick move toward his left as if to evade the larger Boozey, then pivoted on his right toe and rushed directly at him. Caught in midstride, Boozey tried to bend back and block Jackson with his arms, but his body kept going in the direction of the fake. Flailing wildly, Boozey fell on his back with a heavy thud. Paul Stedman and Evan Whyte raced in stutterstep tandem toward the guards trying to push them into a human pocket. For a moment, the strategy seemed about to succeed, then the two young men crisscrossed paths and burst miraculously through the wall of policemen, who promptly piled into each other.

Looking over his shoulder, Fred Jackson smiled as he saw the two men break free, then he let out a little yell. Paul Stedman's red derby had come loose and fallen into the pack of milling guards. For a moment, Stedman hesitated, his hand reaching toward his bare head.

As the three men ran in order toward the open space south of the grandstand, Fred Jackson looked around. Already the police had regrouped and were weaving toward them, but when he spotted a lady wearing a red hat, Fred decided to make a detour. Calling, "Wait!" to his running mates, he suddenly swerved toward the grandstand, snatched the hat from the woman's head, and tossed it to Stedman.

"There they are!" Chance shouted in the cupola. "Green, red, and blue!"

He looked down at the note pad.

Reaching the open spot, the three young men had a brief moment of glory as they bounded into the correct finishing positions, gave a little hop in place, and bowed. A roar of laughter greeted Paul Stedman when he doffed the lady's hat, brought the veil down over his eyes, and twisted his legs and arms into a caricature of a typical matronly position.

Two seconds later, Bill Boozey and his men thundered down on the group, pummeling and shoving the young men to the ground. Gravesend Park swelled with angry boos and catcalls.

"It's official now," Thomas Wynn called out. "The American Stakes has been run. The winner is Puritan, then Marmaduke, and third, Billings Boy . . ."

Waite Nicholson leaned back against the wall of the cupola, exhaled loudly, and took Michael Chance's outstretched hand in his own. "I think," he said, "we could use a nice long drink. What do you say to that?"

"I say, you're fired!" Philip Dwyer shouted over his shoulder, leaving Bill Boozey standing crestfallen in the door of the Brooklyn Jockey Club.

"But why, Chief?" Boozey called back. "Didn't I do a good job?"

The other New York newspapers openly reveled in the "defeat" of *The New York Times.*

Roger Mellon read the *World* editorial with great flowing style. "The forces of hypocrisy have been vanquished by brilliance and cleverness," he said grandly. "Perhaps they assumed that God was on their side merely because they preached with deific arrogance. If so, they erred. We have the distinct feeling that, the Ives Law notwithstanding, the pool sellers and angels were on the same side . . ."

A chorus of cheers greeted his low bow, and the level of liquid in Peter DeLacy's punchbowl descended. A moment later, the tinkling of metal against glass brought the milling crowd of pool sellers, young collegiates, toughs, painted ladies, and average working types to a respectful quiet.

Peter DeLacy stepped onto a chair, smiled at the sea of smiling faces, cleared his throat, and said: "This wasn't meant to be a victory party. I would guess some of you feel differently, but I sincerely believe there can't be a victory in a situation like this. I did want to get all of you together and thank you for the fine job you did. I know you were well paid for your work, but it wasn't easy, going out there knowing that any minute one of Bill Boozey's cops might take a punch at you. That took grit, and you proved you've got it. You helped us prove a point—that it's a whole lot better to use your head when you have a problem than trying to win your point with brute force. You proved we can't be pushed around. Now, this summer I'd like to see all of us—Mr. Humstone of the Ditmas Company . . ." [pause for cheers]" . . . and Mr. Dwyer of the track . . ." [pause for hisses]". . . get together and agree on a mutually acceptable solution for the fall meet. Thank you."

The crowd lavished its applause on Peter DeLacy.

"Your father is a very fine speaker," Waite said to Dottie. They were standing on the edge of the group, each holding a cup of punch in a somewhat formal, uneasy manner.

"Yes, he is," Dottie said. "One always knows which side Daddy's on. Sometimes that's a dreadful handicap."

"Sometimes you can learn things by confusing people about which side you're on," Waite countered.

"And sometimes you can get ahead by confusing people about which side you're on," Dottie smiled.

He raised his glass, sipped from it. She let him drink alone.

At the same time, several miles north, another party was in progress at the home of Philip Dwyer. The conversation was spirited, but more subdued than at DeLacy's as reformers, newspaper writers, and wealthy New Yorkers discussed the events of the past week.

Philip Dwyer himself was watched carefully by everyone. Those who supposed the fiery Irishman would be crestfallen were disappointed, for he carried himself with his old determination, speaking with a voice of conviction that rose high above the muffled tones of the others. Finally, by rapping his teacup with a spoon, he silenced the crowd.

"If you don't mind," he began, "I'd like to say a few words. First of all, I'd like to apologize to Mrs. Ironsides and her ladies, Mr. Roberts of the *Times*, and everyone else, for letting them down after all their good work. When I make mistakes, I'm the first to admit it, and right now I'd like to admit that my handling of things at the park wasn't the best. Bill Boozey is a good guard, but not a sharp thinker, and I wasn't so sharp in expecting him to do the job he was handed. I guess we learned one thing, though. And that is, we're dealing with hardened forces of evil. Why, anybody who would use college boys, women, and children to attain their ends is beneath contempt. But if they think I'm about to quit or compromise even a little bit, they're mistaken." [Pause for cheers.] "I'm going to beat the Ditmas Company. We're all going to beat the immoral, greedy Ditmas Company, led by the deceitful Mr. Humstone." [Pause for hisses.] "Now, I'm going to tell you about the first step. I've replaced Bill Boozey and his crew with people who know how to deal with hardened criminals. I went right to the top, to the Pinkerton National Detective Agency, which recently opened an office here in New York. And, strangely enough, Mr. Robert Pinkerton, after agreeing to take the job, told me he was the one who sent me the note explaining how those college boys were lining up in the horses' places. Of course, the end result of our finding that out didn't turn out so well, but I think it would have been different if we had been able to avail ourselves of Mr. Pinkerton's services right from the beginning. So now, without further ado . . ."

"Without further ado," W. C. Humstone said, "I should like to introduce the young man who, as a result of his ingenuity, energy, and decisiveness, has now earned the right to be called Supervising Chief of All Special Projects for the Ditmas Company . . . Mr. Waite Nicholson."

". . . who will lead us to victory over the forces of gambling and crime because he has the nerve, brains, and experience to deal with master criminals . . . Mr. Robert 'Pinky' Pinkerton."

SUMMER

6

"If you mention that one more time, I'll take after you with my razor strap"

Some called the resort town in the southern foothills of the Adirondacks merely a diversion. Others of the early 1890s, many of them prominent New Yorkers or wealthy Americans from even greater distances, described Saratoga as a spot so delightfully dedicated to pleasant living that it was thought about all year during those dreary days of one's non-Saratoga existence.

A century before, someone had decided that the saline waters of Saratoga, bursting gloriously from underground streams in geysers, possessed healthful qualities. Because the water tasted so undeniably terrible, reeking of iron and other minerals and unidentified gases, no one disputed the fact that it must be medicine of some sort. Eventually an enterprising gentleman even bottled and sold the vile fluid, another man constructed a railroad to the town, and Saratoga was well on its way to becoming the summertime Athens of America. Except for a brief period when reform forces denied the town gambling facilities—a development which threatened to turn the resort into a ghost town but which was quickly reversed by community-spirited leaders—progress had been steady. By 1890, even longtime advocates of Newport, bored by the seaside, were switching to Saratoga as the site of their extended summer vacation.

Attractions in the town, at least during the season, belied its small size. There was, first of all, the natural coolness of upstate New York, abetted by the breeze off Saratoga Lake, perfect antidotes for the steaming sidewalks and manure-smelling streets of Manhattan.

The mineral spring bathing establishments which abounded added a dash of vibrant health to Saratoga's already-pleasant atmosphere. (In fact, one wondered how a person ever died in that salubrious climate—perhaps only through sheer carelessness.) On Philadelphia Street near Broadway that summer of 1891 there opened for business the newest and largest bathing establishment ever built, promising new vitality via "pneumatic rooms," "cow and great milk whey cures," "inhalations," "electricity," and, naturally, exposure to the mineral baths, both internally and externally.

Everyone, of course, sampled the water at least once during the summer—usually on the first day there. This was done by the simple process of visiting one of the many spring buildings scattered throughout and around the town. They were easily identified by their peaked roofs from the top of which flew gigantic flags advertising the particular spring's name— Hathorn, Saratoga Star, Triton, Congress. Inside, past the tables and wicker chairs which filled the barren floor area, was the inevitable rectangular opening, rather like a grave for some huge beast, its sides lined with wood paneling, three or four steps leading down to a lower level of planking. Here, through a series of small openings (square wooden holes cut in the ice), water boys dipped long poles at the ends of which were fixed pieces of wire capable of holding a trio of glasses. Receiving the mineral water, in such a templelike spot and under such mysterious conditions, made an otherwise simple act into a sort of ritual, imbuing the liquid with qualities that if not actually religious were at least cathartic.

On the way to the spring buildings—in fact, on the way to nearly everywhere—one could enjoy the endless music of Saratoga. It began in June when each large hotel's private orchestra arrived for the season. Once started, the musicians seemed to play twenty-four hours a day . . . Lothian's Orchestra at the Grand Union, Stubb's at the United States, Joyce at Congress Hall, the Beacon Lady Orchestra of Boston at the Hotel Balmoral. Walking down Broadway, one often heard the sounds overlap, polkas, marches, quicksteps, graceful waltzes in a variety of arrangements. True, the music was not always as idyllically innocent or uplifting as it might have been, especially when crass songwriters insisted on teasing the public with lyrics that were not only trivial but often went beyond the bounds of normal decency.

> "As we journey all along,
> Thro' life's own busy throng,
> We often meet a maiden gay,
> Who to you'll say,
> Kutch-y, kutch-y, kutch-y, coo!
> Lov-ey me, I lov-ey 'oo!
> Does 'oo lov-ey, lov-ey me,
> As I lov-ey, lov-ey 'ee?
> Kutchy coo! (kiss-kiss), Kutchy coo! (kiss-kiss), Kutchy
> coo!"

Undeniably, Saratoga during the summertime was *the* place for lovers. No one dared try to stop this manifestation of human nature, for it was everywhere, brazen, oblivious to the barely suppressed scorn of older generations. The geography of the region seemed designed for lovers. Large trees, sculptured boxwood, mazes of hedging—the very things giving the town its semirustic charm for weary New Yorkers—were also parapets sheltering the ever-present clinging pair during or immediately following the nightly hops at some hotel or other. Thus, short of reducing the resort into a horizontal wasteland, one could not prevent their hasty meetings. Better to merely hope that good sense, fear of being caught, or the staunch eccentricities of 1890 clothing would allow virtue to emerge triumphant.

Besides deploring the morals of the younger generation, there was much to absorb the interest of the older—that is, married—clientele at Saratoga. The resort was, after all, one of the finest places in the entire East for observing the rich, near-rich, famous, and infamous. Everyone, it seemed, came to Saratoga some time during the summer. The season of 1891 was graced with millionaires such as Jay Gould, the financial wizard whose attempt to corner the gold market had caused a nation-wide panic twenty years before. Now he was not only forgiven but revered. Joining him on the Millionaires' Piazza of the monstrous, quarter-mile long slab of columns and verandas known as the United States Hotel were newcomers John D. Rockefeller and Alexander Graham Bell. The resort that summer also was visited by noted suffragette Susan B. Anthony, Mrs. U. S. Grant, widow of the late president (whose terrible administration, nearly everyone agreed, had not been his fault), President Benjamin Harrison, the current vice-president Levi Morton, and Arthur P. Gorman, the stalwart, gray-haired senator from Maryland who, it was rumored, would shortly be the next president if all went well for him.

In the midst of such sophisticated and intellectual company, quite naturally, brilliant conversation ensued, often miniature debates on burning issues of the day. Was, for instance, the new sport of lawn tennis moral? Would the proposed canal through Nicaragua ever be built? Was Mr. Elliott Roosevelt's so-called illness the result of a mental breakdown or, as some hinted, due to the consequences of strong drink? Would the experiment of mounting soldiers on bicycles really work during genuine battle conditions? Wasn't it terrible that the new tunnel under the Hudson River already had cracks in the roof? Wasn't it even worse how one could go to Sioux City in the infant state of South Dakota and obtain a divorce within three months? What do you think of the Grand Union Hotel's using white boys as waiters instead of coloreds for the first time? Are you in favor of the new six o'clock dinner hour?

Any serious reflections on these pressing problems were probably drowned in the sound of clattering hooves, for Saratoga during the summertime was a showplace for some of the finest horseflesh and horse-drawn vehicles in America. Along Broadway's triple width of dirt road, flanked by giant elms in rows, an endless stream of vehicles moved . . . surreys with fringes round the tops; slender buckboards drawn by long-tailed Morgans; basket phaetons pulled by bobtailed hackneys; heavy victorias with their elegantly heavy ladies; high dogcarts; impudent sulkies using their smaller size and greater mobility to weave a path through the slower vehicles. Here and there a true celebrity could be spotted, such as Miss Nolan, daughter of ex-Mayor Nolan of Albany, showing off her brand new 1891 equipage with its thousand-dollar English patent-leather harness with hand-creased loops. Behind her appeared Colonel Albert B. Hilton, perched on his lofty seat, bandying ribbons over a splendid four-in-hand of bay leaders and black wheelers, rolling along Broadway with a liveried bugler walking the echoes. As the beautiful vehicle paused in front of the hotel, grooms instantly rushed to the foam-flecked heads of the leaders, steadying them as the colonel's trio of handsome ladies, veils swathed about their enormous hats, were lifted down from their exalted seats.

Yes, it was correctly said, Saratoga had everything. It was precisely because Saratoga had so many attractions, because it projected such an aura of fun and opulence that W. C. Humstone objected to Waite Nicholson's going there.

"But Philip Dwyer is at Saratoga for the summer," Waite replied evenly. "If we're going to settle things before the fall meet, someone has to talk with him or at least arrange a meeting."

"Nevertheless," Humstone returned archly, "Saratoga is too far away. And it's a pleasure resort. You're supposed to be working. You can't work in a carnival atmosphere."

"Contortionists do," Waite replied, unable to resist drawing a smile from Peter DeLacy, who was trying to relax on the uncomfortable sofa in Humstone's office.

"Nevertheless—" Humstone continued.

"Sir," Waite interrupted gently. "May I suggest that *you* go to Saratoga and speak with Mr. Dwyer?"

"I?"

"Yessir. I really think someone should discuss the situation with him now that he's more relaxed."

"The boy's right," Peter DeLacy said. "Why don't you go, Warren?"

"You know perfectly well I'm tied up with work here at the office," Humstone shot back.

"Then send Nicholson here," DeLacy urged. "That's what we promoted him for, isn't it?"

"Not to cavort in resorts."

"I won't cavort," Waite smiled. "At least not noticeably."

"Listen," DeLacy said. "If you have to cavort, cavort. Do whatever you have to. Dwyer's hired Pinkerton from out West and the going may not be so easy from now on. I say let's get the problem settled this summer. If it's money that's worrying you," he added, looking at Humstone, "I'm sure the pool sellers will add a few dollars to back the expedition."

"It's going to take more than a few dollars, with him staying at the Congress or United States and visiting the casino every night," Humstone muttered. But in the end he agreed to send Waite on the peace-making journey.

Waite planned his trip so that he would arrive in time for the first day of Saratoga Race Track's gala summer meet. Philip Dwyer, he knew, had several of his own horses entered in races, and the track would be the logical spot to "bump into" the gentleman and perhaps start a meaningful discussion.

He was fortunate in one respect. Dwyer, who might have taken after his younger adversary with a stick under normal circumstances, found himself the owner of two winning horses by the time the meet was four races old. And, except for a last-second spurt in the first race by Schuykill Stable's La Tosca, which carried the filly past Dwyer's Bolero by a head, he might have had a trio of winners and a perfect afternoon.

Waite had spotted Dwyer in the owner's box even before the day's activities began. Yet he deliberately stayed away from him until the first race was run, the better to gauge Dwyer's disposition. When Bolero lost by such a miniscule distance, Waite took it as a bad omen. The very next race, however, went to Dwyer's Eon, and then, following the running of the celebrated Travers Stakes, Dwyer's two-year-old Zorling ran neck-and-neck with Bengal before breaking ahead to win by two lengths. His face creased in a happy smile, Dwyer turned his eyes from the winner's circle and looked directly at Waite Nicholson.

"Congratulations, sir," Waite said warmly.

Dwyer's smile ran down the side of his face. For a long moment, his lips formed themselves into a tighter and tighter circle of purplish flesh, as if he were about to spit. Then, without a word, he walked past the young man in the direction of the clubhouse.

Waite was jostled out of his shocked state by the sound of laughter. It was not the derisive peal of someone intent on inflicting embarrassment, but the kind of involuntary laugh that seemingly squeezes through the tightest-set jaw and mouth.

"I'm sorry," Mary Dwyer said. "It's just that you look so funny, like someone's kicked you."

Waite shrugged, tried to hide his disappointment as he suddenly noticed the young woman seated in the box. "I suppose," he said slowly, "it's a good thing your father had some winners."

"Oh, yes," Mary smiled. "You should have seen him when you made him lose all that money on Snowball. We almost had to tie him down."

Waite laughed, in spite of his situation, and Mary joined him. She was dressed quite pertly in the latest-style yachting outfit— a white flannel skirt trimmed at the bottom with a band of blue linen striped with white, a white flannel chemise with blue collar opening to reveal a sailor's jersey, the whole thing topped with a tiny-brimmed sailor's cap. "You look very pretty," Waite said truthfully.

"Thank you," Mary replied simply.

"There's a hop tonight at the United States," he observed.

"There's also one at the Grand Union," she said. "That's the one I have to go to because of a previous engagement."

"Perhaps if I stood in the male wallflower line, you would take pity on me," he said with just the suggestion of a smile.

"I am not opposed to charitable work," she said, with a little toss of her head.

Later that evening, after waiting patiently while one young suitor after another vied for Mary Dwyer's permanent attention, Waite managed to catch her eye as she glided by in the arms of a tall blond fellow. Mary nodded quickly. Waite cut in and rapidly waltzed her to the other side of the dance floor. After a long moment of silence, Mary's smile widened as she said, "I'll come straight to the point, Mr. Nicholson. Do you want me to arrange a meeting between you and my father?"

He feigned surprise—rather well, he thought—asking, "Why do you say that?"

"Because I know you're up to something," she replied. "Otherwise, why would such a handsome man avoid all these other women just on the off-chance he could dance with me?"

"Perhaps because you're the most attractive young lady here," Waite said.

"Well, all right," Mary said. "I'm convinced. But I still think you'd like me to set up a meeting."

"Could you?" Waite asked.

"I doubt it."

"But as his daughter—" Waite paused. He felt he had been lured into a trap and wished he could find a quick and easy way out. He was thankful that the music ended then. The brief impasse was covered by their applause, but Mary was not inclined to let the topic die. "You see," she said. "That's just it. I'm only his daughter. A woman, and a young one at that. Now I could talk him into something frivolous, such as taking me to a fashion show. But if I were to speak in favor of his doing something that would benefit his business, that's different."

"Would you like to walk?" Waite asked.

"That would be nice," she said.

They paused for a moment at the refreshment booth where groups of teen-agers offered a variety of drinks such as lemonade, ginger beer, and royal nectar to their elders from the big city. "I really don't know what to say," Waite confessed as they sipped and walked. "You're right about the way men look down their noses at women. It's something we do almost without realizing it. We're dead wrong, of course."

"You mean you believe we should be allowed to vote?"

"Yes. Definitely."

"Work in offices? Live in apartments by ourselves?"

"I don't see why not."

"Oh," Mary said. "Oh."

"Is something the matter?"

"Well," she said with a sly smile. "I've found that men who agree with you are the most treacherous."

Waite stopped just long enough to look down at her. "Would you like me to lie and say I think a woman's place is in the home?"

Mary seemed to think about it for a moment. "All right," she said. "Perhaps we can get a good argument going."

"No," Waite said. "I don't want to argue with you. Least of all, when I have no cause."

"I had an interesting discussion with a Mr. Tate last night," Mary continued. "He was very knowledgeable, a treasure house of facts. Did you know that twenty-eight states have granted some kind of suffrage to women?"

"No," Waite replied.

Mary nodded. "Of course, they don't let us vote on really important things, but as Mr. Tate said, it's a start. In Louisiana, we're allowed to vote on whether a railroad line can pass through the parish. In Montana we can vote on matters of taxation. Would you like to kiss me?"

"What?" Waite asked, not sure he had heard her right.

"I was just wondering if you were paying attention."

"Yes, I was. Yes, I would."

"Thank you," she said, but continued walking. "Suppose Mr. Dwyer's daughter had eyes like a fish and a huge wart right on the tip of her nose. Would you still want to kiss her?"

"No," Waite replied.

"Not even if she could put in a good word with her father?"

Waite stopped and grabbed her gently by the elbow. "You really enjoy torturing me, don't you?" he said.

"Yes," she replied, with a little frown. "I wonder why."

"Perhaps because you find me attractive."

"That's probably it."

They started to walk again, but he kept his hand on her elbow. After a minute, Mary slid her arm up so that her hand slipped into his. "That's better," she said. "I felt as if you were leading me off to prison."

"Whipping out his revolver, Pinky turned it on the nine vicious road agents. 'Let's go then,' he challenged. 'Who will be first? There's only six bullets in my gun and nine of you. So three of you will get a chance at doing me in. The rub is, which three? Six of you will be dead, with the odds two to one against you. Got courage enough to try to beat those odds?' As he spoke, a twinkle of amusement crept into his gray eyes. One by one the road agents turned their snarling gazes from his and looked down at the ground. Pinky Pinkerton had defeated the Jennings Gang."

Dottie DeLacy smiled as she put down the book. "Is that the way you really handled it, Mr. Pinkerton?" she asked, placing the garish dime novel in her lap.

Pinky thought for a moment, then replied with a straight face. "Well, not exactly," he said. "Everything checks, except that I told them I had a nine-shooter and they'd all get killed. The Jennings Gang wasn't very smart."

Dottie smiled at his obvious self-mockery. They were seated in her father's office awaiting the arrival of W. C. Humstone.

Peter DeLacy had stepped out to discuss a minor problem in the poolroom with Roger Mellon, leaving his daughter to entertain Pinky for the moment.

When she heard of the upcoming meeting, Dottie had rushed off to do some research on Dwyer's new champion by getting Beadle's novel based on his life and career. She didn't know exactly why she was so intrigued by him, except that she had never met a real western hero and wanted to compare the glamorized myth with the everyday man. Then she had asked her father, "Can I stop by just long enough to meet him?"

Peter DeLacy laughed and said, "Certainly, but just for a little while. I'm sure he's tired of talking about his past, so don't overdo it."

The meeting, which had been requested by Humstone and DeLacy, was to be an informal discussion of ways and means to solve the Gravesend dilemma. They knew that Pinkerton was serving as a consultant to Dwyer as much as he was a security agent. Now he sat just a few feet away from Dottie, but after the first few obvious questions, she hardly knew what to say to the quiet man. Nor he to her.

Woomble.

Goddamn New York doctors were no better than those prairie butchers, Pinky thought as he grasped his stomach by his forearms and exerted a scissoring kind of pressure. The doctors had examined him, pronounced him well and fit except for a dyspeptic stomach, and prescribed a pink liquid called Tanner's Extract. Its chief effect had been to lower the pitch of his inner rumblings and coat the inside of his mouth with something that tasted like tree sap.

Wooloomble.

"Pardon me, miss," Pinky murmured. But the tactful lady was looking the other way and did not seem to hear him. Pinky sighed as he examined the pert chin and nose silhouetted against the light from the window. Dottie bore a marked resemblance to his former wife, Helen, the same Helen who had perished so sadly at the hands of Beadle's dime novel Indians. When he read that, Pinky had flown into one of his few genuine rages, threatening to sue Beadle's for every dime it owned. To the best of his knowledge, Helen was still alive. Very much alive in St. Louis with the same city slicker who had tired of the frontier at the same time she had. When the man from Beadle's interviewed him, the subject of Helen had been a tender one for Pinky. Loath to discuss their differences, he had murmured, "Yes, I was married for a while, but she left. She said she liked the city better, that all she thought about was being murdered by Indians. One day I looked up and she was gone. That's all."

Exercising considerable literary license, Beadle's writer had given Helen her just desserts, but it had not been true and Pinky hated such wholesale perversions of fact. Even worse than the fictional killing of Helen was the fictional retaliation of Pinky against the two dozen Indians who had perpetrated the act. Although he had gunned down more than a few road agents and killers, Pinky had never shot an Indian. He supposed he would have if the situation had warranted it, but the Indians he knew were peaceful unless provoked and, everything else being equal, Pinky preferred their company to that of most white frontiersmen. Beadle's making him into an Indian killer still rankled, so much so that he now found himself saying, "That book you read also claims I shot some Indians, Miss DeLacy. That's not true. I never did."

Dottie looked at him and smiled. "I'm glad," she said.

The door opened and Peter DeLacy came inside. "I'm sorry for this delay," he said. Then, with a glance at the wall clock, he added, "I can't imagine what's keeping Humstone. You can usually set the clock by him."

Woomble. "S'quite all right," Pinky said quickly.

"I see my daughter has been badgering you with that book," DeLacy smiled. "When she told me of some of your adventures, I didn't know whether to come to this meeting with a bodyguard or in a suit of armor."

"If I was meeting the hero in that book, I'd feel the same way," laughed Pinky.

"Well, I'm glad to hear at least some of it is exaggerated. I've never been that good a shot. I probably wouldn't last a week in your former territory."

"I think you'd last considerably longer," Pinky replied. "Out West you survive by thinking quick. I believe you could manage that."

A quick judge of men's characters, Pinky already had decided that DeLacy was strong, resourceful, fair, and decisive, just the type who could not only survive but thrive in the cannibalistic society west of the Mississippi. He looked forward to matching wits with him, for he knew the contest would be fair yet challenging. Of course, he had heard that a younger man named Waite Nicholson actually handled most of the information gathering. Pinky looked forward to meeting him, too. If he were cut from the same cloth as DeLacy, the fall meeting at Gravesend would be a challenge to his mind and body.

But he was already jumping the gun. He had promised himself that he would do whatever he could to settle the impasse peaceably. "One of the reasons I hired you was because of your reputation," Dwyer had said before leaving for Saratoga Springs. "If they've got a brain in their head at all, they'll know that running up against you won't be the same as matching wits with Bill Boozey. So if we can scare them into coming to terms this summer, I'm for it."

Pinky did not believe he could "scare" Peter DeLacy, but he did believe he could help establish a reasonable climate for negotiations between Dwyer and the Ditmas Company. That was, in fact, why he had accepted Humstone and DeLacy's invitation without bothering to consult Dwyer.

Ten minutes later, a messenger arrived with an apologetic note from Humstone. "They're having trouble with the lines from Guttenberg Race Track," DeLacy explained. "Humstone wants to know if we can meet at the same time tomorrow."

"I don't see why not," Pinky said, standing. Then, with a smile, he asked, "What seems to be the trouble? Did someone cut the wire?"

DeLacy laughed. "No, this is an act of God, not Phil Dwyer. A windstorm in Jersey knocked over some poles."

"Well, I'll stop by tomorrow at the same time, then," Pinky said.

"Thank you for being so understanding," DeLacy replied, shaking hands firmly.

"Would you care for a lemonade, Miss DeLacy?" Pinky asked, sliding his glance from the father to his daughter.

"Why, yes, that would be wonderful. We could go to Belle Gardens. You don't mind, do you, Daddy?"

"That you drink with the opposition?" DeLacy smiled. "No, of course not. Have a nice time."

As the couple reached the door, DeLacy thought he heard Pinky quietly say something like, "I hope I can get a glass of milk there."

"He certainly does go the limit to pretend he's a gentle fellow," DeLacy said softly.

As he sipped the sweet tea, Waite had a chance to study Mrs. Dwyer's face, and he concluded that she was more annoyed than angry. She would make him pay for the wound he had inflicted on her pride, but eventually she would allow him to return to her good graces.

He had let Mary talk him into joining her mother at afternoon tea on the back lawn of Albany House, the cottage rented every summer at Saratoga by the Dwyers. Dressed in his best white jacket and striped pants, Waite felt elegant and surprisingly cool. Perhaps it was the influence of the newly watered lawns, which sloped in a perfect concave arc to the edge of a lake, where a single gentleman and lady with parasol drifted in a small boat, very much like an illustration from one of the fashionable magazines. If you did not look too carefully, everything and everyone had a sort of sheen, a posed, otherworld quality of refinement indulging itself. Only when the faces moved close was it possible to see the sweating brow and rivulets of perspiration traveling their fitful route down ladies' necks to secret hiding places behind and beneath lace collars.

Mrs. Dwyer was a fearful sweater, Waite noticed, her broad flat nose being a particularly favorite path for the gathering beads of "dew." Looking at her, he wondered if she had ever been pretty. He decided that she had, and it upset him that the passage of years should be able to coarsen once-pretty features into such gross caricatures of themselves.

Of course, she didn't help her cause by twisting her face into that mock-schoolgirl pout, which was singularly unattractive. "I was so distressed when I found out," she murmured. "Not Waite Nicholson, I said. Not the man who so sincerely told my husband he would cut the telegraph line. But Aurelia—Mrs. Ironsides—was right. I couldn't believe it. For nearly a day I walked around, absolutely stunned. I honestly believe I would have been less surprised if Mary had turned up in the enemy camp."

Waite allowed her to ramble on. It had to come out before he could even begin to smooth things over, so he waited. Only when he was sure she was finished did he speak. "I know what you must have thought, Mrs. Dwyer," he said. "But the fact is

I've been a victim of circumstances. And I've never lied to you. When I told Mr. Dwyer I would cut the line, I meant it. In his position, that's exactly what I would have done. I believe he was morally right to do that, and I admire him for it. I also admire the support you gave him. But when I saw that my employer and the pool sellers meant to fight your husband's blockade, I had no choice but to accept their offer that I oversee the operation. You see, there were elements among the pool sellers which leaned towards violence. There was talk of setting fire to Gravesend Park, or assaulting the patrons—''

"Oh, my!" Mrs. Dwyer gasped.

Waite continued, "And they might have done so if cooler heads hadn't prevailed. So what I was doing may have been against my moral principles in one respect—I don't like to help gamblers. But I decided it was more important to use my abilities, such as they are, to work for peace. That's why I took over the operation, did my very best to get the racing information out peacefully, and will do so again if necessary. The reason I came to Saratoga Springs was to prevail upon Mr. Dwyer, and you, to discuss the problem and solve it by negotiation.''

"Well," Mrs. Dwyer said. "Perhaps I have misjudged you. Of course, I am still opposed to Philip's allowing the wire to be put back, but I had no idea what the true situation was. Do you think they might get violent in the fall?''

"Not if I can help it," Waite replied. "That's my sole reason for wanting to talk to Mr. Dwyer. But knowing what you must think of me, I felt I needed your permission.''

"Oh, isn't he charming?" Mrs. Dwyer smiled.

Mary, standing to the side, smiled also, but her expression was tinged with cynicism. "Just a regular Henry Ward Beecher," she said.

"Of course, I'll see what I can do," Mrs. Dwyer nodded,

patting Waite's forearm several times. "Philip's not quite so angry now, and perhaps you can stop in after dinner Thursday night. I'll let you know."

"That would be wonderful," Waite said. "You're as understanding as my own mother would be."

"Oh, my," Mrs. Dwyer cooed. Then, giving Mary a gentle push by the shoulder, she said, "Please take him away, Mary, before I take him away from you."

Mary raised her eyebrows. "I'm not so sure these afternoon teas couldn't stand something like that," she said. But she took Waite's arm and walked with him down the lawn toward the lake.

"You're really smooth," she said, when they were alone.

"In what way?"

"Listen to the voice of innocence," Mary smiled. "Mother was all set to tear you to pieces and you had her eating out of your hand at the end."

"I just told her the truth," Waite murmured.

"Oh, come now," Mary smiled. "Do you mean you were just standing around when all this happened? Everything just fell into your lap? You didn't, shall we say, make a few things happen?"

Waite stopped walking. "Of course I didn't make anything happen," he said with all the sincerity he could muster. "Do you honestly think I'm a plotter?"

"Yes," Mary replied. "Now don't tell me you aren't because I may be disappointed. You see, some of the tricks you devised were so clever I admired you for them. And it wasn't conceivable to me that you didn't help things along some." As he seemed about to speak, she squeezed his arm and continued. "That would have been all right," she said. "Everybody plots and schemes a little. It's the person who does it and then denies it afterward . . . that's the type I just don't trust or admire."

Waite hesitated just a second or two. Then he shrugged. "Well, I wish I could plead guilty to being a clever plotter," he said, "but I'm not. I just happened to be around."

"That's your story and you're going to stick to it?"

"Why shouldn't I?"

"No reason," Mary said. "Let's drop the subject. There's a great oak tree on the other side of the lake. If you like, you can take me there and kiss me behind it."

That was where Waite had been leading them, but when Mary suggested it, he spoke in a surprised tone of voice. "What a splendid idea!" he said. "I'd never have thought of that."

Mary glanced at his ingenuous features, then looked away and cleared her throat very loudly.

"And how did your meeting with Daddy and Mr. Humstone go?"

"I guess you could say it went well," Pinky said. "To be honest, Miss Delacy, I don't get too concerned about preliminary talks, because I've found that when you get down to dollars and cents, people's opinions often change."

The barouche sped down the road to Gravesend, past Greenwood Cemetery and the rolling farmland and occasional mud flats near Blythebourne and New Utrecht.

For a while, they raced neck-and-neck with a horsecar filled with excursionists heading for Coney Island, Brighton, and Manhattan beaches until the road branched to the right and the horsecar pulled into Union Depot. The area through which they passed was in transition, like a corpse marked for future burial. The population of the flatland, once they left Brooklyn, was sparse, but every so often was a sign indicating future growth. Roads and parkways had been laid out by some enterprising developer and even as they moved through a wilderness of small trees and sandy mounds, suddenly there would be a sign reading "65th Street," standing alone like a grave marker. Pinky wondered what "65th Street" would look like a century in the future. He quickly shut his mind to the thought.

It was too pleasant a moment, sitting here with a young and attractive redheaded beauty at his side. Not that she regarded him as anything more than an elderly folk hero. But with the cool wind against his face, the rattle of the carriage wheels drowning his stomach's low-pitched mutterings, he was reasonably content. Strange, that until he had left the meeting with Humstone and DeLacy, he had completely forgotten his promise of the day before to take Dottie to the race course. A younger man would never have misplaced that thought.

They were nearly at Gravesend before the inevitable subject arose. "If there's no agreement this summer, what do you think will happen at the fall meet?" Dottie asked.

Pinky thought for a moment. "I imagine it will be a larger version of what happened in the spring," he said. "I'll have a lot more men than Bill Boozey and I'll know how to organize them better. And I've got a long list of what I would do if I were your friend Waite Nicholson." With that, he drew a crumpled piece of paper from his coat pocket.

"He's not exactly my friend," Dottie murmured, lowering her eyes.

"Well, let's say that he's on your team," Pinky replied.

Dottie returned her gaze. "I'm not sure what team I'm on, Mr. Pinkerton," she said evenly. "Have you heard of the Anti-Sin Society?"

"The AS—oh, certainly," Pinky replied.

"I used to be a member," Dottie said. "But I was expelled near the end of the spring meet. They thought I had warned Daddy about a raid. Actually, I hadn't said a word."

"That's too bad. About your being expelled, that is."

They pulled into the broad area between Sleight's hotel and the east side of the track. In the bright sunlight and silence, the great deserted, peeling structure seemed about to crumble into a soft mound of sawdust. As the barouche passed by, Dottie remarked at the sight of silhouettes inside the building. "They keep a couple of toughs here all the time," Pinky explained. "I guess they think we might try to blow up the place."

"I suppose you have all sorts of clever schemes ready for them, don't you?" Dottie smiled.

Pinky laughed. "Actually, I don't know what I'll do. But when the action starts, the old mind will begin throwing out ideas. In the meantime, I'll organize everything as well as I can and find ways to buy information about what the so-called enemy's up to."

"Buy information?" Dottie repeated. "You would do that?"

"Of course. That's what seventy-five percent of good law enforcement is, Miss DeLacy. Finding good sources of inside information. If he'd been smart enough to pay twenty dollars to an Indian scout named Red Heel, General Custer might be sitting in Washington this very minute."

As he helped Dottie DeLacy out of the carriage, Pinky could not suppress a slight smile at her expression of sad disillusionment. Partly to soothe her, he said wryly, "Maybe I won't be able to find any good informants this time. In which case, I'll have to rely on my own wits."

"Is that so awfully bad?" Dottie asked.

"Not if the Good Lord drops everything else to help out," Pinky laughed.

"I'd like to be accommodating, but I don't see how I can. You people down there have called me everything from a greedy old skinflint to a damn fool."

"That's not true, sir. Begging your pardon for saying so, but you're mistaken."

For a split second, Philip Dwyer's eyes softened, as if he wanted to believe the young man. Then they resumed their customary steellike anger. "Do you have any idea how much I lost during those three days?" he demanded of Waite.

"No, sir, I haven't."

"About six thousand dollars. Two thousand a day. A thousand a day in lost revenue from the Ditmas Company, a thousand in bets, and more than two thousand in expenses. That doesn't count the suits that have been filed by people who had their clothes ruined or things dropped on their heads." Looking around quickly to make certain the ladies were out of the room, Dwyer added: "One woman claims she has a permanent oil spot on her bosom. You can imagine how much she'll say that's worth."

Waite looked at the floor. For one thing, he wished to appear genuinely contrite. For another, he had no idea what an oil-spotted bosom would bring on the legal market.

"And now you have the nerve to suggest a meeting with your boss—just like nothing had happened."

"I know how you must feel, sir," Waite said. "But I do want to assure you of one thing. Mr. Humstone has never called you a fool or any other name, and I've been with him when he was terribly upset. If there's one thing I can vouch for in this whole mess, it's that."

Dwyer grunted.

Pressing his miniscule advantage, Waite said: "If you would agree to discuss the matter with us, sir, Mr. Humstone would at least have the opportunity to apologize for the trouble he's created for you. Even though much of it was unavoidable, he feels you've been the innocent victim. He'd like to make it up to you, sir, both personally and monetarily."

Dwyer grunted again, not quite so deeply. "He's ready to come up to four thousand a day?" he asked.

"I'm not authorized to discuss money," Waite replied. "But I do know the climate is right to talk peacefully and work something out. I'm sure none of us wants to go through the last three days of the spring meet again."

Dwyer very nearly smiled. "You thought you were pretty smart, didn't you?"

"I was just doing my job," Waite said modestly.

"Well, if we have a repeat of that in the fall," Dwyer said, "this time you'll be up against Robert Pinkerton, who's handled the most desperate men in the West . . ."

"I'm aware of that, sir."

"When does Humstone want to get together?"

"At your convenience."

"I guess it couldn't hurt," Dwyer shrugged. Then, looking at the clock, he suddenly reached out and gave Waite a fatherly pat on the shoulder. "You and Mary had better hurry. You'll miss the first dance," he said. "All right. You can tell Humstone to call me when I get back to New York next week. We'll talk, but I won't guarantee anything."

"Thank you, sir. It's a pleasure to learn firsthand that you're as fair as everyone says."

Philip Dwyer smiled grudgingly. "Everyone?" he said. "Who's everyone?"

"Well," Waite improvised, "Mr. Humstone, Mr. DeLacy. In addition to a lot of people I've talked to who know you from the days when you delivered their meat."

"They still remember me, eh?"

"Oh, yessir. I'm from out of town, but so many people have mentioned your delicious meats and fast service that I feel we've dined together, so to speak."

Mary and Mrs. Dwyer were at the door of the study. "Well,"

Mrs. Dwyer smiled unctuously. "Have you gentlemen finished your little talk?"

"I believe so," Waite said.

"Finished their talk," Mary smiled. "Why, they've just finished dining together, so to speak."

"Have a good time, children," Dwyer said.

After the front door closed behind them, Sophie Dwyer turned to her husband. "He's a very nice young man," she said, "but I hope he wasn't able to charm you into something immoral."

"What in God's name do you mean by that?" Dwyer shot back.

"I'm sure you know what I mean," Sophie replied. "He's trying to arrange a reconciliation between you and those evil men. I admire him as a peaceful influence at the spring meet, but I do not admire his working in the interests of those who would corrupt—"

"Oh, shut up," Philip Dwyer muttered. "If I want a sermon I'll go to church."

"A little more church wouldn't hurt you," Sophie replied. "And if you want my advice—"

"I don't want it," Philip interrupted. "It's rotten."

"Not half as rotten as the you-know-what when you didn't take my advice," Sophie smiled wickedly.

Philip Dwyer reddened. More than a decade had passed and she still twitted him about his "Saint Patrick's Day Special." In March of 1881, Dwyer had been offered a huge shipment of corned beef at a substantial savings. Although she seldom concerned herself with the meat business, Sophie happened to be at the Dwyer brothers' packing house on the very day Philip inspected the beef prior to buying it. Crinkling her nose distastefully, Sophie had muttered, "This smells bad, Philip."

"Don't be silly," he had replied. "It always smells like that.

This is perfectly good meat. I'm going to buy the whole shipment and sell it as my own Saint Patrick's Day special."

"You'll poison the entire neighborhood," Sophie countered. "I tell you, this meat is rancid."

"And I tell you your brain is rancid," Philip replied angrily. "I know what I'm doing."

And Philip had bought the meat, sold it, and saw a large portion of his clientele turn green on Saint Patrick's Day. It had taken him nearly two years to restore his customers' confidence in him. But while they eventually forgave and forgot, Sophie did not. Every chance she got to jab him with the poison dart of 1881's Saint Patrick's Day Special, she did so. It was her trump card, and Philip never failed to respond with barely suppressed agony and rage.

"If you mention that one more time," he threatened, "I'll take after you with my razor strap."

With that, he stormed out of the room, slamming every door between the study and the bedroom.

"Be quiet," Mary whispered as she and Waite approached the darkened cottage. "We don't want to wake up my father, that gentleman with whom you just finished dining, so to speak."

"Will you get off that?" Waite pleaded. But he smiled, secretly enjoying her teasing.

It was after midnight and both of them felt a bit light-headed. Relieved following the success of his mission, Waite had relaxed and enjoyed himself thoroughly at the dance. Afterward, he had allowed himself to be talked into accepting a drink or two at the apartment of a young married couple. He would not have done so, of course, if Mary had not been more than willing. "Let's sin a little," she had giggled.

So they had sinned a little, at the apartment and during the carriage ride home. Now, in the hopes of sinning a bit more, Waite guided Mary into a dark corner of the spacious porch and put his hands on her trim waist. She slid her arms up his chest to his neck and gave him one long, clinging kiss. Just as she pulled away, a voice from above bellowed her name, shattering the silence of the starry night with shocking suddenness.

"Mary! Get the devil in here!"

With a grimace, Mary stood on her tiptoes to kiss Waite quickly on the mouth, then turned and darted into the house.

At the first landing, she was met in the darkness by her mother, who stopped her with an outstretched hand and a finger to her lips. "Just go to bed," Sophie said. "It's no use talking to him."

"What's the matter?" Mary asked, turning her head so that her mother would be less likely to smell the apricot brandy on her breath. "It's not that late, is it?"

"Well, no," her mother replied. "He's just in a horrible mood."

"Is it something I did or said? Or Waite—?"

"No, it's me," Sophie confessed. "We had a little argument and I threw the Saint Patrick's Day Special at him."

Mary sighed. "Mother," she said, in a castigating tone. "You promised!"

"I know," Sophie murmured. "It just came out."

"And now we'll all have to pay for it," Mary said. But she kissed her mother on the cheek and crept softly into bed. She fell asleep wondering if it were really an advantage being the daughter of New York's hottest-tempered businessman.

7

"You miserable swine bastard! I'll kill you!"

". . . because we have dined together, so to speak, I honestly feel there is a bond of friendship . . ."

Mary Dwyer shook her head slightly as she read the message from "A Secret Admirer" to her father. Back from Saratoga, she was straightening his desk, as she did every fall, when the letter struck her eye. Perhaps it stood out because it was unsigned. Whatever the reason, she took it as a particularly strange twist of fate that her eye fell almost immediately on that phrase—"dined together, so to speak," which was such a quaint idea quaintly put.

When she finished reading the entire letter, there was no doubt in her mind as to who had written it.

"That oh-so sincere liar," she whispered. "Do you honestly think I'm a plotter," he had said, his eyes wide and open, nearly awash with innocence. And then he had added the crowning touch by saying that he wished he were a clever plotter but was not.

Just lucky? Hardly. Mary couldn't suppress a smile. The letter must have been devastating to her father, playing so expertly on his pride and exalted sense of virtue. If W. C. Humstone had appeared in person to call Philip Dwyer a damn fool, he could hardly have had more effect than the letter. "Waite, Waite, Waite," Mary said, shaking her head again.

She did not hate him for it. She didn't even dislike him. She only felt cheated because he treated her just like everyone else he needed and used for his own devices. Mary did not particularly mind being used, but she did mind the user thinking he had gotten away with something.

"Well," she thought, "this makes three times he's schemed to use people and gotten away with it—three that I know of. . . . Using this letter to have Daddy cut the wire, using me to get in good with Daddy, and having me agree to find out Daddy's price for the fall meet."

The last-mentioned scheme he had launched just two days ago, expressing concern to her about the upcoming negotiations between her father and the Ditmas Company. "I really have a bad feeling about how things may go," he had said. "You see, Humstone and DeLacy aren't willing to budge an inch."

"Why not?" Mary had asked, knowingly taking the bait.

"They don't believe your father is willing to come down a penny from four thousand dollars a day," Waite replied. "They honestly believe if they move up one cent, he'll take them all the way to four thousand. I've tried to convince them that he's reasonable, that he'll settle for less. But they don't believe me. I wish there were some way to assure them."

"You mean such as being able to say, 'Gentlemen, my secret source says Dwyer will take twenty-five hundred.' " Mary smiled.

"Well, that would impress them," Waite acknowledged.

"I see," Mary said. "Waite, why couldn't you just ask me to spy for you?"

A look of horror came into his eyes. "Ask you to spy on your own father?" he said. "I couldn't do that."

"But I basically agree with you," Mary said. "If Daddy has some figure he's willing to settle for, it's better to just have it out in the open. That would make him happy, and it makes sense from a business standpoint. I mean, why spend money to keep you from having the track information when he can make money by selling it?"

"That's true," Waite nodded. "But I certainly wouldn't want you to—"

"Oh, skip it," Mary interrupted. "If I hear anything, I'll let you know before the meeting."

"Well . . ." he mumbled, "all right. If you hear anything, I would appreciate knowing. But only because it's to your father's advantage."

"Yes, Waite," Mary smiled.

Now as Mary held the letter, she smiled again. Last night she had heard the magic figure—two thousand dollars. She had been on her way out and had walked into the foyer just as one of the group of racetrack owners, who had come to discuss strategy with her father, said: "Of course, if you can get two thousand a day, it'll be a great thing for all of us, Phil."

To which her father had replied: "That's what I'm aiming to do, boys. But two thousand is as low as I'll go."

Later today Mary would give the information to Waite, she decided. Along with some other special information.

Hearing someone coming, she slipped the letter back in its envelope and started shifting papers busily.

It was her father. "I'm on my way to the meeting with

Humstone,'' he announced. "Did you say you wanted a ride downtown?"

Mary nodded. "I promised I'd drop in and see Waite's new office," she said. "Did you know they gave him a place all to himself?"

Dwyer shrugged. "The spring meet at my track was good to him," he growled.

"Well, he's awfully clever, Daddy. Maybe too clever."

"What do you mean by that?"

"Nothing. Well, shall we go?"

Waite smiled and leaped to his feet as Mary rapped lightly and entered. Looking around quickly, he closed the door and kissed her on the cheek, then on the lips.

"It's wonderful to see you," he said. "You look beautiful. Absolutely beautiful."

"Two thousand," Mary smiled.

Waite's eyes assumed a nearly automatic expression of ingenuousness. "What's that?" he asked.

"Never mind," Mary said.

"I thought you just said two thousand," Waite murmured, dropping his voice. "Is that the figure your father will settle for?"

Mary nodded.

"How do you know?"

"I asked him."

"Does he always tell you things just because you ask him?"

"He does if I use the magic word."

"Magic word?"

"Yes. There's a little phrase Mother and I use when he's sitting on the fence and we want him to get off. It never fails to get a reaction from him."

"Amazing—what is it?"

"We remind him about his Saint Patrick's Day Special. 'Only a genius could have pulled off that Saint Patrick's Day Special in the meat business, like you did,' we say. He melts like butter every time."

"Was that one of his big successes?"

"Let's say it was the sensation of 1881."

A rap on the door was followed an instant later by the entrance of W. C. Humstone. "We'll start as soon as Pinkerton gets here," he said, smiling at Mary. "Good afternoon. You must be Philip Dwyer's charming daughter. My name is Warren Humstone."

"I am his daughter," Mary replied. "Sometimes he doesn't think I'm quite so charming." Then, turning to Waite, she said, "Well, I've some shopping to do. Would you excuse me?"

Waite took her hand and nodded. "It was nice seeing you again," he said.

A moment after Mary left, Waite turned to Humstone and motioned him over to the window.

"This morning I spoke with my contact in the Anti-Sin Society," Waite whispered. "She assured me Dwyer will settle for two thousand."

"Excellent."

As he turned to leave, Waite reached out to grab his sleeve. "Oh, Mr. Humstone," he said. "Here's something else. Have you ever heard of Dwyer's brilliant Saint Patrick's Day Special?"

"No," Humstone mused. "What was it?"

"Apparently reminding him of that takes him back to his glory days in the meat business. Perhaps if he seems to be wavering and needs a gentle push, you could remind him of it."

"All right," Humstone smiled. "I'll try to remember."

And as he walked to the office door, he murmured "Saint Patrick's Day Special" to himself several times.

"Remember now, Robert," Dottie DeLacy smiled. "No gun play at this meeting."

"I'll do my best," Pinky said, leaning back in the carriage and stretching out his legs as far as he could. They were headed crosstown toward the Ditmas Company.

Werble.

"Damn it," he whispered.

"Have you met Waite Nicholson yet?" Dottie asked, thinking it best to take his mind off his condition.

"No, I haven't. What's he like?"

"Sometimes it seems he's looking out only for himself," Dottie said. "And then he'll turn around and do something like he did this week—send a letter to the Anti-Sin Society, explaining that I wasn't the source of his information about the raid. He also asked to take me to lunch today," she added.

Pinky smiled wanly. "You mean I have a rival already? Why, I'll gun him deader than a doornail."

"I don't believe you could call him a rival," Dottie replied. "As a matter of fact, he's been seeing quite a bit of Mary Dwyer."

"Philip Dwyer's daughter?"

Dottie nodded.

Pinky, shaking his head, suddenly broke into laughter. "There sure is a lot of mixed company in this case," he said. "Here I am, seeing you, the daughter of New York's biggest pool seller, a fact which I find very pleasant but one which might also be considered against the rules. And there's this boy with the Ditmas Company seeing the racetrack owner's daughter. If there's any suspected spying going on, nobody's going to know where to begin."

The carriage stopped in front of the Lower Broadway Western Union Telegraph Office, which also housed the Ditmas Company. Leaning forward, Pinky smiled at Dottie and said, "When will I see you again?—assuming you're ever going to see me after receiving an invitation from Mr. Nicholson . . ."

Dottie thought for a moment. "How about tomorrow?" she said.

As he strode into the Ditmas Company building, Pinky found himself wishing that Peter DeLacy had not made a last-minute decision to leave the negotiating to Humstone and Nicholson. Despite the basic common sense of such a decision, Pinky felt a bit uneasy. Peter DeLacy, in his estimation, was a force for sanity in this emotion-charged issue, and he had urged him to attend. "Thank you, no," DeLacy had said. "I'd just be in the way. The fewer people involved the better. I'll go along with whatever decision is made."

Werbling fearfully, Pinky asked the secretary for directions and received them. As he started up the stairs, a sharp object struck him in the center of his forehead and sent him reeling back down the stairs. Mary Dwyer had turned the corner at the landing without looking and had barged, elbow-first, into him. Losing her balance, she had started to fall, but Pinky, who had regained his own balance, braced himself against the railing, caught her, and steadied them both.

"Oh, my goodness," Mary stammered, looking into the deep blue eyes of a strong, rugged man, she thought extremely attractive—except for the red welt in the middle of his forehead. Instinctively, her hand went out to touch it, then she removed a handkerchief from her handbag and dabbed at it. "I'm so sorry," she said.

The man did not reply. He did not even look at her. In fact, he seemed miles away.

"I just wasn't paying attention," Mary continued.

He remained silent, his head cocked to one side as if listening to a faraway sound. Actually, Pinky *was* listening. As the first shock of the collision wore off, he had gradually become aware of a curious feeling of peace in the turbulent regions below his belt. Even when silent, the area was nearly always churning, readying itself for its next audible assault. Now, there was only an eerie stillness.

"Well," Mary said softly, "if you're all right—"

Pinky looked at her closely for the first time. Young and pretty, by all rights she ought to have triggered new barrages of sound to confound and embarrass him. But there was only silence—beloved but strange silence. Pinky hitched himself upright, then performed a little motion which caused Mary's eyes to widen.

He hopped in place. Paused. Massaged his stomach. Hopped again. Smiled broadly. Then, as Mary seemed about to slip away from him down the stairway, he reached out to touch her arm. "Would you mind staying just a minute?" he asked.

"Of course I wouldn't mind," she replied.

"Thank you."

He continued to look at her intently, all the while turning and twisting his head as if listening for something.

"It's gone," he murmured slowly. "There's no way to explain it. It's just gone." Then to Mary, he said, "May I ask your name?"

Mary looked at him directly. "If you're the great detective they say you are, Mr. Pinkerton, you'll be able to identify me without any help."

Standing there, it had suddenly come to her that the man must be Pinkerton. She recognized him from the thinner, colder portrait printed that very day in the *Times*. He smiled. "That's two amazing things," he said.

"I'm an amazing person," Mary laughed, looking once more into the blue eyes before starting down the stairway.

Pinky waited until she was out of sight around the corner. "Amazing," he said again, shaking his head.

A few moments later, he entered the office of W. C. Humstone where Dwyer, Humstone, and the young man who could only be Waite Nicholson sat around an expansive desk. They rose as he entered and introductions were made. "I suppose we should begin this discussion by briefly going over the standard contract which has been in force between the Ditmas Company and Gravesend Race Track," Humstone said, reaching for a paper on his desk.

"Excuse me, gentlemen," Pinky interrupted. "Before we settle down to business, may I beg your indulgence by asking if anyone knows the identity of the young lady who just left this office?"

He threw out the words quickly, for already he could experience a weakening of her effect upon him, and it suddenly seemed necessary to solve the mystery as quickly as possible. Like a patient who has found relief in a particular drug, he wanted to know its name, as if that in itself would help him bear the next onslaught of his ailment.

"Why, my daughter just left," Dwyer said.

"Was she dressed in gold?"

"In gold?" Dwyer asked, "Why, I think so—"

"Yes," Waite Nicholson replied. "She was wearing a yellow, or gold, outfit."

"Why?" Dwyer asked.

"No reason in particular," Pinky replied.

"But there must be a reason," Dwyer persisted.

Pinky shrugged. "Let's just say I'd like to get myself an outfit like that," he said softly.

Dwyer looked at him darkly for a moment, then signaled for Humstone to read.

As Humstone droned on, Waite stood and surveyed Pinkerton as thoroughly as possible without being obvious. He was older, experienced, and unpredictable, Waite concluded. His rejoinder to Dwyer indicated a willingness to improvise and perhaps take chances, while his somewhat casual manner of dress could betray a lack of planning ability. But Waite the people-watcher saw no charlatan across the room, no strutting Bill Boozey. If Pinkerton seemed casual, it was only because he had confidence in his own ability. Waite could see that in the strong, intelligent features, and even as he did so, he knew that Pinkerton was sizing him up as well.

A bright young man, Pinky concluded. Bright enough that in a few years he'll realize there are others as bright as he is. But now he's riding the crest of a wave. Defeating him will require total diligence.

For a moment, the gazes of the two men locked, then moved away to Humstone and Dwyer. But only momentarily. Like a pair of gunfighters at opposite ends of the deserted street, their gazes returned again and again to each other, never really concentrating on anything else for more than a few seconds at a time.

"At any rate," Humstone concluded, "that's the standard contract, or perhaps I should say, what used to be the standard contract." Then, looking at Philip Dwyer, he said, "Is there any part of it besides the compensation you might like to discuss?"

"No," Dwyer said. "All I want is four thousand dollars a day. If you agree to that, we can sign the damn thing and all go home."

Humstone cleared his throat. "Phil, there are two things you have to understand," he said evenly. "One is that the Ditmas

Company can't afford to pay four thousand dollars a day—"
Dwyer laughed.

"Wait just a minute, Phil," Humstone urged. "You didn't let me finish. We can afford to pay you four thousand dollars a day, but not all of the track owners. Which brings us to my second point, which is that whether you like it or not, you are now negotiating for those other owners. Thus there's no way we can increase your financial benefits without increasing theirs."

"I'm sure Mr. Dwyer wants it that way," Waite interjected.

"So we have to consider the broad picture," Humstone continued. "It's not just four thousand a day for Gravesend four weeks a year. It would be four thousand a day for dozens of raceways in this section of the country alone. And completely out of the question. Now I've talked with the pool sellers and we're willing to come up to fifteen or sixteen hundred dollars a day."

"It's not enough," Dwyer shot back.

"What would be enough? Can you come down from that four thousand dollar figure at all?"

"I might come down to three thousand, but that's the bottom," Dwyer said.

"Phil, I wish you could do better than that. Look at the long view. If you're an employer and a man does a good job for you, you don't give him a two hundred percent pay increase."

"What's that got to do with anything?" Dwyer charged. "What's a worker's wages got to do with business?"

"I was trying to put our problem in perspective."

"All right, then try this. That last part of the spring meet cost me a bundle of money, but so far no one's offered to pay that back."

"We were coming to that, Mr. Dwyer," Waite replied.

"I'll bet you were."

"Suppose we were to offer a raise to fifteen hundred dollars a day for all of the track owners?'' Waite asked. ''Would they— not you, Mr. Dwyer—would they be happy with that?''

''Sure, I guess so. It's five hundred more than they've been getting.''

''Fine. And it would be because of your efforts. So they surely wouldn't hate you, would they?''

''No. Not unless they were crazy.''

''All right,'' Waite continued. ''Now suppose we increased the track owner fee to fifteen hundred, and then paid you a fee of two thousand dollars? That would pay you back for the money lost in the spring.''

A light crept into Philip Dwyer's eyes. ''Two thousand dollars a day,'' he repeated. ''I hadn't figured on coming down that far.''

''It's a substantial increase, Phil,'' Humstone urged.

Dwyer looked at Pinky. ''What do you think?'' he asked.

''Well,'' Pinky shrugged. ''There's no denying a thousand dollars a day is a nice increase.''

Dwyer nodded.

''That's a hundred percent increase, Mr. Dwyer,'' Waite said.

''Yes, but still—''

Dwyer looked down at the tabletop, his jaw working. He wanted to accept the money, but he knew he would be attacked by the reformers, not to mention his wife.

For nearly a minute, his gaze alternated between the table and the window, as if he could not make up his mind. In his head, though, he'd just about put the do-gooders behind a pile of money.

W. C. Humstone, sensing victory, stood with his face frozen in a slight smile for thirty seconds. Then as Dwyer muttered indecisive phrases to himself, he suddenly decided to take the bull by the horns.

"Oh, come on now, Phil," Humstone said warmly. "Don't try to pretend you're an indecisive man. We know differently. We experienced your decisiveness in the spring when you cut our wire. And everyone here knows how decisive you were on your Saint Patrick's Day Special!"

He tilted his head backward, smiling at Dwyer, ready for the fruits of his praise to produce a decisive agreement.

Dwyer's eyes remained on the floor. In an instant, his neck and face were beet red. A low rumbling sound, like a volcano about to erupt, filled the room.

Pinky looked around. It wasn't coming from him. Where—?

Then, suddenly, he saw the hands of Philip Dwyer flash forward until they were around Humstone's throat.

"You swine!" he roared. "You miserable swine bastard! I'll kill you!"

Humstone shrieked and fell backwards onto his desk, scattering pencils, ink pots, and papers to all corners of the room.

Pinky rushed forward, clasped one of Dwyer's hands behind his back and pulled him off of the thrashing Humstone.

"What did I do? What did I say?" Humstone shouted at Waite, who assisted Pinky with the pulsating Dwyer.

"Not for four thousand!" Dwyer shouted. "Not for five thousand! Never, you bastards! Never!"

"He's lost his mind!" Humstone shrieked. "Get him out of here."

Pinky worked Dwyer toward the door. As he eased him out, he stuck his head back in and murmured, "Unless you gentlemen have something to add, I'll assume the negotiations are over."

NO COMPROMISE WITH EVIL, *The New York Times* headlines proclaimed. "Yesterday afternoon, in a last-ditch effort to induce Mr. Philip Dwyer, head of the Brooklyn Jockey Club and operator of Gravesend Race Track, to allow the Ditmas Company access to telegraphic racing information, representatives of that company offered a substantial increase in payment. To his honor, Mr. Dwyer refused to accept the money and negotiations broke down. In an interview last evening, Mr. Dwyer said he turned down the increase because he felt gambling was immoral, and no amount of money could persuade him to alter his opinion. He vowed to fight the Ditmas Company toughs by employing Robert Pinkerton, of the Pinkerton National Detective Agency, during the fall meet. Mr. Pinkerton, a renowned Indian fighter and lawman, will be responsible for preventing the smuggling of information out of the track when the fall meet begins in September. He is an energetic and experienced officer and his presence will mean only trouble for the gambling element.

"Late last night it was rumored that another meeting had been scheduled but this turned out to be false. It now appears that the final words have been uttered. The next inevitable step is total war."

FALL

8

"I'll keep my nose to the grindstone and my ear to his stomach"

By the 1890s, Coney Island with its three grand beaches—Manhattan, Brighton, and West Brighton—was the most popular resort on the Atlantic Seaboard. On a typical weekend during late summer and early fall, more than sixty thousand visitors jammed themselves into ferry boats, horsecars, steamboats, or dummy railroad cars in order to escape the heat of New York, Brooklyn, New Jersey, and Connecticut. The trip, though not very great as miles go, was, more often than not, agonizingly slow and almost unbearably hot.

Once at the ocean's edge, however, there was no lack of entertainment, not the least of which was the water. Because comparatively few persons actually had the ability to swim (*The New York Times*, in fact, discouraged it, stating editorially that Americans drowned only because they learned how to swim and then took unnecessary risks), the centerpieces of the three beaches were the rope lines leading into the surf, thoroughly anchored to poles marked with flags. Invariably these facilities were the centers of population, places to chat or gaze at one's fellow bather.

The bathing costume worn by men was hardly an innovation or revolutionary change. A two-pieced flannel outfit reaching to the knees revealed no more of the male figure than most Americans were accustomed to seeing. It was the female's outfit that was the subject of shock, dismay, laughter, or admiration, although the latter was extremely rare.

One could generally tell a great deal about a woman's background, however, by the outfit she wore into the surf. The most primitive and prudish bathing suit was a large, loose, flannel gown which enveloped the entire figure, reaching below the ankles. It was, as one reporter wrote, designed to make the female figure as hideous as possible, and if "Venus herself had arisen from the ocean arrayed in such a gown, instead of the mother, she would have been mistaken for the grand-mother of the gods." This garment had a way of expanding and floating to the surface when the wearer was in the water, so that "the lady resembled a blue cotton umbrella with a curiously carved ivory handle."

Less hideous than the full-length gown was the outfit of blue flannel blouse and trousers, which, when water-soaked, seemed to have been made of sheet lead or Brussels carpeting. More daring ladies arrayed themselves in the "opera bouffe" suit from France of short sleeves and low neck, closely fitted with a perforated corset. Some wore trousers which resembled knickerbockers, supplemented with bright stockings, a ribbon about the waist, canvas shoes, and a dainty hat. Others—the most daring of the lot—wore flannel skirts which reached no farther than the knees. No one knew where the trend would stop, but more than a few elderly or middle-aged men cast their eyes toward the water when a young maiden slowly began to pull herself toward the beach, the wet flannel emphasizing her figure in a way that could hardly be described as subtle.

Another attraction of Coney Island, just six years old, was the great Elephantine Colossus. Described as the "eighth wonder of the world," the giant elephant was made of wood, contained a "stomach room" 60 feet long, and was 175 feet high. Every day, thousands of visitors—for fifteen cents apiece—entered it via the hind leg, took a tour, and were treated to a sight of the entire beach from the "eye room."

At night, Manhattan Beach, with its spacious amphitheater, generally featured some kind of pyrotechnical display, complete with band music, battle scenes, and swarms of dancers. One of the most popular was "the Siege of Sevastopol," in which the allied forces were arrayed against the Russians in front of Malakoff and Redan. During the intermission—presumably, while the two armies regrouped—several dozen sailors from the Brooklyn Navy Yard entertained with a cutlass drill, followed by a troupe of Bedouin Arabs and a Highland sword dance. The grand finale, usually featuring Patrick Gilmore's band, included five hundred people, punctuated by the bright and frightening explosion of fireworks.

But a trip to the beach at Coney Island could have its unattractive side sometimes. Occasionally, because nearby municipalities had garbage and the water was the most convenient place in which to dump it, a few undesirable items joined the bathers as they romped in the surf. One of the worst had occurred just a few years before, a solid mass of refuse dumped by the scows. Resembling a combination whale and sea serpent, the scummy mass slowly floated up to the edge of Manhattan Beach, forcing the revelers back onto the sand. They watched, transfixed with horror as the waves lapped at the edge of the island of vegetation which seemed to have a substratum of straw, hay, and weeds, cemented with mud, ashes, and sewage. It carried a miscellaneous cargo in which decayed fruit, grease-soaked barrel staves, old bottles, and an exhaustive assortment of cats and dogs in various stages of post-mortem appealed with staggering arguments to the sense of sight and smell.

But still, New Yorkers loved their Coney Island, in particular because while there, they could also patronize Gravesend Race Track. And never in the history of the cheek-by-jowl existence did they look forward to the track opening as they did in the fall of 1891.

It was, after all, showdown time between the pool sellers and Philip Dwyer, a pyrotechnical display that could make "the Siege of Sevastopol" seem like child's play.

It began, as predicted by *The New York Times*, just as the crowds were largest at the three beaches.

Bonk. Bonk-bonk.

In the cupola of Sleight's hotel, the sound of hammering from the track seemed hollow and metallic. It had started on the first day of September, just two weeks before the opening of the fall meet at Gravesend. First the long vertical poles thrust themselves high into the air; then, like the masts of a sinking ship slipping below water level, the poles slowly disappeared beneath the rising horizontal planking. But before they completely vanished, miraculous extensions occurred to accommodate the growing wall. Twenty, thirty feet it rose; then forty. Not until it reached a height of fifty feet was the wall complete. But still the hammering continued.

"What do you suppose they're building now?" Peter DeLacy asked, leaning against the sill of the cupola window.

"Probably just shoring up the back," Waite said. "That fence is so rickety a strong wind could do it in."

Bonk. Bonk. Bonk-bonk.

"Sounds like code," DeLacy smiled. "Maybe you can use that."

Waite nodded. Everyone, it seemed, had a suggestion as to how to get information out of Gravesend.

"Well, one thing's sure. You can't see a damn thing from here now," DeLacy said. "What do you plan on doing?"

"Going higher," Waite said.

"With the meet starting the day after tomorrow?" DeLacy said. "Shouldn't you get moving?"

"Not yet," Waite smiled. He glanced to his right, where, far off in farmer Young's pasture, his own modest fence had been erected. It was only a hundred feet long and ten feet high, but it was semicircular in shape and before the day was out, it would form a complete circle. Already a half dozen men were smoothing the ground inside the area, an action Waite knew would give Pinky Pinkerton serious thoughts. DeLacy followed his gaze, chuckled a bit, and said: "You aren't really getting ready for a balloonist, are you?"

Waite shrugged. "If worst comes to worst . . ."

The balloon station was, in fact, ninety percent decoy. Sending a man aloft would be not only tremendously expensive, but would create moral problems for both sides. An observer in the cupola could be blocked by a fence or obstruction; a signaler within the park area could be arrested; balls laden with information could be intercepted. But there was only one way to deal with a balloonist. He would have to be shot down. Waite wasn't even sure he could entice an aeronaut into the danger zone above Gravesend Park, or that he wanted to. But he did want to give Pinky something to think about. So he had also rented a steam winch, which sat in the pasture, covered with a large section of canvas. And if worst came to worst, Waite thought, hoping it would not . . .

Inside Gravesend, crews could be seen working on several

small circular platforms about six feet in diameter. "This is like the world's biggest chess board," Peter DeLacy said. "I'm rather enjoying it. If it weren't for the other pool sellers, and Humstone, I'd enjoy it even more."

"Are they getting nervous?" Waite asked.

DeLacy nodded. "This has become a holy war for them. A holy war of dollars and cents. Frankly, I think they're taking it too seriously, but then I've got the restaurants and my other investments. I can see their point."

Waite swallowed. He knew he could not afford to fail, knew also that his rival Pinkerton would not be panicked or tricked by obvious devices. The contest would go to the man who thought faster, reacted quicker, or was more ruthless.

"What do you think he has in mind for the odds board?" DeLacy asked. He looked at Pinky's new wall, which even now blocked about half of the track interior from view.

Waite looked at the quartet of men grouped about the large board between the infield and grandstand on which a series of movable panels and blocks provided race information for the track's bettors. The men seemed more than a little concerned about the base of the board, which led Waite to reply, "They're probably devising a method of putting it on tracks or runners so they can shift it from side to side."

"Good Lord," DeLacy laughed. "I was wrong when I said this was a chess game. It's more like a shooting gallery."

"Let's hope not," Waite said.

His eyes were drawn from the odds board by a familiar figure entering the track through the main gate. It was Mary Dwyer. As she went through the gate, she turned, shaded her eyes with a gloved hand, and looked directly at the cupola. Then she waved. Waite returned it.

Waite watched her go up the ramp into the main office. For a week or two, after the fiasco in Humstone's office, he had avoided her, not trusting himself to speak. Then, unexpectedly, she had dropped by his office.

"I've just been shopping and thought I would drop in," she said. "I hope you don't mind."

"No," he said stiffly.

"I've missed you," she said. "Is something the matter?"

"You know perfectly well what's the matter," he said.

"Well, I know the negotiations didn't go well," she replied. "But that's no reason to turn against your friends." Her smile was disarmingly attractive. "Have you just been frightfully busy in general, or have I done something specific?" she asked.

"All right," Waite returned. "You've made your point. And you had your fun, I presume, with your little Saint Patrick's Day special surprise."

"Surprise? I don't know what you mean. Wasn't the two-thousand-dollar figure right?"

"Oh, that was a reasonable figure, I suppose," Waite smiled. "What wasn't right was soothing him with that Saint Patrick's Day reminder."

Mary's hand flew to her mouth. "You didn't mention that to him, did you?"

"Of course," Waite murmured. Then he looked her directly in the eye. "You really didn't do that deliberately?"

Mary returned his gaze. "I don't think that even deserves an answer," she said.

"What does that mean?"

"It means I'm no more guilty of tampering with the situation than you are. I'm just a bystander, too."

After giving it some more thought, Waite decided that at the very worst, she had played a cruel joke on him. Along with the piece of accurate information, she had given him a red herring, and like a voracious shark, he had snapped it up. It was a valuable lesson, he supposed, and after a few days, he began seeing her again, although because of her father's objection, their meetings were always discreet. But their relationship became somewhat cooler. Waite attributed it in large part to the growing tension between rival forces as the fall meet at Gravesend approached.

"That's a most attractive young lady, Waite," said DeLacy.

"Yes indeed, she is that, sir," said Waite, "almost as attractive as your own daughter."

"Don't tell me, tell Dottie that," DeLacy smiled. "What do you think of this Pinkerton fellow?" he then added.

Waite didn't want to get into a discussion of the crisscrossed quadrangle that Mary, Dottie, Pinkerton, and he were becoming involved in. His own head was buzzing with ideas and anxieties, schemes and counterschemes, and though he relished Peter DeLacy's attention and esteem, he decided to play dumb. "He seems cool and efficient," he finally answered.

"Dottie says he has nervous stomach problems."

"Pinkerton?"

"Yes."

"Well, I don't see how that can help us."

"I didn't expect it could. I only mentioned it so you'll know that he's human, just in case you ever start figuring otherwise."

"Thanks," Waite smiled. "I'll keep my nose to the grindstone and my ear to his stomach."

"I wouldn't advise doing that in public," DeLacy laughed.

Twice she had done it to him, Pinky thought, looking into Mary Dwyer's dark eyes and listening to the silence within himself. He wondered about her power over him, but whatever it was, she was young, pretty, and made him feel comfortable. He would relax and enjoy her company, never forgetting, of course, that she was still seeing Waite Nicholson and capricious enough to be a spy.

"Your father's down at the paddock," Pinky said. "He should be back in a minute or two."

"Thank you," Mary smiled. "Is he pleased with what you've done?"

"He seems to be," Pinky said. " 'Course, we haven't done anything yet."

"I'd call that towering wall something."

"Well, Miss Dwyer," Pinky said, "that's just an object. The true measure of what we do will be seen in the poolrooms. If they continue getting their information, it doesn't matter if we build a wall to the moon. We'll have failed."

"Do you expect to fail?"

"No, they'll win some, and we'll win some. But we only have to stop them enough so that they'll have to give up eventually; and that I can assure you we'll do."

"What makes you so confident?"

"A man's got to be confident. If you think you're going to miss your mark, chances are you'll miss. If you worry about saying the wrong word, that word will probably come out." He almost added, "If you think your stomach's going to break into song, it sure as heck will."

Mary marveled at his casual strength. No doubt his mind was busy with plans to combat the Ditmas Company and pool sellers, and she was the farthest thing from his consciousness. Such a situation did not appeal to her. If he were hostile, she could have tolerated it. But his matter-of-fact politeness disquieted her. "What do you think of me?" she suddenly asked.

"In what way?" Pinky smiled, "Mentally, physically, emotionally, intellectually?" He almost added: "Gastrically."

"I mean," she said, "are you suspicious of me because I'm a friend of Waite Nicholson? Do you think I may be a spy for the Ditmas Company?"

Pinky nodded. "Mostly, I guess I'm suspicious of you because you're a beautiful woman, and when I look into your eyes something inside of me just seems to stand still."

"Thank you," Mary said with a lightly sarcastic smile. "But I seem to have heard of that ailment before."

"Really?" Pinky replied. "I didn't know it was that common."

POOL SELLERS DEFEATED, *The New York Times* headlined as the day of the fall meet dawned. "The giant wall opposite Sleight's hotel is now complete. Except for a few trees, which are far removed from the track, there seems to be no way the forces of illegal gambling in New York can gain their evil information. While it is true that a few runners may find ways to signal, without a single strong point with good visibility, the pool sellers are doomed. We look forward to their demise with eager anticipation. Patrons of the track are warned that the gates will be closed at the beginning of the first race and no one will be allowed to leave until the last race without special permission from the management. This regretful inconvenience can be blamed directly on the evil forces of the pool sellers."

Unfortunately for the *Times*, the hopeful editorial was written before new construction atop the cupola began.

It was five o'clock in the morning when the heavy trucks loaded with lumber, men, and tools rolled up to the hotel. Hopping off the back of the lead truck, Waite motioned the carpenters out and watched them file into the ramshackle building with their designated equipment. It had all been carefully prepared, the wood measured and cut beforehand. Some nails had even been partially driven into the wood, awaiting only their companion pieces and several hard whacks for completion. Waite's smile was confident as lanterns were lit and the first sounds of construction echoed across the flat ground between the hotel and Gravesend Park.

W. C. Humstone was at his elbow, his thin face etched with nervousness. "Why did you wait until the last minute?" he asked.

"Because we wanted to hide our plans as long as possible," Waite replied. "And we want to show them how organized we are."

Within minutes, neighbors of Gravesend had collected in knots and were admiring the efficiency of Waite's carpentry crew.

Their open-mouthed admiration was justified, for no circus tent ever went up faster. *Bonk-bonk. Bonk.* Ten feet into the air above the cupola rose the latticework of a staircase. Then, even before the staircase was filled in, a landing was built. Then another staircase extended itself still higher. Carpenters swarmed like ants about the base and sides of the structure, hammering, passing material, hardly a motion of their bodies or blow of their hammers wasted. Soon it was daylight.

Bonk-bonk-bonk.

The third staircase rose to sounds of, "No! No! It will fall!" But it did not fall, for Waite had discovered that despite its rickety appearance, the support foundations of the cupola at Sleight's hotel were massive and sound. At least the high-priced builder he had hired weeks before had assured him that was the case.

By midmorning, however, the hammering atop the cupola was already being answered by equally frantic hammering from behind the fence at the track.

"Damn," said Waite, "he's right with me. Keep going!" he exhorted his men. Even as he spoke, the fence at the track started to rise again. From fifty to fifty-five feet. Then to sixty.

In response, another landing was added above the cupola, then still another. Soon the huge ugly derrick of white pine began to tremble beneath the carpenters' weight. A sudden breeze from Sheepshead Bay blew the men's hats off, but they continued hammering, pausing only to take several deep breaths before fastening another brace or section of planking into position. Cheering first for one side, then for the other, the residents of Gravesend came and left, then returned with members of their family or friends who maintained the vigil until midmorning, when the wall stopped growing at sixty-six feet. But the platforms above the cupola did not. Not until an hour later was the last nail driven. Although swaying lightly but visibly in the breeze, the tower was nearly fifteen feet higher than the fence opposite. Holding his hammer above his head, the carpenter who drove the last nail waited for the applause, smiled broadly when it greeted him, and clambered down the rickety stairway.

As he did so, Ditmas Company men were already extending the telegraph wire from the cupola upward. When a team ascended with a table and two chairs, a precarious feat, the crowd reacted with spontaneous cheers. One of the men bowed and nearly fell.

"There!" Waite said triumphantly.

"There!" Dwyer stormed. "Do you see what they've done?"

"Yessir," Pinky replied evenly. "I can see that it's higher than our wall."

"If you can see it, why didn't you build the wall higher?"

"Because it's too shaky as it is. I don't imagine you want that thing to fall down on your customers, do you?"

"No, of course not. But—"

"Don't worry about it then, we'll take care of it soon enough," Pinky said. "Let's just see how things go till we do."

"But the first race starts in less than an hour!"

"Fine. Why don't you take a nap until then?"

Dwyer shook his head. He was beginning to wonder if Pinkerton acted casual just to infuriate him.

Ten minutes before the start of the first race, Pinky walked over to the odds board for a consultation with Harvey Kittering, one of the few park policemen he had retained. "How's she moving?" he asked.

"Fine. We got it greased real good. Takes us only half a minute to move all the way down there."

"All right," Pinky said. "They can read the board from here, but after we send up the canvas, it'll be up to you to position yourself so it's between you and their platform."

"Right. When do you think the sails will be ready, Mr. Pinkerton?"

"If we're lucky, some time today. I'd never of thought that ramshackled ruin could support all those platforms. Guess it's sounder than it looks. Anyway, you can't win them all, Harvey. But when we set sail, they'll be biting the bullet."

High atop the Ditmas Company tower, Michael Chance frowned. "They can move that odds board," he called down to Waite. "I just saw it move."

"I know."

"What are we gonna do?"

"There's nothing we can do. Or have to," Waite yelled back up. "We'll just wait till they move it to where we can't read it."

"I guess you're right," Chance said. Swaying slightly, a situation that caused an uneasy sensation in the pit of his stomach, he trained his spyglass on the line of starting horses. It was just one o'clock.

"They're off at Gravesend!" Thomas Wynn shouted. The crowd in Peter DeLacy's poolroom cheered boisterously, for it had been rumored that betting might be curtailed as a result of the fence constructed at the track. But shortly before noon, the young men who distributed odds, scratches, weights, and jockey information appeared as usual outside DeLacy's and the other pool selling establishments. Word soon spread that bets were being taken and the regular customers, along with many curiosity seekers, crowded inside.

"It's Chesapeake taking the lead at the quarter pole," Wynn continued. "He's followed by Eclipse, Trinity, Dennis Dunn, Rinfax, and Refraction Filly. That's the latest information from the Ditmas Tower, eighth wonder of the world!"

The crowd laughed appreciatively and continued to laugh and wager with very few delays, until the fifth race. That race began smoothly enough, in Wynn's usual impeccable style, and continued until midway through when he announced: "At the half, it's Dennis Dunn followed closely by—"

The crowd waited silently, tensely.

"Followed by . . ."

Thomas Wynn licked his lips nervously. The news had stopped coming.

"Jesus, I can't see a thing!" Michael Chance shouted.

Braving the warnings of his heaving stomach, he actually stood on the platform. It didn't help.

Just before the fifth race, the poles had appeared, growing like giant plants atop the fence. Waite immediately waved the pennant which signaled the first wave of auxiliary help in the park to go into action. "Something is up," Waite said. "We'd better be ready." He was right, for just as the horses sprinted into the far straightaway, the spires blossomed with huge sections of canvas. Caught by the heavy breeze off Sheepshead

Bay, the cloth billowed and flapped until the horses could be seen only accidentally. "It's like trying to look through a goddamn schooner!" Chance cried helplessly.

"Can you see anything?" Waite called up.

"Yeah! Sails!" Chance replied.

Waite was annoyed. Not because he was incapable of circumventing Pinky's sails, but because he had gotten so little value out of his platform. Less than five races! His hope had been to get at least a full day's information before Pinky found a way to stop him. Now, glaring at the fluttering sail cloth, he felt new respect for his opponent. The obstruction to his view was not merely a quick reaction, Waite knew. The raising of his cupola platform had been anticipated and plans made to combat it. What else had Pinkerton planned? Waite was not sure. He was sure only that the man on the other side of those sails was a cunning, methodical adversary.

Michael Chance rushed back to reply to Wynn, who was desperately seeking new information.

"Say whatever you like," Chance clacked back. "Just keep the horses close together, because we're having trouble."

Taking a deep breath, Wynn closed the field, bringing all eight horses into a fictitiously even line as they neared the stretch.

"How about Archie?" an assistant asked Waite. "Can he see the finish?"

"Right you are," Waite nodded. Grasping a green pennant, he waved it out the side window of the cupola.

A half-mile north, Archie Wethering, perched in the top of farmer Young's locust tree, set his jaw as he trained his spyglass on the horses pounding toward the finish line. Gradually their numbers came into view and he called them to his assistant on the ground.

"Trinity breaks away and is first across the line," Wynn

called out a minute later, after the information had been relayed from the telegrapher at the foot of the locust tree to the cupola and thence to New York. "Rinfax is second . . . then . . ."

"Who's third, Archie?" Archie's assistant asked.

"I don't know, dammit!" Archie shouted back. "I couldn't see him. We're too far away. He was blocked by another horse . . ."

"Can you see the odds board?"

"Yeah. Wait a minute."

As he spoke, Archie swung his spyglass farther down the track. Focusing his eyes on the board which posted the odds and winning numbers, he immediately recognized the first and second horses as being the same as he had called out. Then . . .

Then, suddenly the odds board was gone!

"It's gone!" he yelled in amazement.

"What's that?" his assistant yelled back.

"The board moved," Archie whispered.

It was true. No sooner were the horses across the finish line than Harvey Kittering suddenly spotted the tall figure of Pinkerton coming toward him. "Move it to your right!" Pinky shouted, gesturing in the general direction of the large locust tree peeping up over the north end of the grandstand.

"Right!" Kittering called back. "Right you are!"

Jerking his head southward, Harvey shouted directions to his men, who put their shoulders against the base of the odds board and shoved mightily. To the crowd's amazement, the board slid gently along the edge of the infield until the locust tree could no longer be seen. "That ought to do it," Harvey smiled.

The crowd in Peter DeLacy's poolroom began to grow restless, many staring at the wall clock with angry expressions. "Any word on that third place horse?" one of the milder customers asked.

"We're still working on it," Thomas Wynn replied.

"Have we got anything yet?" Michael Chance called down to Waite in the cupola.

Waite took the slip of paper from the breathless runner, who had managed to retrieve a desperately thrown blue ball from the very fingertips of one of Pinky's men. "Third is Eclipse!" Waite shouted through cupped hands. Then, turning to the runner, he said, "Thanks a lot, Willie."

"It's all right," the man panted. "But if we have to go through that more than a couple times, we're finished."

Waite nodded, knowing the man had a point.

At Peter DeLacy's, the announcement of the third place horse was greeted with mock jubilation. Thomas Wynn waited until the noise died down, then added his usual, "Next race starts in fifteen minutes, folks."

"Any idea who's in it?" a wag asked.

"No, but we're working on it," Wynn replied sardonically.

With his view of the odds board blocked from outside the track, Waite decided to signal his second band of auxiliaries inside the park in an effort to obtain information about the next race. But as he reached for a pennant, he suddenly realized that Pinky's schooners blocked the auxiliaries' view of the cupola. "Send out Paul Revere with the signal that we need all the help we can get," he called down the stairway.

A moment later, from farmer Young's pasture, a solitary horseman broke into view. Galloping at full speed, he seemed about to collide with the Gravesend fence until the very last second when he suddenly veered to his left and began circling the gravel road outside the park at breakneck speed.

Philip Dwyer slammed down the telephone, glared at Pinky. "The *Times* men at DeLacy's say they got the results," he said curtly.

"Well, maybe they did," Pinky replied. "But they sure paid for them."

"We got to do better than that!"

"Mr. Dwyer," Pinky said evenly, "in a war of attrition, patience is a virtue. We'll wear them down. Don't worry."

Still grumbling, Dwyer jammed his hat on his head and stalked back outside. Pinky followed.

When they walked from under the grandstand, they could hear the crowd noise swell into a mixture of laughter and cheers.

"What the hell's going on now?" Dwyer muttered.

The answer came when they spotted the object which was amusing the crowd—a man on horseback galloping about the track's outside perimeter. In his left hand, tucked under his arm, was a long pole, from the end of which dangled a massive piece of red material.

"Looks like knighthood's back in flower," Pinky smiled.

"It's not funny," Dwyer retorted. "That's probably a signal."

Pinky nodded. "Probably."

"Well, don't just stand there. Do something!"

"What would you like me to do?" Pinky asked. "Shoot him?"

"Stop that man!" Dwyer shouted, swiveling his head wildly and pointing from the horseman to the various Pinkerton deputies. The deputies in turn looked at Pinky.

"Calm down, Mr. Dwyer," Pinky said, holding up a placating hand. "Whoever he's signaling has gotten it by now. It's too late."

"I don't care. Arrest that horse!" Dwyer fumed.

With a sigh, Pinky turned to one of his men. "Jake, go arrest that horse," he said. "And don't forget to take the extra large cuffs."

———————

"All right."

Waite leaned back against the wall of the cupola. "All right," he said again, as if to reassure himself. "It's up to the people inside the track now. Whatever means we rehearsed."

He was disgusted with himself. Had he anticipated Pinkerton's quickness, he could have had his next major scheme in operation by now. But setting up the winch would take a couple of hours at the very least. It could be readied by tomorrow, but in the meantime, Waite and his cohorts would have to rely on piecemeal methods. Without a good observation point, they were virtually helpless, however, and the results of the next three races, delivered by ball throwers, runners who managed to slip through gaps in the fence, and signalers who were able to remain in contact with Archie Wethering before Pinky's men got to them, were slow and often incomplete.

At DeLacy's poolroom, several customers took the time to complain. Roger Mellon heard them out, apologized, and promised that the situation would improve. "This Nicholson fellow is clever," he said. "He's promised us that he'll keep the information coming, and I believe he will. Anyway, why are you complaining? We had to pay off on two horses today that ran fourth and fifth."

At Gravesend, Waite held a conference with his men following the last race, discussed plans for the next day, and finally accepted Michael Chance's offer to buy him a beer at the Kensington Tavern on the way back to New York.

When they arrived there, Waite immediately noticed a broad back that seemed familiar. It was Pinky. Hunched over the bar with a glass of milk in one hand and a whiskey in the other, he did not seem to notice them. Grabbing Chance's sleeve, Waite whispered: "There's Pinkerton. Pretend you don't notice him and don't act surprised at anything I say."

As they passed to the rear of Pinky, Waite said in a soft voice, "When Johansen gets here, have him outfitted at . . ." and then he dropped his voice even lower, as if suddenly aware that they were in a public place. When they got to the end of the bar, Waite paused, called out "Two beers" to the bartender, then allowed his eyes to travel half the length of the bar to where Pinky stood.

"Who's Johansen?" Chance whispered.

"Shut up," Waite replied, raising his eyebrows and nodding elaborately at Pinky.

With a slight smile, Pinky picked up his glasses and strolled down to their end of the bar. "You fellows out at the track today?" he asked.

"Manner of speaking," said Waite.

"Tomorrow's going to be an interesting day," Pinky smiled. "First race has twenty-six horses in it. And that's the baby of the card."

Waite laughed. "It's the first three or four across the line we care about. I guess as long as we get those we can stay in business."

"Well, I wouldn't count on Professor Johansen if I were you," Pinky said. "He's in Copenhagen."

"Sorry, I don't know who you're talking about," Waite replied.

"Oh," Pinky said. "I thought I heard you mention the name Johansen. You know—the great balloonist."

"Never heard of him," Waite said.

"Fellow like that could probably get a lot of information out of the track before we turned him into a Roman candle," Pinky smiled.

"I heard that Pinky Pinkerton never shot a defenseless man, didn't you, Michael?" Waite said, wide-eyed.

"That's right."

"That's the only kind I shoot," Pinky deadpanned. "Do you honestly think I'm going to take on a man who can shoot back?"

"Well, it doesn't matter. We don't need an aeronaut. You caught me a bit short today with those sails, but tomorrow's a different day. Even a moving odds board may not help."

"Sounds bad for me," Pinky said, shaking his head. "Can't you give me just a little hint of what's in store so I can get myself an excuse?"

"If a horse fifty feet high knocks on your fence, don't let him in," Waite said.

"A horse fifty feet high," Pinky repeated, scratching his head. "What color?"

"That's all the information you're going to get," Waite said. "See you tomorrow." On the way out, he said to Chance, his voice a bit louder than usual: "Send Johansen to me as soon as he gets here."

POOLSELLERS DEFEATED, *The New York Times* headlined. "Yesterday the opening of Gravesend Race Track's fall meet was greeted by the erection of an enormous platform atop Sleight's hotel in an effort by the pool sellers to gain information. The plan was thwarted when lawman and noted Indian killer Robert Pinkerton hoisted sails, which the crowd soon dubbed "Pinky's Schooner," opposite the platform and rendered it useless. For the remainder of the day, the pool sellers were forced to get their information by means which were mostly ineffective. Most of the poolrooms displayed signs which read, 'Not responsible for errors in weights and jockeys.' In one instance, the scratches for the sixth race were not known until after the seventh had been run. And the winner of one race was not announced until 56 minutes after the race was completed. As a result, great were the howls of protest at the pool sellers.

"At the end of the day, a rumor was heard that Laurits Johansen, professional balloon pilot at Tivoli, Copenhagen, had been hired by the Ditmas Company to fly his ship *Montebello* over the track, but this has since been discounted.

"Racing will resume today at the track with the Speculation Stakes being a highlight."

By noon the track was jammed. Enticed by the possibility of seeing aerial warfare—despite the *Times*'s denial—more than ten thousand persons, including theatrical producer Charles Frohman and leading lady Maude Adams, entered the park well before racing began. The pair immediately sought out Philip Dwyer and Pinky.

"We'd like to compliment you on having the best show in town," Frohman said, extending his hand to Dwyer.

Dwyer didn't take it. "Show?" he said. "This is serious business."

Miss Adams, meanwhile, sidled up to Pinky. "How many Indians have you killed, Mr. Pinkerton?" she asked, turning the full charm of her person on him. "Exactly now."

Pinky thought for a moment, then said: "One and two-thirds."

Miss Adams laughed huskily.

"Next year it goes up to one and three-quarters," Pinky continued. "You know how legends grow."

"Would you have time to take me on a tour of the track, Mr. Pinkerton?" the actress smiled. "I'd so like to know what's going to happen today."

"So would I."

"Oh, you're so modest, Mr. Pinkerton, pretending you don't know."

"I don't."

"Well, maybe not exactly, but I'm sure there's an inner voice that's telling you something."

"That's right, Miss Adams," Pinky said, massaging his stomach gently. "Which is why I'm going to let my assistant take you on that tour."

Two other visitors to Gravesend Race Track drew considerably less public attention than the theatrical duo of Frohman and Adams, but for the relative few who recognized and followed the rotund figures of Richard Canfield and John W. Gates, the day was a rewarding one.

Richard Canfield, owner of the Hoffman House, a gaming club near Delmonico's, had a round, somewhat blotchy face the color of corned beef, but his ready smile made him seem even younger than his thirty-six years. Dressed severely in a dark suit, matching vest, and bowler hat, he invariably puffed on the stub of a dead cigar before responding to questions from three reporters who accompanied the two men and their small entourage of friends. Already known as The Prince of Gambling, Canfield was rumored to have his eyes on no less an establishment than the Casino at Saratoga.

His companion was an older, larger man with a gray fuzzy brush mustache who wore a slouch hat and equally casual clothes. But if his appearance was unimposing, John "Bet-a-Million" Gates's bankroll was exactly the opposite. It was, in fact, enormous, and he used it judiciously as a prop to impress the impressionable, and sometimes to pay smaller wagers or debts. The truth was that the slab of ten- and twenty-dollar bills carried by Gates in his right-hand pocket was usually too small to cover his average bets. For that reason, he had hired a private secretary to accompany him and keep a running account of his winnings and losings on paper so that he would be able to pay them by check at a later date.

"What brought you to the track, Mr. Gates?" one of the newspapermen asked.

Gates smiled. "Just wanted to look at the fortifications." He glanced at the fence which had been constructed opposite the hotel cupola. "Bet you ten thousand that fence is sixty feet high, Dick," he said to Canfield, pausing to survey the structure.

Canfield shrugged. "Not worth taking the time to have it measured or find out," he replied. "Is it?"

"You're right," Gates murmured. "Any bet that can't be settled in two minutes or less just ain't worth the time."

He looked reflectively at the roll of money in his hand. "Someday, Dick," he said as they resumed walking, "the government's going to find a way to take most of this from people like us. But I'll be dead and gone by then, thank God." He smiled and doffed his hat to a pair of painted ladies who sauntered by. "What a great time to have lived!" he exuded.

At the corner of the grandstand, they paused while Canfield made a new attempt to light the cigar stub. "I'll bet you ten the next person who comes round the corner is a woman," Gates said.

Canfield nodded. "Odds are against you, John."

"That's the way I like it."

No sooner were the words out of his mouth than a pair of men turned the corner. "That's twenty thousand you owe me," Canfield laughed.

"Like hell," Gates replied, turning to his secretary. "Put Mr. Canfield down for ten, unless he'd like to double up for the next customer."

"Sure," Canfield said.

Still another man appeared. Gates's secretary made a nota-tion on his pad. The group then turned toward the paddock. On the way, Gates and Canfield made a variety of wagers. Once, spotting a woman with a closed parasol at her side, Gates bet she would open it before one minute had elapsed. When she did so, he promptly doubled the stakes on how long it would take a huge black ant to reach a crack in the cement. He also wagered successfully on the number of papers—odd or even—a news-boy was holding, and his winnings shot to fifty thousand dol-lars. But he then lost all he had won, and more, betting on how many orange ices—versus lemon ices—would be sold at one of the refreshment booths. "Don't worry, it's only money," he assured one of the newsmen who continued to shake his head at each wager.

At the paddock, Gates's losses reached one hundred thou-sand dollars when a specified horse failed to flick its tail more than three times during a thirty-second interval. Hardly had the loss been duly noted than Gates fairly shouted: "Quick, which drop of water do you want, Dick? Double or nothing!"

He pointed to a pair of water droplets at the top of a newly washed window of the paddock. "It's a hundred thousand on which gets to the bottom of the pane first," he said.

Canfield, nodding, pointed to the somewhat larger bead of water.

The men stood back and began to root for one drop or the other. A small crowd collected, wondered what the devil the commotion was all about, then joined in the fun when they found out. For a while, it seemed that Gates's drop, which moved steadily downward, would be the winner, but Canfield's choice, although moving more sporadically, continued to draw in molecules from nearby sources, becoming larger and larger until it suddenly plunged downward at a great rate. A roar from the crowd went up, causing heads to turn a hundred feet away.

Less than three inches from the wooden pane, however, Canfield's bead ran into a piece of dirt and abruptly stopped its downward movement. Again the crowd cheered. Slowly, inch by inch, Gates's bulb of water slid downward until it was closer to the edge than Canfield's. But its pace was agonizingly slow. "The hell with it," Gates said suddenly. "Let's call the bet off."

"But yours is ahead now," Canfield said.

"Yeah, but it's liable to take all night to get there," Gates replied. "I don't have time for that."

"For a hundred thousand, I'd wait till Doomsday," one of the observers said.

"Well, you win it," Canfield said as they turned away.

"Oh, no," Gates shook his head. "It's a no-contest. I'm a hundred behind. But I warn you, I'm going to get that back tonight at faro, my friend."

"But, sir," one of the reporters said, as the two gamblers made their way toward the exit gate. "Sir, the first race hasn't even started. Aren't you going to stay and bet on the races?"

"Oh, no," Gates said, his expression solemn but a twinkle in his eyes. "I promised my dear departed mother that I'd never risk my soul by doing that."

"You?"

"Yes. Me. What's so funny about it?"

"Did Pinkerton ask you?"

"No. It's my own idea."

Peter DeLacy leaned back in his chair and tried not to laugh. For a moment, it was difficult not to, until he slowly began to see his daughter's point. It really wasn't so outrageous after all. What did bother him was that the imbroglio at Gravesend had brought him and Dottie together, despite their philosophical differences, and now they would be separated again if she had her way. Still, he realized she was old enough to know her own mind, so he did not try to exert parental authority.

"What makes you think Pinkerton would want a lady cop?" he asked.

"I reasoned it out for myself," Dottie replied. "Sooner or later, something is going to happen at Gravesend that a man won't be able to handle."

"But can't you wait until that happens?"

"Yes, but it may be too late then."

"Nonsense."

"It's not nonsense, Daddy. I'd like your permission to go to Robert and volunteer my services."

Peter DeLacy stood up, walked slowly to the window, and looked out. "What you don't realize," he said after a moment, "is that this isn't some charming romantic episode. It's liable to get dirty, even violent."

"That's all right. I've thought about it, and I would like a career of adventure."

"Is there anything between you and Pinky?" DeLacy asked suddenly, hating himself even as he said it.

"We're good friends," Dottie replied. "I've been inspired by him, perhaps. After a lifetime in this city of corrupt policemen, I finally saw a lawman who is honest. I would like to follow in his footsteps."

"Do you mean that even after this thing at Gravesend—"

"I would like to continue in law enforcement."

Peter DeLacy sighed. "Do me a favor," he said softly. "Don't rush into anything. At least wait until something happens. Until there's a definite need for a woman. Will you promise me that?"

Dottie nodded.

"There!"

"Over there! To the right of the big tree!"

One by one, the patrons at Gravesend Race Track became aware of the phenomenon behind them, and one by one they turned to gaze with awe and amusement.

It began with the sound of a steam winch. For an hour before the first race, its *chuck-chuck-chuck* could be heard in the distance, but the noise was largely unnoticed except by those persons in the topmost rows of the grandstand. Those few hundred, however, were treated to a panoramic view of another spectacular bit of carefully rehearsed Ditmas Company efficiency. First, dozens of men appeared from behind the circular wall which had been constructed in the north end of farmer Young's pasture. They carried sections of pole, rather like the mast of a ship, which they proceeded to place on the ground and fit together. Longer and longer it grew until it reached a length of 90 feet. Considerably thicker at one end, it tapered almost to a point before a crossarm was nailed into position at that end. Then, fastening chains from the gigantic pole to the winch, the crew stood back and watched as the object was quickly hauled into a vertical position.

"Oooh!" the Gravesend crowd sighed.

It stood like a giant serpent, its head peering over the north edge of the grandstand, twice as high and much closer to the park than Archie Wethering's locust tree position, higher even than the cupola platform.

"Look!" grandstanders cried in unison.

Suddenly all eyes were on the thin man in a red sweater who, after fixing a set of spikes to his feet, slipping a rope about his waist and the pole, and gathering a bagful of equipment, started to climb to the top. As he did so, a ribbon of telegraph wire trailed down behind him. Hand over hand, foot by foot, but with amazing speed, he lurched toward the crossarm. When he got to it, he threw his leg across, reached into his bag, withdrew a small American flag, and fastened it to the very top of the mast above him.

The Gravesend crowd roared its delight.

"Get that man!" Philip Dwyer shouted, grasping Pinky's arm. "Stop him! Do something!"

It was too late. Within seconds, the polesitter had relayed information from the odds board at the track and the horses were off.

"It's Long Knight, Pearl Set, and Lepanto at the quarter pole," Thomas Wynn called back at Peter DeLacy's. "Bringing up the rear is Ma Belle and Ballyhoo."

Thirty seconds later, more information came, then even more, until the very end of the race. "The winner," Wynn said with an authority that was almost unknown to him, "is Lepanto. Second is Pearl Set, then Long Knight and Ballyhoo."

"Next race is in twenty minutes," Roger Mellon said, clapping his hands as he walked among his customers. He accepted their congratulatory comments with a good-natured smile.

"Shoot him!" Philip Dwyer said to Pinky back at the track.

"Take it easy," Pinky replied. "You can't kill the man for sitting on a pole."

"Well, we've got to do something!"

Pinky frowned as he strode toward Harvey Kittering and the odds board. Anticipating him, Harvey had instructed his men to move the board as far south as it could go. It was not enough. "He can still see us," he said when Pinky came over.

Pinky nodded. He still had those "funny little things," as Mary Dwyer called them, which were nothing more than smaller, portable versions of his canvas obstruction. But he doubted that they would extend high enough. If necessary, he could mass them to block the finish line, or at least part of it, but it was the odds board which bothered him. Returning to

Dwyer, Pinky said, "I'd like to discontinue using the board."

"Why?"

"Because we can't hide it from them while making it visible to the patrons. It's an impossible situation."

"But the people need that board to make bets. This is a business, Pinkerton. If no one makes bets, we go out of business."

"Well, if I may make a suggestion, why not post the information under the judges' stand? That way, it will face the infield and at least that polesitter won't be able to see it."

Dwyer was livid. "The firms which have their advertisements on that board pay me handsomely," he said. "If you insist on covering it, I'll lose the money."

"I didn't say cover it, Mr. Dwyer. I merely suggested we don't use it anymore."

"That's the same thing. If it's not being used to post information, people won't look at it and the advertisers won't pay. Good Lord, man, don't you understand the basic rules of commerce?"

"No sir," Pinky replied evenly. "Now can we stop using that board or not?"

"We will not."

By the end of the fourth race, however, Dwyer's temper had been cooled by the sobering news that every bit of racing information had been reported accurately in the New York poolrooms.

"Very well," he said to Pinky. "If you've got to stop using the board, go ahead."

Pinky nodded. "With your permission, I'd like to put some false information up there after the last race."

"All right," Dwyer muttered. "But be sure to instruct my men at the windows. We don't want to pay off on losers here."

"All right, when is it going to happen?" Waite asked, a light smile playing over his features.

"What?" Michael Chance asked.

"The bad information from that odds board. I can't believe they're going to let us have honest stuff all day."

From their perch in the cupola, they could actually see the board better than Arne Thorsland atop the pole, for in sliding the board as far south as it would go, away from the polesitter, Harvey Kittering had caused it to become visible to the men in the cupola. For the first four of Gravesend's eight races, the information on the board coincided with that passed along by Thorsland and signalers inside the track, but Waite expected that situation to change dramatically. "We'll be on the lookout for a trick during these last four races," he said. "So let's not be in a hurry to pass the results along to Wynn until we check them."

It was time, Pinky decided, to play one of his trump cards.

He had spotted Wally Kunstler yesterday, but had not had him arrested for a couple of reasons. First, Wally's position had not been good for the type of signaling he was doing and thus was not damaging to Pinky. Yesterday, the pool sellers' best point of visibility had been the locust tree, which was quite a distance from the grandstand, but today was different, and Wally was going full blast. Standing just on the edge of the crowd, well in view of the flagpole sitter, he buttoned and unbuttoned his coat, mopped his brow, shaded his eyes with a paper, and otherwise signaled the airborne telegrapher, largely to confirm what Arne Thorsland could see from his high perch.

But after the third race, when Pinky positioned his "funny little thing" so that a close finish would be difficult for the man on the pole to read, he noticed that Wally became even more active. "Good," he thought. "It looks as if they're depending on him now."

The second reason Pinky had left Wally alone was that he was a crook on whom Pinky had something, and crooks on whom he had something were like money in the bank. Now he decided to make a withdrawal.

Between the sixth and seventh race, he sent a small boy to Wally with a message. Glancing nervously at Pinky, who was out of sight near the edge of the grandstand, Wally hesitated at first, then slowly walked over as instructed.

"You want to see me, mister?"

"That's right, Wally," Pinky smiled.

"Wally? My name is Peter Goldsmith."

"Maybe. But you're Wally Kunstler to me. How's Henrietta?"

"I don't know any Henrietta."

Pinky sighed. "Wally, be honest with me, will you? I recognized you right away. You were one of the best dice men at Carson City, and Henrietta is your wife. Do you know she's still out West, looking for you? That was a pretty smart idea, coming all the way East. Henrietta didn't figure that. Of course, if she found out . . ."

"Aw, Pinky, you wouldn't do that to a fellow, would you?" asked the suddenly familiar Wally Kunstler.

"Do me one small favor, Wally, and I won't send off a telegram to my brother Bill tonight, saying where you are."

"What kind of favor, Pinky?"

"Make a little mistake on the last race."

"How big a little mistake?" Wally asked, his eyes narrowing.

Pinky smiled. "All you have to do is get the first and last horse mixed up."

"But they're paying me twen—fifty dollars. If I make a slip like that, they won't pay me."

"Do a good job on this and I'll pay a hun—seventy-five. Deal?"

"Deal. Second and third horses the same?"

"Same as on the board."

"All right, but dammit, Pinky, you're making a crook out of me."

"They're off," Thomas Wynn cried. "It's the last race of the day at Gravesend. At the quarter, it's Piccalilli, Panhandle, and Billet Doux in that order. Captain Brown is coming up on the outside . . ."

He couldn't believe it. When this race was completed, it would be a perfect day.

Tick-tick.

"Watch out for a trick," Waite cautioned again. As he waited for the results from Arne Thorsland, he thought about the morrow. Pinkerton would probably discontinue using the board and find a way to block at least the finish line from Thorsland's direct view. But he couldn't block his view of the entire park. Or could he?

Tick. Tick. Tick-tick-tick.

"It's Piccalilli, Captain Brown, and Airplant as they head into the stretch."

Waite heard the roar of the Gravesend crowd swell in anticipation of a close finish, then trail off as the horses crossed the line. . . . A few moments later, the result came from Thorsland:

"He says Airplant, Captain Brown, and Piccalilli," Michael Chance said. "Shall I send that to Wynn?"

"No," Waite replied. "I want confirmation from inside the park."

"Right."

A half-minute later, Thorsland's message came over the wire. "Correction. Order of finish is Enid, Captain Brown, Piccalilli."

"Who says which?" Waite asked. "Have him give me the sources."

Chance sent the message to Thorsland and a moment later the answer was telegraphed back.

"He says the board lists the final as Airplant, Captain Brown, Piccalilli," Chance said. "Our man inside the track says Enid, Captain Brown, and Piccalilli. Looks like you were right, Waite. They probably waited till the last race to cross us up by posting a phony winner on that board."

Waite wondered.

"I'll send Wynn Enid, Captain Brown, and Piccalilli—all right?" Chance asked, his fingers poised over the telegraph keys.

"No," Waite said. "Give it the way the board has it."

"Are you sure?"

"Yes."

With a shrug, Chance clicked out the final result to Thomas Wynn. "First, Airplant, second Captain Brown, third Piccalilli."

"Now let's hope I guessed right," Waite murmured.

A quarter hour later, a runner who had raced from the west end of the track returned with the official result. Airplant was the winner.

"Wow!" Michael Chance said. "How did you figure that out?"

Waite laughed. "I don't know, exactly. It just seemed too obvious for Pinkerton to post the wrong information on the board. I guessed that he'd be looking for me to suspect something, so he'd try to trick me from inside the track."

"But suppose he had just used the board?"

"Then we'd be paying off on another loser," Waite replied.

"That was pretty good going, young man," Pinky said, looking down at his glasses of whiskey and milk as if trying to decide which to drink first. Deciding on the milk, he drank, made a face, then sipped blissfully at the whiskey.

"Thanks," Waite smiled.

The two men were again seated at the bar of the Kensington Tavern. Both thought it natural to return after they had concluded their business at the track, although neither knew exactly why he enjoyed or craved his rival's company.

"Of course," Pinky said, "I had a feeling you wouldn't take the bait. I don't know why. Well, there's always tomorrow."

"That's right," Waite agreed.

"You have any more hints like yesterday? The fifty-foot horse didn't show up."

"He stopped by to have his picture taken with P. T. Barnum. But don't worry. He'll get there."

"I thought Barnum just died."

"Yes, but he doesn't know that."

"Who doesn't?"

"The horse."

"You know what?" Pinky said with sudden seriousness. "I think we both could use a good night's sleep."

Waite would have liked to sleep, but he had agreed to meet Mary Dwyer for a late dinner. When he arrived back at the Ditmas Company in New York, Mary and Rochemont were already waiting for him in the Dwyer carriage.

"Bravo!" cried Mary when she saw him approaching. "You

had a perfect day. Daddy was furious.'' Waite just gave her a weary smile.

"I took the liberty of borrowing Rochemont,'' Mary said. "I assumed you'd be tired. He's trustworthy and won't tell Daddy.''

"Thanks. I am tired at that.''

He leaned back in the barouche and tried not to think of Gravesend Race Track for a few minutes. It was difficult under normal circumstances, impossible when Mary broke into his reverie.

"I have an idea you might use at the track,'' she said.

Waite exhaled wearily. Everyone, of course, had a foolproof method of circumventing Pinky's precautions. Some were obvious, most were fantastically expensive, and others hadn't the slightest chance of working unless all the laws of nature were suddenly repealed. Beginning in September, when it became known that there would be a fight to the finish and word got out that young Waite Nicholson was in charge of the information-collecting mechanism of the Ditmas Company, he had been barraged with suggestions. If he never heard another elaborate scheme, he would be happy.

Mary noticed his annoyance. She did not expect him to be wildly grateful, of course, but it did seem reasonable that he would appreciate her thinking of him.

The sigh was followed by a long pause. Then, with a visible effort, Waite forced a smile to his lips as he said, "Yes? What is your plan?''

"Never mind,'' Mary replied, looking straight ahead. Actually, her idea was not that exceptional and she knew it.

"Come on,'' Waite said dutifully. "Tell me.''

"No.''

Waite shrugged, too tired to humor her. "It's probably been thought of already, anyway,'' he said.

"No doubt," Mary snorted. "Whoever heard of a mere woman concocting an idea that could confuse men."

"Please don't start that again," Waite said.

"I'll bet I could think of something far better than any of your obvious schemes," she said hotly. "If I just sat down and gave it some thought."

"I'm sure you could," Waite replied, his voice heavy with condescension.

"You have absolutely no respect for my mind."

Waite couldn't resist. "I've said all along your mind's your most remarkable attribute," he smiled.

"Are we fighting?" she asked.

"I'm not. Maybe you are, but I'm too tired."

All of a sudden, Mary realized what she was doing to him. "Waite, I'm sorry," she said. Noticing that they were only a couple of blocks from his flat, she said, "Why don't I have Rochemont drop you off and we can see each other Sunday? A good night's sleep will do you a world of good."

He did not protest, so she gave Rochemont directions to Waite's apartment building. When they arrived, he got out, squeezed her hand, and as he stood by the side of the barouche, Mary said: "I want you to make me a promise. If and when I perfect an idea, I want you to hear me out."

"Fine," he agreed, his eyelids heavy.

"Do you believe a woman could have a reasonable plan?"

"Of course," he said.

He was obviously tired. One hand held hers, the other leaned against the top of the barouche near Rochemont's pedestal. As he looked at her, Waite nodded once again and tapped his hand absently. "Yes," he said again. "Absolutely yes."

"All right," Mary said. "Have a good night's rest."

"Good night."

He walked off. As he did so, Mary heard a light chuckle. It could have come only from Rochemont.

"Did you laugh, Rochemont?" Mary asked.

"Well, a little," the dapper chauffeur replied. "I'm quite sorry."

"Don't be sorry. Just tell me what's funny."

Rochemont turned to look at her. He had been with the Dwyers for as long as Mary could remember. "I really wasn't eavesdropping," he said earnestly. "You know that I've trained myself to shut my ears to conversations, Miss Mary."

"Then what were you laughing at?"

"The gentleman," Rochemont replied. "He was standing right next to me, saying yes, yes, yes, with his voice, but no, no, no, with his hand."

"With his hand?"

"Yes, miss. Unless I'm mistaken, that young fellow knows Morse code."

"That's right."

"Well, that's what's so funny, miss. Maybe it was force of habit, but his hand and voice were saying different things at the same time."

"And where did you learn Morse code?" Mary asked.

"During the war, miss. I was the youngest telegrapher in Grant's army."

"I don't suppose a person ever really forgets something like that once they've learned it, do they?"

"No, miss."

Mary thought for a moment, then smiled. "Take me home, Rochemont," she said. "You've just given me a much better idea."

POOL SELLERS DEFEATED, *The New York Times* headlined. "Yesterday, the second day of racing at Gravesend Race Track started out in favor of the pool sellers, who erected a giant praying—or perhaps one should say 'preying'—mantis next to the track. Although the forces of Robert 'Pinky' Pinkerton and Philip Dwyer could have disposed of the man with one accurate shot, Christian morality bested the temptation to score a quick victory at the cost of human life. Thus, despite the fact that much information got through to the poolrooms of New York, Detective Pinkerton, the noted lawman and Indian killer, contented himself with blocking the finish line view of the polesitter. By the end of the day, he had accomplished this aim, and the pool sellers will find no easy method of obtaining results today.

"Near the end of the day, it was rumored that Laurits Johansen, the celebrated Danish aeronaut, was on his way to Gravesend with a balloon capable of carrying an entire telegraph station in its passenger compartment. This has since been discounted.

"The highlight of today's racing will be the Culver Stakes."

9

"That was Dottie DeLacy who did your dirty work in the ladies room, wasn't it?"

It was barely ten o'clock in the morning, but Peter DeLacy's bar had three customers drawn up to its edge when Waite Nicholson entered. "Glad you could stop by on the way to the track," Peter DeLacy said, putting his arm around Waite's shoulder. "I've got somebody here I want you to meet."

He guided Waite toward one of the customers, a chubby, red-faced bald gentleman of about seventy-five. Waite examined him closely as he turned to smile at them. His face seemed familiar but its origin eluded him.

"Waite Nicholson," DeLacy said, "I thought you and my old friend Jack Schultz ought to meet, seeing as how you have so much in common."

The man's name, like his face, was also familiar, tantalizingly so. DeLacy allowed the puzzle to continue for a moment while the men shook hands, then guided Waite's eyes with his own to the portrait above the bar. A younger, more cosmetically perfect version of the man smiled down at them above the small plaque which read: "Jackson S. Schultz, Health Commissioner, City of New York."

"This gentleman's a man after my own heart," DeLacy said, "a real bluenose-buster. A man of action, like you, Waite."

Schultz smiled to reveal a set of crooked, tobacco-stained teeth, but the effect was somehow pleasant. "I asked to meet you, son," he said. "You're doin' a hell of a job. People all over town are talkin' about it. Wanted to shake your hand."

"Thank you," Waite smiled.

"Tell him about the time you invaded Staten Island, Jack," DeLacy urged.

Schultz grinned broadly, apparently needing little urging. "It was back in '66," he said. "Well, you think we have cholera now. You ought to have seen it then. Ships was comin' from Europe two, three, four a day, just filled with immigrants. And the ships was filled with cholera, too. So nobody wanted to let the folks off."

"I recall reading something about that," Waite said, nodding. He hated to refer to an incident in the man's past as "history."

"Anyway," Schultz continued. "The city of New York, of which I was health commissioner at the time, owned this piece of property down on Staten Island near Seguine's Point. Perfect for a quarantine hospital. Except that nine or ten years before the folks on Staten Island decided they didn't want sick folks around, so they dragged 'em out of the hospital and burnt it to the ground."

Waite looked appropriately horrified. "What happened to the patients?" he asked.

"Most of 'em died," said Schultz. "And naturally, that scared hell out of some New Yorkers, so much that when I suggested takin' those folks from the cholera ships onto Staten Island, they nearly fainted. 'No, no,' they says, 'there'll be trouble again.' Well, I could see that, but I didn't figure we had a choice.''

"And that's when you invaded?''

"Yessir! Got myself a steam launch—one of them Revenue cutters, named the *Cuyahoga*. Then I took just five men each from every one of the seventeen police precincts so nobody'd get wind of what was goin' on and we set out about eleven o'clock at night.''

"Sounds like fun,'' Waite said, genuinely amused at the old gentleman's enthusiasm. "What happened?''

"Well, it was a complete surprise. We took over our own land and before the natives was awake we had carpenters startin' to work on a hospital.''

He slapped Waite's arm. "Can you imagine what would've happened if we'd announced we was comin'? Why, it would've been debated and kicked around and those folks in the harbor would've kept on dyin' like flies.''

"He's a man who took the bull by the horns,'' DeLacy said. "That's why I have his picture up there in the place of honor.''

Waite smiled. "It's a pleasure to have met you, sir,'' he said.

"Same here, son,'' Schultz replied. "In a way, you're doin' the same thing I did, you know. Kickin' dirt on them that say 'You can't do that!' like that's their only pleasure. That's why I'd like to be in your place . . . give it to the *Times* . . . yessir.''

"Well, if you have any ideas for me—'' Waite began.

"I do. I have one you won't believe.'' He put his gnarled hand on Waite's sleeve. "Listen, if you get stuck sometime durin' this meet and really need a whopper, you can count on Jackson Schultz.''

"Thank you," Waite said genuinely. "I certainly hope we don't *need* to use you, but it's a comfort knowing you're on our side."

A few minutes later, Waite's feeling that literally everyone in New York was involved in the Gravesend imbroglio was further strengthened when Dottie DeLacy approached him.

"That window at the back of the grandstand," she said.

"Yes?"

"It's the ladies' room," she said. "And there's a very nice view of your station from there."

Waite looked at her admiringly. She had done what so many had failed to do—given him a new weapon.

"Thank you very much," he smiled. "You've really been a help. Your father will be real proud of you."

"Oh, no," Dottie said. "You must promise me that you'll never tell him what I've done. It's important to me."

"Very well, I promise," Waite said, bowing with mock gallantry. "If necessary, I'll take your secret to my grave."

When Waite arrived at the track, Michael Chance and a man named Dean Bergen were busily opening crates of softly cooing pigeons. "Well, today your birds might get their chance," Waite said, slapping Dean on the shoulder. "You're sure this will work, aren't you? Because I'd hate to see you lose your birds."

Dean, a thin and intense eighteen-year-old native of Yonkers, nodded seriously. "Most pigeons have to be trained over a long period of time to come back to one spot," he explained. "But mine just seem to come back to wherever Warren and Virgie are. I don't know how they do it. They just seem to know."

As he spoke, he patted the cage which held a pair of extra-large pigeons.

"This is Warren and Virgie," he said.

"Welcome to the team," Waite said, bending at the waist to look closely at the birds.

Just then the fluttering of wings was heard, followed a few seconds later by the noisy entry of a third pigeon through the cupola window.

"Good boy, Barney," Dean cooed, reaching out to grasp the pigeon and put him in a nearby cage. Then, looking at his watch, he said, "I told one of your helpers to set him loose from Gravesend at noon. He's right on time."

"Any special instructions for our pigeon carriers?" Waite asked.

"No," said Dean. "Just tell them to be gentle."

"They will. You have my word."

"And don't let Warren and Virgie out or they'll all fly back to Yonkers."

"Right."

After reviewing the method of tying the small messages to the pigeons' legs, Waite poured himself a cup of coffee, took out his checklist, and began to plan his day. "We're going to make him move today," he said softly as he ran his finger down the list.

Frohman and Adams were again back with what seemed to be the entire cast of a New York play, and their presence infuriated Philip Dwyer. If only they would keep to themselves, he thought, it would not be so bad. But they insisted on dropping by the Jockey Club to stare at him and Pinkerton as if they were part of a menagerie or freaks at the circus. When Dwyer admonished them about the Gravesend situation being serious business, they invariably laughed in a condescending way which told him they didn't believe a word of it. They even gave the impression that Dwyer had created the battle as a piece of entertainment. That was the unkindest cut, although Dwyer did have to admit that attendance at the track had never been better.

Sophie Dwyer, on the other hand, enjoyed meeting the actors and had gotten into the habit of visiting the clubhouse before the day's activities in order to see them. Mary Dwyer accompanied her mother, as was her custom. Sophie assumed she was enchanted by the actors, too, and for a time so did Mary. Then she began to question her own reasons for coming. Was it to see Frohman and Adams and their crowd? Or was it to see Pinky? She had to admit that she liked a lot of little things about him, the way his eyes crinkled a split second before he released a droll remark; his generally patient manner with everyone; the way he downplayed his own importance, yet refused to knuckle under to her father. She even sensed a feeling of respect in him for her, not especially because she was an attractive woman, but for some other deeper, perhaps inexplicable, reason. He seemed to enjoy being around her. At first it made her feel somewhat uncomfortable, until she suddenly realized that he demanded no conversation from her. Simply being there was enough. Mary was touched and somewhat awed by their relationship, but did not agonize over her situation. It was natural for her to be at the track, so she began to spend more and more time there. Having challenged herself to devise a foolproof method of gaining betting information, her presence at Gravesend was even more important. She did begin to wonder if she was more interested in proving something to Waite or in outwitting Pinky. Fascinated by his coolness, she wondered if that were possible.

When the chattering actors finally left the clubhouse, Pinky looked at Mary for a long moment, then said finally: ''Would you like to have dinner with me tonight?''

Mary hesitated long enough for a chill to traverse her spine.

Had he read her mind? Somehow it didn't matter. "Yes," she replied simply.

"Assuming," Pinky said, "that after today's cat-and-mouse session, I'm still able to walk."

"Run!"

"Fly!"

It was the best day of the fall meet, from an entertainment point of view. "Oh, if only the great Barnum were alive to see this," Charles Frohman gushed to the cast gathered around him. "He would have found some way of taking it on the road."

The festivities began immediately, for patrons saw as soon as they entered the track that Pinky's "funny little things," which had partially obscured the finish line the day before, had been replaced by an inclined partition erected on the infield side of the raceway. Fifty feet long and eighteen feet high, it supported a slanted roof which projected out over the finish line like a covered bridge sliced lengthwise. While patrons in the grandstand could see the track perfectly, it was obvious that a large portion of the roof blocked the view from Arne Thorsland's 90-foot pole. Scattered applause greeted the structure as various knots of spectators realized the purpose of the awkward-looking addition to the track.

"Just what I would have done," Waite murmured, watching from the cupola platform.

It was barely forty-five minutes before the first race. Yet, with their view even more obscured than yesterday, Waite did not seem particularly upset. Looking at his pocket watch, he smiled, then called down to Michael Chance. "Now," he said.

Less than a minute later, the Gravesend crowd was treated to a bigger and better version of yesterday's performance. Two hundred yards north and slightly west of the 90-foot pole, a new pole, 120 feet tall, arose. As soon as it reached an upright position, a telegrapher, clad in a blue sweater, started toward the top. When he was a third of the way to his destination, Arne Thorsland, wearing a red sweater, raced for his shorter pole and spurted upward. The crowd cheered as the men propelled themselves in a dead heat toward their separate summits.

The *World* later reported that more money-per-second was wagered on the pole race than at any other time during the fall meet.

The cheers of the crowd amused Waite, but he knew the second perch would have only limited value because of its being so far from the track and almost head-on to the finish line. Still, he hoped to get some use from it.

In fact, he got practically none, for just as the first race began, Pinky gave a signal to his man near the finish-line partition. The man waited until the horses passed under the north edge of the roof, then pulled a heavy cord releasing a curtain of sail cloth affixed to the edge. This cut off still another five or six feet of the finish line from the polesitters' view. Now even the man on the higher perch realized he would have to content himself with using his telescope to watch Waite's signalers inside the track, a difficult job that was made even worse by the swaying of his pole in the typical Gravesend breeze. Despite these difficulties, race number one went to the pool sellers. Ever resourceful, Arne Thorsland had located Hannah Brown, who sat on a blanket on the infield grass, fanning a baby. From her position, she could see the information board beneath the judges' stand and simply passed it along by wig-wagging her fan in code.

During the middle of the second race, however, Hannah suddenly felt a gentle hand on her wrist and heard a voice say, "Allow me."

It was Pinky. Removing the fan from Hannah's fingers, he

swung it gently back and forth over the sleeping baby. "Your wrist must be awfully tired by now," he said.

The horses crossed the finish line.

Ten minutes passed.

In the cupola, Waite swung his head back and forth. "What's happening?" he asked. "What happened to Arne and Hannah?"

Chance took down Thorland's message. "Hannah's been nabbed," he said.

"So soon?" Waite muttered, checking her off the list. "Damn that Pinkerton."

"What now?"

"We'll go with the birds," Waite said. "Give the signal."

By the time a runner reported with the second race results, the third race had already started and chaos reigned in the New York poolrooms. "You'd better do better," Thomas Wynn telegraphed back.

Meanwhile, at the track, patrons were treated to the sight of Hannah Brown kicking her Pinkerton captor in the shins as she was led off following the second race. After the third race, the crowd gaped as a pair of pigeons suddenly flew out of the grandstand, circled high above the track, and flapped off toward the cupola.

As they departed, however, a piece of folded paper drifted down in their wakes.

"Carrier pigeons," Pinky said, watching the birds fly off. "I was wondering when he would get to that." Pointing to the fluttering paper, he shouted, "Get that message, Charles!"

A minute later, Waite grasped the first bird and muttered a curse as he discovered its leg was bare. "Damn it," he said. "I spent half the morning showing them how to fasten those things."

His anger lessened a moment later when the second pigeon arrived with the necessary order of finish.

"I would say it's now two races for the robbers and one for the cops," Charles Frohman announced sagely.

Pinky's men immediately started a thorough search of the crowd to find out which patrons had smuggled in pigeons. One man inadvertently identified himself just after the fourth race by suddenly bursting into laughter, clutching at his chest, and falling to the ground. When he was apprehended, it was discovered that a pigeon hidden in his coat pocket had clawed its way through some torn lining and suddenly made an appearance beneath the man's underwear.

"What'll we do with this?" one of Pinky's men asked, holding the captured pigeon carefully with both hands.

"Hold on to it for now," Pinky said. "Meanwhile, keep looking, and send for Snapper Garrison."

"Right."

As the assistant turned to leave, Pinky once again scanned the crowd for suspicious characters, keeping a particularly keen eye for stragglers at the fringes. Almost immediately, he noticed what seemed to be a furtive signal given by a man in a tan duster to a stout woman clad in a large bustle and hoop skirt. Judging her to be about fifty years old, Pinky was a bit surprised to see her wink at the man and nod toward the rear of the grandstand. His eyes followed them as they slipped behind the structure, then reappeared less than a half-minute later, the man buttoning his coat and glancing about as if to make sure no one had seen them.

"No, it can't be . . ." Pinky muttered.

As soon as the man was gone, the woman reappeared, smoothing her skirts briskly, and promptly took up her old position.

"I'll be damned," Pinky chuckled. "That's about the quickest . . ."

No sooner were the words out of his mouth, however, than a repeat of the previous scene occurred between the woman and a different man. "Oh, hell!" Pinky shouted, starting to run toward the grandstand. As he did so, he gestured to one of his men to follow, but slowed down as the woman reappeared suddenly. Catching her eye, Pinky repeated the high-sign he had seen the other two men use. The woman winked in response, spun on her heel, and started right back behind the grandstand again.

"Well, here's hoping she's working for the pool sellers and not herself," Pinky said, following her.

When he turned the corner, he was met by the sight of the woman bending over and fussing with her skirt. Straightening herself quickly, she brought her hands toward Pinky. There was a pigeon in them.

"Thank you kindly," Pinky smiled, taking the bird.

Something in his tone of voice caused the woman to look at him as if for the first time. "Damn," she said suddenly, snatching the pigeon from his hands. "You're Pinkerton."

"At your service, ma'am. Now may I have that bird back, please?"

"Sure, if you can fly, copper," she said.

With that, she threw the bird into the air, where it disappeared in a flurry of thrashing wings.

Just then, Pinky's man arrived. "I'll be danged," he said in amazement. "It's Penelope Pockets, the most notorious shoplifter in New York. I'd know that face and skirt anywhere. What's she got under there, Mr. Pinkerton?"

"Pigeons."

"Pigeons, eh?" said the man. "Well, if I know Penelope, she's got enough to stock a good-sized loft."

"Here," Pinky said. "Take her other arm and help me escort her to the office."

"I don't need no escorting," the woman said.

As they started up the steps to the grandstand, Penelope

flapping her elbows like a wounded chicken in an effort to keep the men's hands off her, a familiar voice suddenly said, "Robert, can I be of some service?"

Turning in the direction of the voice, Pinky spotted a woman beneath a huge hat covered with rose blossoms. A heavy veil, also covered with rose blossoms, nearly obscured the face behind it.

Pinky managed to suppress a laugh. "What the deuce are you doing hiding behind that rosebush, Dottie?" he asked instead.

"Oh," she said. "You saw through my disguise."

"I recognized your voice. Why are you wearing all that?"

"Well, I wanted to come here today, but I was afraid if they knew who I was, they wouldn't let me in," Dottie explained.

"I see," Pinky said sardonically. "So you thought you'd make yourself as inconspicuous as possible."

"That's right. Isn't it a good disguise? I looked in the mirror and even I couldn't tell it's me."

"Only a honeybee could tell."

"Thank you, Robert," Dottie said gaily. Then, in a voice suddenly grown serious, she added: "I see you've apprehended a female suspect. Could you use my help?"

"Thank you for your offer," Pinky smiled. "But this is man's work, despite what it looks like. All we're doing is escorting this lady to the office where she wants to give us some pigeons she has . . . tucked away. Then she has to leave. Don't you, Penelope?"

"Eat your hat, flatfoot," the disgruntled woman sneered.

Dottie sighed. "Well, Robert, perhaps there will be some time when you do need me," she said. "If that happens, will you let me help?"

"You have my word on it," Pinky said. At the office they found two pigeons left in the trick pockets of Penelope's skirt, which seemed capable of holding three to four dozen birds.

"Been a busy little girl, haven't you?" Pinky said.

"I hope you find out the first time you turn those blue eyes up to the sky, honey," Penelope smiled.

"Thank you. You can go now."

Pinky next turned to a small man at his desk who was waiting with an eager smile. "Did you want to see me, Mr. Pinkerton?" the man asked.

"That's right, Snapper."

"Will I get a chance to do my stuff?"

"Yes."

The small man smiled broadly. He was known as "Snapper" Garrison, a top jockey also reported to be an expert shot. "I sure love shooting pigeons," he said.

"Well, don't shoot this one," Pinky replied, showing him the tan bird he had in hand. "I'll be releasing him from the paddock after the next race. Let him get through, but if any others head for that cupola, bring them down. This one's got a little love note from me, written up just like the one we lucked into after the third race."

"Right, Governor," Snapper said, giving a little salute with his small-caliber repeating rifle.

With that, the little man went off and stationed himself in the runway directly opposite the cupola. Shortly after the fifth race ended, when Pinky's bird passed overhead, he pulled off two shots at it but was careful to miss with each. The Gravesend crowd immediately started buzzing and glancing about for the source of the shots. It was even said that Pinky had shot a Ditmas man until Snapper was spotted.

Snapper himself was too busy to notice the crowd's growing attention. His eyes were riveted on the pair of circling pigeons which a half-minute before had sprung from the park and now began to flutter toward the cupola. Those persons who could see the little man with the rifle immediately sensed what his mission was. As the two birds moved into range, some spectators shouted "Get 'em!"

"Fly faster!" others urged, taking the opposite cause.

"Duck!" one man yelled somewhat incongruously.

Garrison waited. At the precise moment when the pigeons were closest to him, he squeezed off one shot, then another. A split second apart, the pigeons faltered and pitched downward into the runway.

The crowd issued a mixed cheer and booing sound.

"Ben! Martha!" Dean Bergen gasped from the cupola, his hands flying to his mouth.

The safe arrival of Edgar was scant consolation. "You didn't tell me they'd—" he whined, clutching Waite's shirt front.

"I didn't know," Waite replied. Though genuinely contrite, he took a moment to pass the paper with the race information to Michael Chance. Barely glancing at it, he turned his attention back to Bergen. "It never occurred to me that they would shoot—he's some shot—two out of three."

"Please," Bergen begged, "get them out of there."

"Look, I'm sorry, but we've made a deal."

"No, no," Bergen muttered, nearly in tears. "They're like my family. Get them back for me. I shouldn't have been greedy. But when you offered me so much money—I'll give it all back but please, get them back."

"Forget the money, that's water over the dam now," Waite said, giving in to the boy's tears. "The problem is I don't have a signal to stop their being released once we've started. The only two signals I made up beforehand is one to release two birds after each race and another to release all the birds simultaneously."

"Oh, God," Bergen nearly cried.

"All right, I'll give the signal to release them all after the next race."

A moment later, the Gravesend crowd applauded the appearance of a blue and red rocket which suddenly appeared and exploded a hundred feet above the cupola. "Fireworks!" they shouted. "Who's celebrating what?"

"What do you think that means, Governor?" Snapper Garrison asked Pinky.

"God knows," Pinky smiled. "Maybe that's the signal for all those pigeons to come dump on you."

"Well, at least the flowers will grow on my grave, Governor," replied Snapper with an unexpected show of wit.

As the sixth race approached, Dean Bergen began to perspire heavily. There must be another way, he thought. He was being punished for being greedy, but surely he had paid his debt by seeing Ben and Martha killed before his very eyes. Now, in his mind's eye, he could see the rest of his friends flying toward him, some twitching and falling behind the fence, others veering off. How many would die? Tears of remorse and misery clouded Dean's eyes as he tried to think of a way out.

In the midst of his living nightmare, a runner scrambled into the cupola with a slip of paper. "Here's the fourth race results just in case you want to check," he said.

Waite took the paper. "Jee-zuss," he said finally.

"What is it?" asked Chance.

"The one pigeon that got through had the wrong horses on it. Find out if they've paid off already."

Chance tapped out the message to Wynn, his expression a reflection of his knowledge that there was no hope. "They've paid off," he replied, when Wynn tapped back his reply.

A moment later, still another pigeon flew into the cupola and nestled itself next to Warren and Virgie.

"Nona!" Dean Bergen cried joyously.

Waite took the note from the bird's leg, read it, and promptly doubled up with laughter.

"What is it?" Chance asked.

"A message from Pinky," Waite replied, then read it aloud. "How does it feel to be kicked by a fifty-foot tall horse?"

"I don't get it," Chance muttered.

"Never mind. What it really means is he's damn quick. One race in and the next he's got me. Well, let's see if he can get all of the pigeons this time."

The sixth race started precisely at three o'clock. A quarter-hour before, large numbers of spectators started assembling near the runway where Snapper Garrison was stationed with his rifle. By post time, almost as many fans crowded near the marksman as were in the grandstand opposite the finish line and nearly as much money was bet on the number of birds Garrison would pick off as was wagered on the actual horse race itself.

A half-minute before the race ended, Dean Bergen made his move. Stepping quickly to the cage that held Warren and Virgie, he flung it open, reached inside and grasped the two pigeons. Stumbling toward the window of the cupola, he then threw the birds outward, crying, "Go home! Fly home, Virgie! Go, Warren, and lead the others!"

The pigeons circled nervously for a moment, then began to fly away toward the north.

"What the hell's going on?" Michael Chance yelled.

As he said it, the race ended and a minute later, dozens and dozens of pigeons rose simultaneously from the grandstand, paddock, infield, and other sections of Gravesend Race Track. Standing in the runway, Snapper Garrison took a deep breath, blinked, whirled his head like a top, then made sure his rifle was cocked and ready.

Circling, diving, rising, the pigeons seemed more nervous than usual. For a brief moment, they seemed about to fly en masse toward the cupola, and Snapper Garrison's rifle moved quickly to his shoulder. But at the last minute, the birds pitched off to his right and headed dead north.

A moment of complete silence was followed by a low groan of disappointment from the crowd, mixed with scattered laughter.

"The pigeons outfoxed them!" one man shouted gleefully.

"I'm sorry," Dean Bergen said miserably, tightening his neck into his shoulders as if he expected Waite to pummel him. "I just couldn't let any more of my birds be killed."

Waite shrugged. "Well, it's too late now." As he spoke, he caught sight of a quick, flashing movement from the window at the back of the grandstand. Then he remembered telling Jane Anderson, a noted lady confidence man, to go to the ladies' room and check with him about halfway through the racing card. Michael Chance already had his glasses on her and had translated the hand signals. "It's Jane," he said. "She wants to know if we want the sixth race results."

"Yes, you bet we do," Waite cried.

Chance moved his hand up and down several times, then began writing as the small figure in the faraway window began a series of finger manipulations. "First is King Cadmus . . . then Dagonet . . . Yorkville Belle . . . Alcina Colt . . . Curt Gunn . . . Silver Fox . . . Lamplighter . . . and Phil Dwyer."

The news that Dwyer's colt had run last brought a cheer to Peter DeLacy's poolroom, but otherwise the place was gloomy. "It just don't seem the same," one customer muttered to Thomas Wynn.

"Cheer up," Wynn said. "We got that last race pretty fast, and I have a feeling things are going to get better."

Things did get better, or worse, depending on which side of the fence a person was. At the end of the sixth race, one of Dwyer's assistants rushed up to his boss and Pinky. "They got the fifth and sixth results perfect," he said. "Not much else after the start, but the end was right there."

"And the end is what really counts," Pinky said. Before the seventh race, he called his men around him. "I want everybody to keep his eyes open during this race," he said. "Just look. You men patrol the outside. You the inside. They're still getting the information and we've got to find out how."

The men assembled again after the seventh race. Danny Higgs, patroling the roadway between Sleight's hotel and the park, had spotted Jane Anderson. "Looked like somebody in the ladies' room," he said. "She was using hand signals."

Pinky frowned. "I guess whoever it is comes out to get the results, then goes back in and passes them along."

"That's easily fixed," Dwyer said. "We'll close the room."

Pinky shook his head. "Mr. Dwyer, if you think you had troubles at the main gates when we locked them, you haven't seen anything. There's no way we can keep those ladies out of their room."

"Then somebody's got to go in there and make sure whoever she is don't signal."

"Well, let's get up there and see what we can do," Pinky suggested.

They climbed the stairs and waited outside the room. Several ladies entered and left, each of them fastening a faintly quizzical, angry look on the knot of patrolmen. Pinky stood at the head of them, wondering if he had the disposition to just break into the room and interrupt the woman standing next to the window following the eighth and final race.

Werbleerblelerblelerblelerblelerblelerbleerberberberberble.

His stomach gave him the answer. And his stomach was right. It was simply not the proper thing to do.

"May I be of service?"

Pinky recognized the familiar voice of Dottie DeLacy, who had quietly approached him following his noisy confrontation with himself.

It was tempting. Quickly, he explained the situation to her. When he finished, Dottie nodded.

"I will go inside, if you like," she said. "But only if I'm properly deputized."

"Deputized?"

"That's right. I would like this to be my first official assignment for the Pinkerton National Detective Agency. If I am successful, I would hope there could be more opportunities for a young lady in an organization such as yours."

Pinky had to smile. The rush of words, delivered in a semiformal manner, told him she had planned them beforehand. But he really did not mind. She was probably right, and while he wouldn't recommend a detective's life for a woman, he could always speak with her later.

"All right," he said finally. "Raise your right hand."

The ceremony was appropriately brief, but when it was concluded, the rest of the force broke into applause. Bending low so that only Dottie could hear, Pinky then said, "All right, Officer DeLacy. Go in there and flush her out."

Dottie blushed just a bit, threw her hand to her forehead in a quick salute, and disappeared into the ladies' room.

The final race was over. Michael Chance focused his glasses on Jane Anderson, took down the letters E . . . N . . . G . . .

"Goddamn," he muttered.

Waite could see the second figure at the window and the beginning of the scuffle. Leaping to his feet, he grabbed another spyglass and trained it on Jane Anderson's fingers. With one hand, she was trying to hold the intruder at bay; with her second, she was forming letters. "Take them down, take them down!" Waite shouted, grabbing a pad himself and scribbling with a pencil.

Before she finally gave in to the harassment of Dottie DeLacy, Jane Anderson was able to form several recognizable letters. "What did you get?" Waite asked Chance.

Chance looked at his crumpled pad. "E.N.G.B.O.Y.S." he replied.

Waite looked at his own paper. "I picked up B.O.Y.S." he said.

"The E.N.G. must be English Lady first," said Chance, glancing at the list of horses in the race. "B.O.Y. must be Boy of Battle. That leaves the letter S."

"Strathmeath?" Waite asked.

"Or Stage Whisper."

"I'm pretty sure Stage Whisper was scratched," Waite said. "Send Strathmeath."

Only when he sat down with a sigh of relief a moment later did Waite's mind begin to re-form the picture of the two women struggling. Slowly the features of the intruder came into focus, belatedly, like a dream sequence returning after the sleeper has been awake for hours. She was . . . Dottie DeLacy! Shaking his head, Waite closed his eyes and looked again.

It was Dottie! "Goddamn," he said slowly. "You just can't trust anybody these days." Then, deep down inside himself, he felt a dull, aching sensation which slowly spread over him. It puzzled him, for he had never felt anything like it; nor could he recognize the pangs of injured love, because he had never been in love before. "Goddamn," he repeated.

He was still in a pained and depressed mood ten minutes later when W. C. Humstone came panting up the stairway. "Well, at least you got most of the results near the end," he said grudgingly. "Although the carrier pigeons certainly didn't work out.'' He looked at the perspiring face of Waite. ''What do you have planned for tomorrow?''

Waite shook his head. ''I don't know.''

''You mentioned something about hiring a balloonist,'' Humstone said.

''That's right,'' Waite said. ''I talked with John Allen and found out all of the ins and outs. He'll do it. We've even built a launching enclosure for his balloon the way he told us. But that was mostly to unnerve Pinky . . . Pinkerton. I'd really rather not use him.''

''Why not?''

''Because that will put us both in a terrible spot. If it works, the only thing Pinkerton could do would be to shoot down the balloonist. If it doesn't work, it will use up all of our budget for the meet and we'll still have a week to go.''

''Do you really believe Pinkerton would shoot Allen down?''

''No.''

''Good. Why not?''

''Because I've sized him up and don't believe he could kill a defenseless man.''

''Excellent,'' Humstone smiled. ''Then it's perfect. I'll use my influence to have the budget stretched to include the balloonist.''

''Well, sir,'' Waite said. ''If you don't mind, I'd like to find another way.''

''Why, for God's sake?''

''Mr. Humstone,'' Waite returned, ''I don't believe you should force people to the wall this way.''

''Nonsense. They forced us to the wall when they cut the wire. The responsibility is theirs.''

''Please, sir, give me another day or two.''

''Well,'' Humstone replied, ''it will take a day or two to get John Allen here. I'm going to wire him immediately. In the meantime, you can try to devise some other methods, although I'm sure you've used every conceivable trick man could imagine. If you've not improved on the system of getting information by tomorrow afternoon, Allen will ascend the day after.''

Waite sighed. "Yessir," he said.

An hour later, when he dragged himself into the Kensington Tavern, he was in an even darker mood. He needed to talk the problem out, but of course Pinky was not the person with whom to discuss the dilemma. He was, in fact, the last person from a practical standpoint, but he was the only one. Pinky noticed the younger man's depression and tried to jostle him out of it.

"What's the matter, young fellow?" he said. "You look like Snapper Garrison when he didn't get the chance to kill all those pigeons. Hell, you got more than half the races. That's not bad, you know, considering all the preventive devices we have at the track."

Waite shrugged. "The answer to your question is, 'It feels like hell to be kicked by a fifty-foot horse.' '' Then after a moment he asked, "That was Dottie DeLacy who did your dirty work in the ladies' room, wasn't it?"

"That's not very well phrased, but yes. That was her."

"Is she sweet on you?"

"They all are, son, they all are. It's my rustic charm," Pinky said with a wink. Then seeing Waite's pained expression, he added, "Look, she's just a friend and she was only doing what she thought was right. Anyway, she helped me out of a jam today, but I convinced her that, what with her father and all, it would be better for her to stay away from the track until this is over." Seeing Waite's relieved smile, he added, "But don't get your hopes up, young fellow. Thanks to Dottie, there'll be a half-dozen lady Pinkertons at the track from now on. Never thought I'd see the day." Standing up and downing his drink, he said, "See you at the track, young fellow."

"Do you have to leave so soon?" Waite asked, not wanting to be alone. "It's still early and I'd like to ask you a few questions about how you brace a tunnel."

"Sorry," Pinky said, hitching at his belt. "I've found a rare woman who wants to have dinner with me, so I've got to grab the opportunity. Then later I have to rehearse Finley's Fusiliers. We're going to entertain the crowd between races tomorrow with a little balloon shooting."

POOL SELLERS DEFEATED, *The New York Times* headlined. "Yesterday, the third day of the fall meet at Gravesend Race Track was highlighted by a desperate attempt to collect information via carrier pigeons, two of which were shot down and the rest frightened away. Following the defeat of this system, the pool sellers then stooped to their lowest ebb yet by violating the sanctity of the ladies' room. For several races, the final results were obtained by a female confederate who sent coded messages from the window of this room. Robert "Pinky" Pinkerton, the noted Indian killer and western lawman, was a perfect gentleman, however, and did not thwart the plan in person. Instead, he enlisted the first lady Pinkerton to prevent the further use of the room as a message center.

"Later in the day, it was rumored that Laurits Johansen, the celebrated Danish aeronaut, was in Boston on his way to Gravesend Race Track. This rumor was later proved false.

"The fourth day of the meet will continue today. It is expected that the pool sellers may try to tunnel beneath the track, so patrons are warned to be careful."

10

"Sorry, young fellow, it's either a bullet or the ax!"

Warned of the likelihood of danger, people flocked in even greater numbers to the scene of the potential disaster and almost certain entertainment. It was the most prosperous day in the history of Gravesend Race Track, a fact much-lamented by Mr. Engeman of the Ocean Hotel, whose aquarium, with its sea lions and three mammoth turtles, usually drew excellent afternoon audiences. The Elephantine Colossus stood silently, lonely. Even the sausage stands, cheap amusement booths featuring Negro minstrels, gambling, and envelope games were largely deserted. "All we can do," noted one entrepreneur sadly, "is wait for that terrible impasse to pass."

For the first day since the fall meet began, Waite Nicholson arose without a feeling of hope, without the certainty that this would be his day of triumph. In fact, he knew that the only luxury left him was desperation. He knew also that desperation did not fit his character. He played the game best when he dealt the cards, when he was ahead so he could afford to fall back a bit to see how the land lay. Now he was not an attacker but a burrower, a whale suddenly beached.

Peter DeLacy met him in the cupola.

"That aeronaut's in town," DeLacy said. "Humstone said he arrived this morning and that his balloon will be here tonight."

A muscle flexed in Waite's jaw as he stared out over the track. "I suppose Mr. Humstone told you I'm against using him."

"Yes," DeLacy said. "And I agree with you."

At the end of the third race, they heard footsteps on the stairway and a moment later saw Humstone enter with a large, round-faced man in his early fifties.

"Gentlemen," Humstone said, when Chance and Waite had finished piecing together the scanty information from the track, barely managing to transmit the first two horses' identities, "I'd like you to meet Mr. John Allen, the celebrated aeronaut."

The men shook hands all around. When the silence was broken, it was Waite who asked: "What kind of gas do you use in your balloons, Mr. Allen?"

"Hydrogen," the aeronaut replied. "On occasion I've used illuminating gas, but it's heavier and doesn't rise as quickly as hydrogen."

"Hydrogen is more inflammable, isn't it?"

"Somewhat. Why?"

"I presume Mr. Humstone has told you that there may be some danger in this job," Waite said.

"He said that the man in charge was not likely to fire at my ship," Allen replied. "In any event, there's always danger. I'm used to it. Immune, you might say."

Humstone cast a sharp glance at Waite. "One man's cowardice is another's pleasure," he said meaningfully.

As if to punctuate their conversation, an excited cheer from the Gravesend crowd greeted the martial sounds of a drum and bugle corps that accompanied the launching of a pair of small unmanned balloons from the track's infield. On the bottom of each balloon was a dummy figurine, holding a spyglass, and below the gently rising objects paraded a half-dozen blue-clad men with rifles followed by four more men pulling an old-fashioned cannon. Moving with casual deliberation, the cannoneers raised their weapon to a high trajectory position while the riflemen formed a line so that their direction of fire was away from the grandstand and over Gravesend Bay. Then, in response to a staccato order from one of their number, a fusilier lit the cannon's fuse as the riflemen threw their weapons upward in unison and pulled their triggers. There was an almost simultaneous deafening roar of cannon and rifle fire. The two balloons, by now several hundred feet in the air, promptly broke into twin meteors of blue flame, their dummies carrying them quickly downward into the bay. A cheer rose from the crowd as the squad of marksmen re-formed their line and paraded off to the accompaniment of march music, the still-smoking cannon behind them.

After a moment of embarrassed silence in the cupola, W. C. Humstone cleared his throat and said, "Well, of course, you'll be a good deal higher than that, won't you, Mr. Allen?"

"No," Allen replied. "But it doesn't matter. The Ditmas Company is paying me a handsome sum, in advance, and I shall undertake the mission despite the element of danger."

"I don't recall saying it was payable in advance," Humstone said, with a weak smile.

"It is now," Allen replied.

"Of course," Humstone agreed. "And I assure you, Pinkerton will not be so heartless as to fire at your airship. That little demonstration was only to unnerve us. Wasn't it, Nicholson?"

Waite nodded briskly.

"It sure as hell unnerved me," said Peter DeLacy. "Listen, Humstone, I have the pool sellers' agreement to negotiate for them. They said if ever I decided to pay Dwyer the figure he wants, I can do so. I am now deciding. Whatever he wants, he can have."

"Now look here, DeLacy," Humstone said angrily. "This is Mr. Allen's decision. I'm glad Pinkerton staged this little pyrotechnical demonstration for us. Now there's no possibility of delusion. If Mr. Allen wishes to accept that display as an accurate statement of Pinkerton's intentions, then I suggest he go home this minute. But if he's willing to take a small gamble, he can make himself a considerable sum."

"In advance," Allen added.

"In advance."

"Then, thank you, gentlemen. And good day," Humstone said meaningfully.

"Hey, Thorsland got all three horses that race," Michael Chance cried, peering through his spyglass.

Humstone stiffened. "We need to show them we can get more than final race results," he said. "Come along, Mr. Allen."

The two men descended the stairway.

"What the hell," Waite said, when they were gone. "The way Mr. Humstone figures it, it's only the fellow's life. How important can that be compared to Ditmas Company money?"

"In advance," DeLacy added.

"That's right," Waite said. "If that man goes down, someone will have to keep Mr. Humstone from searching the body to get his money back."

It was a bad day all around. Except for a couple of races, obtaining the track information was an agonizingly slow process.

Waite decided not to go to the Kensington Tavern that evening.

The work began late that night with the laying out of a criss-crossing network of ropes and sandbags as directed by John Allen. At the center of this network, the fabric of the balloon was placed down and attached to the hose of a portable hydrogen generator. About ten feet high, the generator resembled a miniature steam engine of the 1830s, consisting of two large upright boilers and a pair of smaller containers, all interconnected with pipes through which water and sulfuric acid were passed over iron filings to produce hydrogen. The gas was then cleaned in a kettle, dried, and fed directly into the balloon bag. Nearby also was a steam winch, its thousand feet of cable neatly rolled on a six-foot-long spool. By daylight, the balloon resembled a soft egg clinging to the ground, not yet having risen to half its capacity.

"Three or four hours more, gents," Allen said. "Then we'll be ready to take her up."

At the edge of the smooth grassy circle, Waite and Humstone watched the bag fill slowly. Humstone's face occasionally broke into a broad smile, rather like a proud father showing off his new offspring. As the pasture began to fill with curiosity seekers eager for a glance at the airship, Humstone supervised the placement of toughs outside the wooden fence. "Keep those people out of here," he ordered. "We can't take the chance that one of them's a Dwyer man."

Intimidated by the presence of street brawlers, who stationed themselves around the circumference of the circle, the crowd remained at a safe distance, but by midmorning there were more than a thousand onlookers, including every young boy south of New York City.

Shortly before noon, when the plump gas bag stretched to its full size, John Allen announced that he was ready to go aloft. "Where's my telegrapher?" he asked.

Waite stepped forward. He had held a meeting with the

Ditmas Company men the night before to discuss who would go
aloft as a spotter and telegrapher. Despite being offered a large
bonus, none of the men, all of whom had either seen or heard of
the fusiliers' display, seemed particularly enthusiastic, except
Arne Thorsland, who was needed in the pole station, and one
other man with a wife and five children. Even Michael Chance,
Waite's young and seemingly carefree assistant, wanted no part
of the airborne spy mission. "You may be sure he's not going to
put a hot bullet in that bag," he said, "but I'm not."

Thus, purely as a matter of necessity, Waite nominated
himself. He even managed to put on a brave front, affecting a
certain casualness, but inwardly he was terrified.

My God, he thought, as he walked toward the wicker passenger compartment of John Allen's ship, they're actually
going to let me do it.

"If you don't do it, by God, I will!"

Philip Dwyer's face was red again.

Standing at the north end of the grandstand with Pinky and a
dozen of his men, he watched as the balloon slowly ascended to
the accompaniment of a chorus of faraway cheers. Beneath the
ship was its captive cable, which was being let out by the winch
operators on the ground, a heavily wire-meshed rope holding
the balloon to mother earth. Using a captive cable had been
Allen's idea. At the end of each day, the balloon would simply
be hauled in by the winch; thus it would not have to be re-
inflated the next day.

A half-hour before the first race of the day at Gravesend,
Allen's ship, a golden orb resplendent with large paintings of
exotic places, reached the end of its tether nearly a thousand feet
above the track. But the wind was blowing lightly from the west
and it remained well to the east of the track at an ineffective
spying distance.

Nevertheless, Philip Dwyer was angry. *His* patrons were cheering the ascension; *his* patrons were openly pleading for the wind to shift; *his* patrons waved in response to the waving figures in the basket. It would not do.

"I want that thing shot down!" he shouted to Pinky.

"What for? It's too far away now."

"Don't you understand—I'm ordering you to shoot that down."

"I understand, but the men at this park are taking orders from me. And I won't have them firing at that balloon. For one thing, there are people up there, and for another, the town of Gravesend is over there. Do you want our shots to land on people's homes?"

"No," Dwyer replied, "but I won't be made a fool of, Pinkerton."

"Nor will I, Dwyer. This operation is my responsibility and so far we've made Ditmas pay a lot of money for damned little information. The bettors at the pool halls are getting fed up. We're winning, I keep telling you. But if you can't leave the decisions to me, fire me."

Dwyer glared at the tall detective for a moment, then stalked off. When he was out of sight, Pinky scratched his chin thoughtfully. If the wind shifted enough to bring the balloon over the race, the observers in it would be able to see nearly everything. And, short of blasting it from the sky, Pinky would be powerless to retaliate. With a sigh, he glanced back at the balloon. Somehow he had believed that Waite Nicholson would never resort to that. Their battle throughout the first days had been classically cat-and-mouse, with neither side bringing forth the ultimate weapon. Pinky knew he could have enlisted sufficient forces to attack the Ditmas strong points, such as the hotel or observation pole position. But that would have been an invasion of someone else's property. Worse, it would have signified desperation, and probably resulted in people getting hurt. When you deal with a road agent holding a gun on someone, violence can be condoned. Here, Pinky felt, there was no need for it.

He had discussed the problem just the other night with Mary. "I'm sure that the minds on both sides are clever enough to continue coming up with nonviolent ideas," she said. "I hope so, anyway. Tomorrow, I'm going to the track and watch every race. That's something I haven't done since I was a little girl. So if you need encouragement, just look my way. I'll be in our carriage right in the middle of the infield."

He could see her now, sitting in the barouche behind the chauffeur, Rochemont, and she was watching him. Tentatively, she waved.

He nodded, then also waved in response.

As he did so, he thought he felt the wind shift.

"How do you like it now—better?"

Waite looked at the proud, vibrant face of John Allen and suddenly realized that aeronauts are born rather than made. The man actually loved it up here!

As for himself, Waite began to think he might make it after all. The height was somewhat terrifying, but it did give him a feeling of being safely removed from the rest of the world. Intellectually, he knew that Pinky's fusiliers' bullets could reach them, but a feeling of emotional euphoria contradicted the logic. Or perhaps he was merely light-headed. Perhaps all balloonists were light-headed. At any rate, he wasn't sure whether he liked being in the air or not. "Let's see if this thing still works," he said, busying himself with the telegraph keys. He sent a message. Far below, the little knot of men spread their arms and flapped them like birds, the signal that everything was fine.

"Damn," Waite muttered. His secret hope had been that the telegraph would not work and they would have to descend. But then he shrugged. As long as they were here, they might as well succeed.

He chanced a panorama view. To his rear—the east—was the town of Gravesend and the flatlands leading off toward Sheepshead Bay. Directly below was the cupola; a hundred yards or so to the west was the track, looking quite small; to his left, Coney Island; straight ahead was Gravesend Bay and a thin strip of land far in the distance. Was it Staten Island? New Jersey? Texas? Waite tried not to think too hard about it. "Is there any way of steering this thing?" he asked Allen.

In response, Allen merely laughed. "You pray," he said.

Of course, they did not have to worry about being adrift, thanks to their captive cable. That was one worry off Waite's mind. But they were in a very poor position to see the horses, nor could they see the information and odds board beneath the judges' stand. Waite looked through his spyglass at the horses being led to the starting line for the first race. To his amazement, their numbers were plainly visible. "We should be able to get the start and finish pretty well," he said happily. "That's better than nothing."

"Now! Can you feel it?" Allen said, his voice rising with barely controlled excitement.

"What?"

"The wind. It's shifted from west to east."

"Shifting" hardly seemed the word for what was happening to them. A strong breeze whipped through the ropes, causing strange twisting sounds, like a ship in a storm. Beneath them, the captive cable groaned and lurched; above them, the fabric of the gas bag fluttered menacingly. Waite had a momentary feeling of sickness, but he forgot all about it when he finally could get up his nerve to look directly below them. No longer were they above the circular launching position in farmer Young's pasture! Instead, the infield of Gravesend Race Track and judges' stand were plainly visible. "Good Lord, it's perfect!" Waite shouted.

"I told you we'd soon have a favorable wind," cried Allen.

Waite trained his glass on the board with one hand and sent back information as quickly as he could with the other. From a telegraph station on the ground, the data were quickly relayed to Peter DeLacy's and the other pool sellers.

"Holy Mother!" one patron of DeLacy's shouted above the excitement. "It's a jockey's weight! You sure you're not making it up, Tom Wynn?"

"Cross my heart," Wynn smiled.

For the first race of day number five, it was like old times in the poolrooms. After the first race, however, the information board at the track was not used. Instead, young men circulated among the spectators distributing leaflets which listed which horses were running. They were followed almost immediately by Ditmas Company runners, who spread the news that the first leaflet thrown over any part of the fence that was used by the Ditmas Company would earn the sender twenty-five dollars. The next several races were marked by near-panic inside the park as patrons scurried to find pencils, pens, and small rocks around which they could wrap their autographed leaflets.

By the end of the fourth race, Pinky was worried, and Dwyer was nearly apoplectic. "They're getting nearly everything!" Dwyer shouted. "It's all that damn balloon's fault. Get rid of that balloon!"

Pinky glanced up at the drifting object. Dwyer was right, unfortunately. His men stationed near the fences, outside and inside the track, had been able to retrieve most, if not all, of the patrons' thrown leaflets. His problem was the balloon, in clear view of so many potential signalers. It was just about impossible to prevent information leaking out.

"That balloon is trespassing," Dwyer raged. "According to the law, I own the air above this track, clear on up to Heaven. Now you get those fusiliers out here and let them have it!"

"I don't know who those men are up there," Pinky replied. "But if you hit that gas bag, they'll be dead men thirty seconds later."

"I don't care," Dwyer said.

"Well, I do," Pinky said.

"And I'm telling you—" Dwyer started. He never completed the sentence. A monstrous gust of wind blew his hat from his head and took his breath away, so violent was it.

Waite felt as if he were standing on nothing but air as the basket was nearly ripped from beneath the two men. Reaching outward, he quickly grasped one of the side ropes, but not tightly enough, as he fell to the floor of the compartment. John Allen, wiser to the whims of the air, steadied himself and offered a hand to Waite.

Below them, they could see the wind whipping up small cyclones of dust mixed with paper, scarfs, and men's top hats. A vicious downdraft suddenly caught the balloon, dragging it lower and lower until the aeronauts were actually beneath the level of the grandstand roof.

"Jee-zuss!" Waite cried, then pointed and grasped Allen by the sleeve. "Look!"

The captive cable was on the top of the grandstand, not caught on any obstruction, but sawing back and forth where it met the eastern edge. "Signal for us to be pulled in," Allen shouted.

Waite literally attacked his telegraph key with the message.

As he did so, Pinky was off and running toward the grand-stand, shouting at his own men to follow. With surprising speed, he charged up the four flights of stairs at the back, scattering patrons as gently as time permitted. Once he paused long enough to grasp one of his men by the shoulder and yell, "Fire ax!" before continuing up the steps. When he arrived on the roof of the grandstand, the cable of the balloon was already moving slowly, grinding backward in the direction of the steam winch in farmer Young's pasture.

"You men!" Pinky shouted, gesturing toward the cable. "Get it!"

A half dozen Pinkerton men suddenly flung themselves as one. Grabbing the pitching cable, they wrestled it to the roof, several of them even entwining their legs about the thick rope. Even so, it continued to inch its way through their grip as the toughs in farmer Young's pasture heaved on their end of the cable in an effort to add to the meager power of the winch. When more of Pinkerton's men arrived on the rooftop, a desperate game of tug-of-war began. Meanwhile, hundreds of track patrons burst from their seats toward the side and back of the grandstand in order to get a better view of what was happening.

In the basket of the balloon, Waite looked at John Allen anxiously. "What the hell do we do?" he asked.

"Our only chance is to get ourselves higher!" he shouted, grabbing a couple of sandbags and throwing them over the side.

"Why?" Waite shouted back. But he also threw several sandbags over.

"Got to pull ourselves out of their grip," Allen gasped, pointing to the band of blue-clad men only a couple of hundred feet below them.

Waite tossed another sandbag overboard.

On the roof, Pinky made a quick decision. "The ax!" he

yelled to one of his men. "We can't seem to haul this devil in. So we'll cut it loose!"

The balloon was exerting almost incredible force. Ten of his men could barely hold their own against it, and as the sandbags rained down on them, Pinky knew it was only a matter of seconds before the balloon freed itself from their grasp. When the wooden handle of the ax was placed in his hand, he let go of the cable and ran to the edge of the grandstand.

Waite spotted Pinky, ax in hand, racing toward the point where cable met roof. "Pinky!" he cried out, just as he raised the ax over his head. "Don't! It's me! Waite!"

Pinky paused in midswing, his head turning toward the solitary voice from the balloon. Not more than twenty yards away, his arms waving and hanging half out of the basket, was Waite. For a long moment, the glances of the two men locked.

Then Pinky yelled up, "Sorry, young fellow, it's either a bullet or the ax!"

On the word "ax," he brought the instrument down hard against the cable. But the thick cord was squirming so much, it was difficult to strike more than a glancing blow. Again and again Pinky swung, but with only minimal effect.

"We're getting free!" John Allen cried joyously. "In a moment, we'll be free!"

As he said the words, however, Pinky landed a crushing blow ripping nearly halfway through the tough cable, which then proceeded to shred itself even more against the rough edge of the rooftop.

"You're right," Waite yelled miserably. "We're going to be free, all right!"

Seeing that the cable was about to break clean through, Pinky shouted, "Let go!" to his men and stepped back. The heavy rope parted with a loud pop, sending Pinky's men in all directions like toy soldiers scattered by a petulant child. The balloon rose rapidly, its torn telegraph line and severed cable twisting behind it like wildly flapping kite tails.

Pinky looked up at the forlorn face of his rapidly retreating adversary. Raising his hand in a half-salute, he whispered, "So long, young fellow. So long." He thought he saw Waite wave back.

POOL SELLERS DEFEATED, *The New York Times* headlined. "Just when it seemed that the forces of illegal gambling were about to triumph yesterday at Gravesend Race Track, nature lent a hand by bringing the captive balloon of John Allen into a position where its cable could be severed by the alert forces of 'Pinky' Pinkerton. The information-collecting team ended its brief career by sailing off toward the west. When last seen, they were just north of Norton Point and quite low to the water.

"By a late dispatch yesterday, it was reported by several persons at the Upper Quarantine Station on Hoffman Island that they had seen a balloonlike object sailing to the north, heading toward the Fort Tompkins Light.

"Still another report states that the balloon passed over Poughkeepsie late last night."

11

"This is just a trick! Well, it won't work, you Ditmas snake-in-the-grass!"

"Can you swim?" Allen shouted.

"A little," Waite shouted back.

"Better make yourself ready," Allen said. "Take off your shoes and grab that life ring. We may be coming down."

Waite did as instructed, but once out to sea the balloon played a maddening game of tag with the water. At one point, they were not more than a couple of feet from the choppy surface when a sudden gust of wind lifted them fifty feet in the air before deserting them. The balloon promptly fell nearly straight down half the distance. Waite staggered to the floor of the basket. His shoes went overboard.

Allen laughed. "I've landed in the water twenty-six times," he said, almost proudly. "There's really nothing to worry about."

"Except the twenty-seventh," Waite said.

A couple of minutes later, they spotted a sandy beach and seemed to be headed directly for it. A light breeze teased them away from the shore, which caused Waite to curse but Allen to smile. "It's all right," the aeronaut said. "If my calculations are correct, that should be the quarantine island. We wouldn't want to land there, anyway. There might be cholera, and it could take us days to get ashore."

"But we'd be alive," Waite protested.

"There's a much more likely spot to land," Allen said, pointing off to the west. "Yes, that's quite nice."

Almost as Allen said the words, the balloon veered even farther from the island and headed toward their ultimate destination. Soon the beautiful expanse of Staten Island loomed before them and Allen reached up to allow even more hydrogen to escape. A minute later, they bounced to a halt on a deserted section of beach. Leaping out of the basket, they secured the ship to a tree. Waite then sat down, legs outstretched, and placed both hands flat on the ground. "I don't know about you, Mr. Allen," he said, "but this feels just fine to me. Yes sir, just fine."

"Nonsense, my boy," replied the hearty aeronaut. "A few more flights like this and you'll be one of us."

Waite knew better, but didn't argue the point. After thanking Allen for all he had done and reassuring him that he would send help as soon as he could, Waite shook hands with the aeronaut and started his barefoot journey back to New York.

Waite really had no idea where on Staten Island they were or in which direction to head. Walking to his left up the beach, he struck inland until he spotted a thick Dutch-style house atop a knoll of well-manicured grass. As he approached the building, he passed dozens of Oriental vases and pagoda-shaped ornaments set out on the lawn, which gave him the sensation of walking through an outdoor museum. At the house when the butler spied him, he latched the door before giving Waite directions to Fort Wadsworth. There Waite first bought a pair of shoes, then boarded the train, a smoke-belching local trailing three open cars, for Jersey City and the ferry to Manhattan. It seemed an agonizingly long trip. When he finally arrived home, it was well after dark, he was famished, and his feet ached and burned from the chafing of new shoes.

A small crowd awaited him at his flat. First in line was Peter DeLacy, who rushed forward to clasp Waite's hand as if he were a conquering hero. Michael Chance added his congratulations on Waite's brave feat, as did Dottie DeLacy with slightly downcast eyes. "We received a report that the balloon had landed safely, so we thought we would wait for you," Dottie said. "I fixed you something to eat."

"And here's a bottle of wine which I'm sure will go well," DeLacy added.

Waite smiled. "Thank you. Thank you all." Catching Dottie's eye, he said, "Especially you, Officer DeLacy," and winked.

He led them inside and they discussed the events of the afternoon while they ate. In the background, smiling vacuously but adding nothing to the congratulatory nature of the conversation, was W. C. Humstone. After an hour, when the others got up to leave, Humstone remained behind. "I'd like to talk with Mr. Nicholson for just a moment," he explained.

"Of course," Waite said. "But first I'd like a quick word with Mr. DeLacy."

He walked to the door with DeLacy, waited a moment until the others were out of earshot, then said: "I can use your friend now. Honest to God, I was thinking about it during the whole trip back. My brain is drained. If there's another good way of getting information after what happened today, I want to hear it."

DeLacy looked at the floor. "You mean Jack Schultz?"

"Yes, of course," Waite replied.

"I'm sorry," DeLacy murmured. "He died this morning. If it's any consolation, having that conversation with you made his last few hours happy."

Waite shook his head ruefully. "It would have been a pleasure having him with me in the cupola."

Dottie had returned. She looked at her father and he nodded to Waite. "See you tomorrow," he said, moving down the hallway.

"You don't hate me?" Dottie said earnestly.

"Of course not," Waite replied, somewhat self-consciously, for he could almost feel Humstone's eyes boring into his shoulderblades through the narrow door opening.

"Good," Dottie said. "You see, I'm not like most other girls. I like adventure, and this was my way to find some. In a way, we're a lot alike."

With that, she reached up, gave him a quick kiss, turned, and ran to catch her father.

"Well, I'll be damned," Waite said, going back into the flat. Humstone had obviously seen the quick kiss for he smiled slightly and harumphed before getting to the point.

"I understand you've been talking to Pinkerton at the Kensington Tavern," he said.

"That's right," Waite replied, kicking off the tight boots with a sigh of relief. "But they weren't compromising conversations, if that's what you think. Pinky . . . Pinkerton stops there on the way home the same as I do, and we ran into each other. It wasn't deliberate and he never got any information—"

Humstone held up his hand. "I did not say that. I merely wanted to check that he goes there."

"Yes, he does. Why?"

"Because I intend to be there tomorrow. We're beaten. Our only chance is to find out what Pinkerton's price is."

"I don't think he has a price," Waite said. "He's being well paid by Dwyer."

"Then we can double it. Besides, I have a friend who's quite close with Pinkerton's older brother Bill, the real boss of their agency. He says that Pinky doesn't like it here in the East. He also says that he can persuade Bill to bring Pinky back West. That could be quite an inducement, couldn't it?"

"Well, if you want my advice—"

"I don't," Humstone replied. "All I wanted was confirmation that Pinkerton goes to that tavern."

"He does," Waite said.

After Humstone left, Waite flung himself across the bed and tried to sleep. For the first time in weeks, his mind did not even think of Gravesend Race Track. He was free of schemes and counterschemes. Dwyer and Pinky had won. Waite had done his best and would continue to do so as long as the Ditmas Company wanted him to, but he knew there were no more tricks that could succeed. Forcing his mind into a state of almost total blankness, he slowly dropped off to sleep.

There was a rap at the door.

Dragging himself to his feet and pulling on his robe, he opened the door and saw a messenger boy holding out a large bottle of champagne with a pink ribbon about its neck. Sleepily, Waite started to fumble in his robe as if looking for a coin, but the boy said, "Don't bother, sir, it's already been taken care of." Handing Waite the bottle and a note, he left.

Stumbling over to the bed, Waite opened the note. It read: "Sorry to be so late with this. Bon voyage. Pinky."

"Well I'll be damned," Waite moaned. With that, he dropped back on the bed and was nearly asleep when still another rap sounded on the door.

Shaking his head, Waite again staggered from his bed and opened the door. In front of him was Rochemont, looking quite miserable. "I hate to bother you at this hour, sir," he said, "but Miss Mary is in the carriage downstairs and she says that it's time to tell you of her plan to get the information you need from the track."

"Oh, God," Waite said miserably.

"No," Pinky said.

"That's all?" Humstone asked, almost plaintively.

"Except that if you weren't so old, I'd push your ears together."

Humstone got up and walked dismally out of the Kensington Tavern.

POOL SELLERS DEFEATED, *The New York Times* headlined. "Near riots in the poolrooms added a note of sadness to the triumph of morality at Gravesend Race Track yesterday, where practically no information of value was collected by the gamblers. Faced with complete failure during the sixth day of the meet, it seems likely that the Ditmas Company will now abandon its plan to gain track information by elaborate spy systems.

"At last reports, aeronaut John Allen had quit this area."

"They're off," cried Thomas Wynn. "At the quarter post, it's Jabuka, followed by Saucy Sally, then Gondolier. Fourth is Dream Waltz. Beau Brummell, Prohibition, and Cottonade bring up the rear. Now jockey Andy Covington on Saucy Sally is bringing her to the front. . . . At the half mile, it's Saucy Sally . . ."

The customers at Peter DeLacy's cheered, even those with

tickets on horses other than Saucy Sally. Once again the con-
glomeration of clerks, businessmen, and professional gamblers
had something to believe in, and they gave vent to their happiness like schoolboys at a football game. Everything was coming
through right on schedule—weights, jockeys, scratches, odds,
and results. Not only that, it had started on the seventh day of
the meet and continued right through the eighth. Sixteen con-
secutive races without a hitch or delay!

"It's Saucy Sally hanging on as they head into the stretch.
Dream Waltz is making a good run of it. . . . Here they
come . . ."

Even Thomas Wynn seemed back in old form, customers
agreed.

"Dream Waltz wins it! Saucy Sally fades to third as Gondolier flashes by for second place. Fourth is Cottonade . . ."

The cheers that followed were louder than usual, the groans
softer; even the beer tasted cooler. "See you tomorrow,"
"Look out for King Mac in the second," "I'll make it up
tomorrow," were the good-natured comments as the customers
at Peter DeLacy's poolroom slowly filed out or meandered over
to the bar after the final race of the day.

One of the regulars managed to buttonhole DeLacy as he
moved past. "Hey, Peter," he said. "How's your boy doing
it?"

"Sorry, Joe. I can't say. I've been sworn to secrecy."

The customer walked away, complaining good-naturedly.

DeLacy smiled as he checked the receipts with Roger Mellon. Even after two days, he was amazed and amused by the
number of people who at least partly believed the "big telescope" ruse. Two days before, at the same time he started
receiving information by another system, Waite had dispatched
Archie Wethering to the top of his locust tree with a huge
telescope that had a Z-shaped bend in it. Then the story was

circulated that the new device could be directed so as to see around corners and obstacles, indeed that it was so powerful it could read the writing on one of the track leaflets. The New York *World* even circulated the story that the entries in one race were picked up by Wethering reading a leaflet held by none other than Philip Dwyer. Although nearly everyone scoffed at the idea, it was noted that Mr. Dwyer, from that day forth, held his entries card in the manner of a very suspicious poker player.

The telescope act was an adjunct to Mary Dwyer's bonafide scheme. "If you give people a fantastic enough lie," Waite had explained to her, "chances are they'll believe it. Anyway, we need a good solid distraction, and the telescope should do the trick."

Now, seated in the cupola with Michael Chance, Waite smiled a contented smile. Two days of perfection! He decided to return Pinky's favor with a little present of his own. After all, turnabout was fair play.

Mary Dwyer had laughed when Waite told her of Pinky's present. By that time, he could afford to laugh with her, for she had outlined her proposal, and he had been forced to agree that it could work. They had tested her system for one day, then put it in operation on the seventh day of the meet. It came just in time, too, for the sixth day had been a near-disaster for the pool sellers. Waite had been forced to use all of his persuasive powers to get Humstone and the pool sellers to give him another day and one more try.

Mary's system was simplicity itself, at least on the exterior. All anyone at the park saw was another lady, accompanied and driven by her chauffeur, enter the infield with the family barouche. During the races and between them, the young lady would eat a picnic lunch, mingle with the crowd, and occasionally return to speak with her servant. He, in turn, dressed in handsome livery and tall top hat, sat stiffly at his post during the afternoon, not even getting down to stretch his legs. By the end of the eighth day of the meet, Pinky's men were so suspicious of everyone and everything that they even scrutinized Mary and Rochemont for indications that they were signaling to someone. If they were doing anything, it was impossible to detect. Meanwhile, Philip Dwyer turned from a gloating victor into a madman. "I've been betrayed!" he kept shouting over and over. "Someone inside this park is spying for them!"

"Of course," Pinky said. "There have been spies in here from the very first day."

"That's not what I mean," Dwyer countered. "Someone who works for us is spying for them."

"I've checked our people out a half dozen times," Pinky replied. "They're all reliable. But if you like, I'll check them again."

"I like," Dwyer said. "And while you're at it, check yourself, too."

Pinky's eyes narrowed. "What do you mean by that, Dwyer?"

"That you met Humstone the other day. The day before all this started."

"I didn't meet Humstone," Pinky said. "He came to the tavern where I have a drink on the way home. If he had asked for an appointment, I'd have told him to wait until this meet is over."

"Nevertheless, they're saying you sold out—"

"Who's they?"

"Rodney Roberts of the *Times*. People in general."

"And what are you saying?"

Philip Dwyer tried to stare Pinky down, but he could not. Finally, he looked away with a scowl. "I'm not saying you made a deal," he muttered thickly. "I'm just telling you what people are saying."

Pinky walked back to the Jockey Club and held a brief meeting with his men. They were as disconsolate as he. Not a single man had the vaguest idea where the leak was, or even how to go about looking for it. "Maybe there's something to that big bent telescope," Harvey Kittering said weakly.

Pinky had to smile. The idea was ludicrous, of course. After a half hour's discussion of the day's events and tomorrow's strategy, Pinky dismissed his crew and left for the Kensington Tavern.

When he got there, the first things he spotted were a pair of bottles on the bar top neatly tied together with a huge ribbon. One of the bottles contained milk, the other an excellent brand of whiskey. "The fellow at the end of the bar said these are for you," the bartender grinned. The attached note read: "Better keep looking for that fifty-foot-tall horse. W."

Nodding, Pinky took the bottles and walked down to a smiling Waite Nicholson. "I suppose you think this entitles you to the first and last dances," he said.

"Plus a trip in my airship," Waite said.

"If I had known you were in that balloon, I'd have taken Dwyer's advice and shot it down," Pinky said.

"I gambled you wouldn't do it, but I think Dwyer would have."

"Yeah," Pinky laughed. "A couple of days ago, he wanted to send you to hell. Today he wants to send me."

Mrs. Ironsides' cheeks flapped vigorously as she pounded her fist on Rodney Roberts' desk. Her normally mottled-white complexion had changed to the color of overripe rhubarb; her voice was a full octave higher than her normal baritone; the veins at the side of her thick neck jutted out so far Roberts thought they were going to burst and spray his desk with molten blood. "Please calm yourself, Mrs. Ironsides," he cautioned.

"That's easy enough for you to say. All you have to do is sit here and write stories about how the pool sellers have been defeated. If you would remove your . . . your . . . yourself from that chair and get out to Gravesend, you would see that the forces of evil are winning."

"Yes, we've heard there's a leak," Roberts admitted. "But if we exaggerate its importance, it's liable to encourage the criminal element."

"Exaggerate its importance?" Mrs. Ironsides shouted. "How can you exaggerate a disaster? The ship is sinking and you're telling the passengers it might be nice if they signed up for swimming lessons sometime soon. We need action now!"

"But what can we do?" Roberts murmured. "They've got scores of men at the park. Pinkerton—"

"Pinkerton is either an idiot or has accepted a bribe from the Ditmas Company. I intend to find out which. This very afternoon."

"How?"

"By going to Gravesend and observing a race. I'm sure it won't take me but a race or two to find out how the Ditmas Company people are doing it."

"That's a pretty tall order."

"And I am a tall person, Mr. Roberts. If you would like to accompany me, you are welcome."

"Perhaps I shall."

Pinky sat in his office, hands over eyes. He could hardly believe it. And yet it was true. As he had said to Waite Nicholson only the day before, "It just goes to show you can't trust a soul." The observation had been thrown out partly as a jest. He never believed it would become so sharply and so quickly a fact of his life.

Learning that fact had been such a blow to him that he had left the track at the end of the day. Ironically, he fled not because he had failed to discover the source of information from track to pool sellers. He fled because, after many days of futile searching, he had broken the code at last. Breaking it, however, brought not joy but a sort of stunned misery.

"It's hard to believe," he said, standing alone on the top of the grandstand roof. "It's a great scheme. Somehow I should find a sort of happiness in that, but I don't feel a thing except disappointment."

And so he fled—not to the seclusion of the Kensington Tavern—that would have been too ironic for him to bear—but to the quiet of his office. He needed time to think, but about what he was not sure. Perhaps he just needed to have a talk with himself. "The truth is," he said aloud, "you're too old to be surprised by this sort of thing. And being discouraged and upset by it isn't very smart, either. People are people. If you don't put too much faith in them, you won't be disappointed."

But he had been disappointed. He could not deny it. "Mary Dwyer," he said slowly. "Why you?"

At first, he had hoped that the glint of flashing light from Rochemont's top hat had been some kind of reflection. But after he had spotted it, he looked more carefully and saw it again. Sitting in an upright position, with his head tilted just slightly to the rear, the top of Rochemont's hat formed a direct line with the man stationed on the lower pole erected in farmer Young's pasture. Slowly Pinky put the puzzle together. In his mind's eye, he even saw the wire running down from the hat to a battery hidden beneath the seat of the barouche. But was Mary—his Mary—responsible or even aware of the scheme? Perhaps, he tried to tell himself, Rochemont was the sole perpetrator of the ingenious plan. Then he realized it was just not possible for the unmoving chauffeur to collect all the information with his eyes alone. Mary was supplying it. Her trips back and forth to the carriage seemed haphazard until one watched her carefully. Then they assumed a regularity that could mean only one thing.

By the end of the sixth race, Pinky was sure Mary was a part of the scheme. He could have put a stop to it then and there, but he did not. He wanted time to think and compose himself. When he faced her tomorrow, he would be free of emotion, disappointment, sorrow. Perhaps not love, but even that would pass with time.

Far away he heard a rapping sound. The office was closed. Whoever it was, couldn't the idiot read?

The rapping continued, so Pinky went to the front door and threw it open.

"Bob," Mary Dwyer said. "I've got something important to tell you."

"Come in," he said.

Her confession was brief but all-inclusive, even to a description of which type battery was used. "I only did it to show that a woman could think," she said. "Then, today I heard them saying things about you. I couldn't stand to hear them, so I decided to tell you."

She looked directly at him, a furtive tear near the corner of one eye. "I'm sure you must hate me now," she said.

"No," he replied. "I couldn't do that unless I worked at it."

For a moment, he was about to tell her that he had discovered her system. Then he choked back the words. Why say anything? Wouldn't it be a nice present for her to know that she had outsmarted the Great Detective? And by telling her he knew, would he not downgrade the courage she had shown by coming to him? No, he decided, whatever happened, he wouldn't take that away from her.

"I promise you that tomorrow—" she began.

"Tomorrow you'll keep right on doing the same thing," Pinky said, reaching out to take her hands in his.

"Why?" she asked.

"Because thanks to your honesty in telling me, you've given us the means to put an end to this nonsense once and for all," he said. "You see, there's a very, very long shot in the sixth race. No matter what that horse does, your Rochemont will tell the pool sellers he's the winner. We'll spread enough money around to darn near wipe out the pool sellers and end this thing. That's a little trick your daddy tried back in the spring, but this time we're going to make it work. You and me."

"You and me," she repeated. "The grammar is bad, but the idea has a nice sound. Bob, I wasn't really trying to hurt you. It's just that it all seemed like such a game and I wanted to play. I never dreamed it would go so far. Thank you for being so understanding."

"Your confession has been good for my soul," Pinky smiled. "Thank you for telling me."

"You're welcome. Would you like to kiss me?"

"I guess I can," he smiled. "I'm off duty."

By the third race, Aurelia Ironsides was shaking with frustration. Hours of peering into faces, watching people's arms, hands, manner of dressing, walking, talking, standing, and even spitting had nearly worn her out. Worse, her pilgrimage of failure was made even more unbearable by the presence of Rodney Roberts, who had decided to accompany her on this, the tenth day of the Gravesend fall meet. Although he was every bit as depressed as Aurelia by their inability to discover how the pool sellers were getting their information, at least Roberts had the satisfaction of seeing Mrs. Ironsides' boast turn to vinegar.

Then, suddenly remembering what someone had said about the roof being a good observation point, Mrs. Ironsides' eyes took on new excitement. "To the roof," she said, bounding off toward the grandstand.

Roberts followed, muttering to himself.

Getting past the guard who was stationed at the stairway, ostensibly to protect patrons from going up to the roof and possibly falling, was a simple matter for the rotund warrior. "Mr. Pinkerton has given me permission to go anywhere I want in this park," she said authoritatively.

The guard let them pass.

The third and fourth races were run. Although watching the area beneath them with the intensity of a vulture waiting for its prey to breathe its last, Mrs. Ironsides saw nothing suspicious. There were, of course, deliberate plants in the crowd, persons whose express purpose was to feign elaborate signals, but even the impetuous Mrs. Ironsides did not take the bait of such overt activity. Just before the sixth race, however, she spied the same glint as had Pinky the day before. "Look," she cried to Rodney Roberts. "What's that?"

"It's a man in a tall silk hat," Roberts replied.

"No, I mean the way it's shining."

"All silk hats shine."

Aurelia snorted: "Silk hats shine on the side. That one shines on top."

"I can't see it," Roberts said curtly.

Nor could Aurelia. Had it been a figment of her imagination? No. Yes! There it was again. This time there was an unmistakable series of irregular short and long blinks of light emanating from the top of the hat.

"Do you see it now?" she triumphantly demanded.

"I certainly do," Roberts answered.

Abruptly, the lights stopped, for Rochemont had suddenly

realized he was allowing himself to slump and had pulled himself into a more nearly upright position. Thus when the light inside the hat blinked and shone through the small hole at the top, the angle was such that only Arne Thorsland could see it.

But Mrs. Ironsides' suspicions had been confirmed. "Come on," she said to Roberts. "We're going down and put a stop to this at once."

Only moments before, Pinky had a brief conversation with Mary. "Cerberus is going off at 110 to 1," he said. "He's number five. When you send back instructions, be sure to keep him in the running, so it doesn't look like a fix. Our men in town have about five thousand dollars bet on him, scattered from poolroom to poolroom."

"Number five," Mary repeated.

". . . is Cerberus, at 110 to 1. Jockey is Ed Midgely," Thomas Wynn intoned. "Number six is Verbena, at 6 to 1. Jockey Walt Seegren. Seven is Contribution, 3 to 1, with Booth Sladden up. Eight is WBH, 4 to 1, Doc Garbus up; number nine is Apollo, 6 to 1, Don Gadseen up; and number ten is Johnnie Lackland, ridden by Adam Sumner. Race starts in two minutes."

Peter DeLacy wondered why the rest of the leading pool sellers of New York did not appear happier. They met at his establishment once a month to discuss matters of mutual interest, and today was the September meeting. They were all here—Oele Pearsall, Paddy Reilly, Jumbo White, Shang Draper, Mike Minden, Alf Baker, and a dozen others. Last week, as the race information trickled in, they would have been miserable. Today, with the news flowing, they ought to be happy, DeLacy thought. But they weren't. Instead of circulating among the customers and patting a few backs, they stood huddled against DeLacy's bar like condemned men. "What's the matter with everybody?'' DeLacy asked Mike Minden in a low voice.

"They're scared," Minden replied. "Things are goin' too good."

DeLacy laughed. "You fellows can't be satisfied, can you?" he said. "If things are going bad, you're miserable, and if things are going well, you're miserable."

"It ain't that," Minden said. "The boys feel that things aren't in their hands anymore. What I mean is, we're not payin' off anybody. Somehow that don't seem right. Couple of them think we're bein' set up for something."

"By who—Pinkerton?" DeLacy asked.

"Maybe. Or even that kid—"

"Nicholson? No, I tell you, he's all right," DeLacy said. "He's got his faults. He pushes too hard. But he's playing us fair."

"There's talk he's been seein' Pinkerton."

"Maybe he has. He's sociable. Look, my daughter wants to be a lady Pinkerton now. Do you think I'm setting you up?"

"No, 'course not," Minden said. "Not you, Pete. It's just that the boys are suspicious of this Nicholson kid 'cause they don't know him, you understand?"

"I understand," DeLacy said, "but I trust him."

"Sixth race about to start," Thomas Wynn announced, leaning forward in his chair.

As she clomped through the crowd, Mrs. Ironsides collected a band of her ASS followers as well as a small force of Pinkerton men via the simple process of crooking her finger at them and thereby ordering them to follow. Daring not refuse, they collected behind her until, like an invading army, she and her minions cut a wide path through the Gravesend crowd. The destination of the broad-shouldered woman was the infield and the black barouche which sat almost squarely in the middle of it.

Pinky spotted her just as she descended from the grandstand and began to make her way through the area adjacent to the track. His own steps in her direction were as firm and purposeful as hers, and he confronted her right at the edge of the infield.

"Where are you going?" he asked.

"To that barouche," Mrs. Ironsides replied.

"The Dwyer one?"

Pinky's tone seemed to indicate that she was out of her mind, but Mrs. Ironsides was not intimidated. "Yes," she said.

"Why?" Pinky asked.

"I saw that man's hat flickering Morse code," Mrs. Ironsides said. "Didn't I, Mr. Roberts?"

Roberts, at her elbow, nodded. "That's right."

"Well, this race is about to start," Pinky said, gently taking Mrs. Ironsides by the sleeve. "Why don't we wait until it's over? In the meantime, we can stand over here and observe."

Mrs. Ironsides shook her head vigorously from side to side. "Are you mad? We've got to stop them right now."

She took a step forward, but Pinky stepped in front of her. "No," he said. "I'm sorry, but you can't."

A victorious smile crossed the fat woman's features, then turned to a scowl. "I thought so," she said. "You're in league with them. Advance!" she commanded, starting forward so forcefully that even some of Pinkerton's men found themselves moving with her.

"Halt!" Pinky barked, placing himself in front of her. The rest of the officers stopped.

"Mr. Pinkerton, I demand that you let us through, this very minute," Mrs. Ironsides threatened.

"Since you're so persistent, Mrs. Ironsides, I'll tell you why I want you to stay away from that barouche—"

"Aha! So there is a reason!" Mrs. Ironsides cried triumphantly.

"Yes," Pinky replied, again taking her sleeve. "Come here and I'll tell you."

"No," Aurelia replied, tearing away from him. "This is just a trick! Well, it won't work, you Ditmas snake-in-the grass! I'll turn that carriage over with my bare hands! Forward, ladies! Forward!"

With that, the resolute reformer rocketed ahead, her followers immediately behind.

Seeing that Mrs. Ironsides was in no mood to listen to reason, Pinky acted quickly. He could not permit her to upset his plans for the sixth race, so he placed his hands on her shoulders and shoved backward, calling, "Kittering! Farber! Bracken!"

When his three best men rushed up, Pinky said, "Arrest this woman! Put her under the grandstand until this race is over."

"Arrest?" Mrs. Ironsides shrieked. "For what?"

"For sending information to the Ditmas Company," Pinky replied.

The three young men managed to pinion the struggling woman's hands to her side and began to lead her off. "Ladies!" she cried over her shoulder. "Are you going to allow this to happen? Attack!"

"Push them back!" Pinky countered.

At first, his men retreated under a wave of flailing parasols and handbags, but slowly they regrouped. Hands over their faces to avoid the jabs of the women's weapons, the guards formed a solid wall and managed to break through the violent but disorganized mob. Not, however, before Officer Tracy received a solid uppercut from a husky matron that lifted him a foot off the ground and rendered him unconscious on the track infield. Two other officers suffered parasol cuts and one man was bitten on the end of his nose. Throughout, the Gravesend crowd shrieked with delight.

At the end of ninety frantic seconds, it was all over. Pinky's men were battered and bruised, but the ladies finally retreated in a disarray of burst handbags and broken parasols. "Escort these ladies to the gate and show them out," Pinky ordered.

As the women were being led off, Rodney Roberts stepped forward, a sudden look of resolution on his features. "This is an outrage, Pinkerton," he said. "You know Mrs. Ironsides wasn't sending information. I believe what she says is true. You are in league with them."

A substantial crowd had gathered. Pinky decided that the situation was simply not right to explain his stratagem for the sixth race. In fact, so many people were closing in on them, that a real Ditmas Company spy might overhear any explanation or guess what was being whispered. Rather than risk detection, he put an arm on Roberts's shoulder and gestured to another Pinkerton man. "Take this gentleman and lock him under the grandstand," he ordered.

"You can't do this, Pinkerton!" Roberts shot back, as he was being led off in the wake of Mrs. Ironsides. "I'll use the *Times* to bury you!"

"Fine," Pinky replied. "Just stop calling me an Indian killer."

Philip Dwyer arrived on the scene just in time to see a red-faced Rodney Roberts being escorted off. "What the hell's going on here, Pinkerton?" he demanded. "What are you doing? Those ladies belong to the finest families in New York. You've lost your mind! Isn't that Rodney Roberts your man's got his hands on?"

"That's right," Pinky said. "Listen, I don't have time to

explain now. Just trust me and I assure you everything will be all right.''

''Trust you! After what you've done? You're fired, Pinkerton! I mean it. Get your arse out of this park.''

Pinky suddenly reached forward to grasp Dwyer's arm in a viselike grip. ''Come here,'' he ordered, herding the older man toward the back of the grandstand.

''Let go of me, you idiot!'' whined Dwyer. ''I won't go.''

Pinky dragged him toward the detention room, the pair arriving there just as the doors closed behind Rodney Roberts and Aurelia Ironsides. ''Now you listen to me,'' he ordered, pointing a thick finger at Dwyer. ''You stay still and I promise you that when this day is over, you'll thank me for this. Just stay out of my way for the next half-hour and we'll win this crazy shootout. Do you hear that? We'll win. It'll mean money. Money, Dwyer! Think! Money!''

With that, he shoved Dwyer through the door which Harvey Kittering opened for him, slammed it shut, and locked it. ''Harvey,'' Pinky said. ''No matter what they or anyone but me says or does, nobody's to come out of there until twenty minutes after this race is over. Understand?''

''Right!'' the beaming Kittering said.

''They're off!'' Thomas Wynn shouted. ''Jumping into the lead is Verbena, followed by WBH, then Cerberus. Fourth is Apollo. The rest of the field is spread out, with Forest Master in the rear.''

''You see, everything is going just fine,'' Roger Mellon said. The rest of the pool sellers collected around the bar nodded or grunted, depending on their particular moods.

''Shall we go upstairs now so you can get back to your places by closing?'' DeLacy suggested. ''We've only a couple things to talk about.''

Several of the pool sellers moved away from the bar in the direction of the door leading upstairs.

''At the half, it's WBH, with Cerberus second, followed by Verbena and Apollo,'' Thomas Wynn interjected.

''Cerberus?'' Mike Minden said. ''Second? That nag should be dead by now.''

''She'll fade,'' Shang Draper muttered. But the group of men did not move.

''At the three-quarters, it's WBH and Cerberus sticking right together,'' Thomas Wynn called. ''Apollo and Verbena are neck and neck right behind them, with Contribution making a late challenge . . .''

Wynn felt the perspiration start to break out along his upper lip. He was aware that the assembled pool sellers were suddenly quite interested in the race, as was he. Cerberus, of course, had no business running such a strong race, but strange things often happened at the track.

''It's still WBH and Cerberus, followed by Contribution. They're in the stretch.''

''Come on, Contribution!'' several of the pool sellers called out.

''Come on, WBH!'' another added. ''Anybody!''

''They're in the stretch,'' Wynn called. ''It's Cerberus by a head, then WBH and Contribution, and here comes Forest Master making a late bid.''

''Come on, Forest Master!'' the pool sellers cried, violating the silence rule of their own establishments.

''It's Cerberus and Forest Master!'' Wynn cried out. ''Cerberus and Forest Master!''

''Shoot the nag!'' Shang Draper hissed.

"Cerberus! It's Cerberus! The long shot of the fall meet wins it!''

Cheers and confused talking filled the room. As bettors stepped to the payoff window to collect their winnings, panic struck the pool sellers.

"I got to get back to my place," Mike Minden said. "If there are as many winners there as you got here, I'm outta business!"

As his cohorts scattered, Peter DeLacy walked over to the cashiers' windows, where Roger Mellon was going through the ticket stubs with downcast eyes. "We're going to be out forty-two thousand on that nag Cerberus," he said. "It'll clean us out. Do you think there's something phony going on?"

DeLacy walked over to Thomas Wynn. "Check with Waite and make sure he sent the right information."

A moment later, the repeat message came back over the wire. "Winner: Cerberus. Second: Forest Master. Third: WBH. Fourth: Contribution."

"All right," DeLacy said. "That's good enough for me. Every once in a while, lightning strikes, you know. Pay them off, Roger, and close up for the day. Tell the customers we'll post a notice letting them know about tomorrow."

POOL SELLERS DEFEATED, *The New York Times* headlined. "Yesterday was the high point of the fall meet at Gravesend in that it saw the ultimate downfall of the illegal gambling forces in our city. For three days, the pool sellers thought they had discovered a way of getting information from the track, but they were actually being led astray by Robert Pinkerton, the clever lawman. By making the gamblers believe that the ruse of a blinking coachman's hat was working for them, Pinkerton built up their confidence in the method until he was able to convince them that Cerberus, a nearly crippled horse which finished dead last, had won the sixth race at 110 to 1. Many pool sellers lost such enormous sums of money that they were forced out of business. Even the infamous Peter DeLacy has decided to close his poolroom indefinitely. Pinkerton, using his own money, had his agents deliberately bet on Cerberus and then generously donated the winnings to the American Indian Society, his favored charity. Even worse for the pool sellers was that those who bet on Shamrock, the actual winner of the race, returned to the poolrooms an hour later after they found out they had been cheated. Riots followed at several establishments when there was not sufficient money to pay these genuine winners.

"Late last night, it was rumored that many pool sellers were in such an angry mood that a price had been placed on the head of Waite Nicholson, the Ditmas Company employee in charge of the information-collecting systems at the track. As soon as the gamblers discovered that Cerberus had run last rather than first, a thorough search of the area at the track was instigated but no trace of Nicholson was found. It is believed he escaped to Canada."

12

"Not so much the sad departure, but ever the happy arrival!"

Waite pulled air into his lungs, held it there, and listened as the carriage ground to a halt. His face was next to a can of paint and the piece of sailcloth covering him smelled of old beer. But the grimy cocoon was heaven, for it represented a form of safety. As the low voices began to mingle, Waite could feel his forehead throbbing so loudly he thought surely they must hear it outside, like some distant dismal drum.

The events following the catastrophic sixth race at Gravesend had become a blur. He first saw the look of panic on Michael Chance's face, heard the threat that "They're coming for us because they think we set them up." Next he saw the face of Humstone, scowling fiercely but with a certain malignant satisfaction as he methodically blamed one failure after another on Waite, carefully disassociating himself with the balloon episode or other of his recommendations. On the other end of the telephone, he could hear the angry hysteria of another voice. Then he remembered Humstone's final directive. "There will be a meeting here at six o'clock, Nicholson. I'll expect you to be here."

"Stupid me," Waite thought. "I was actually going to stay around till then." But fortunately, a hurried call from Peter DeLacy had gotten through to him. It had been blunt but, under the circumstances, more than kind: "Get your arse out of there as soon as you can."

It had come none too soon. As Waite tried to slip out the back way of Sleight's hotel, a fist struck his forehead and he went down. The next objects he saw were two pairs of feet. "Oh-oh," he thought. "Here it comes."

But the beating he expected never arrived. Instead, he heard a hard slapping sound, a gutteral cry of pain, and saw Badger Wilson, one of the Ditmas Company toughs, drop next to him. A pair of hands, one with a missing finger, reached down and quickly stuffed the man's mouth with a scarf and bound his hands. "There's a carriage outside, young fellow," Pinky said. "Make sure the way's clear, then hustle to it and get yourself under that piece of sailcloth in the boot."

Waite hardly needed a repeat of the instructions. After quick looks in both directions, he raced to the barouche and did as directed. Although he was aware that Mary Dwyer was in the carriage, for the moment she was just another part of the landscape as far as he was concerned. Bolting into the boot, he thrust himself under the canvas and into his musty haven.

A half-hour later, after several long pauses during which he heard muffled angry voices mixed with Pinky's cool tones and Mary's mocking laughter, Waite felt a tap on his shoulder. "All right," Pinky said. "You can stick your head out for some air now. I think that's the last of them."

Waite could imagine to whom he was referring. As soon as he

thrust his head into the cool evening air, Pinky threw a crinkly, ticklish object at him. "Here," he ordered. "Put that on and you can sit up here with us society folks."

"What is it?"

"Some false whiskers. I also got you a slouch-hat and coat."

Waite tried but couldn't fasten the disgusting device. "You have them upside down, I believe," Mary said.

He finally slipped the whiskers on, donned the other gear, and crawled out from beneath the sailcloth. "What's happening?" he asked.

"They're out to get themselves a scapegoat," Pinky said, tapping Rochemont's shoulder, who responded by whipping the horses ahead with even greater speed. "That's you, of course. Being opposed to murder, which is not only immoral but makes an awful mess, we decided to give you a lift."

"Much obliged."

"Humstone saved his own skin by blaming everything on you. At least that's the story I picked up."

"It sounds believable," Waite murmured.

"How is your head?" Mary asked.

"Fine."

"I guess you're wondering what happened to Rochemont's hat," Pinky said. "Well, the long and short of it is I found them out. Mary here was darned clever, but you know this old Indian killer is smarter than anybody."

Mary opened her mouth as if to speak. Pinky was covering up for her by pretending to have discovered the ruse. That was sweet of him, but for a moment, she wanted to confess to Waite as she had done to her Bob. The words, however, did not come. Perhaps, she rationalized, it was because no good would be served by it now. At any rate, there were more important things to consider, among them what would happen to Waite. Looking at him, she asked, "What will you do now?"

"I'm not sure," Waite replied. "It's all so sudden. I guess the only sure thing is that I've lost my job."

"But not your head," Pinky laughed. "That's the important thing. What you'll have to do is get out of town. It's going to take a while for those pool sellers to forgive and forget. In the meantime, you'd best be somewhere else."

"I suppose you're right." As he said the words, Waite looked at Mary in a way that caused her to smile sadly.

"Bob and I are going to be married," she said.

"Bob?"

"Pinky," she smiled.

"Oh, yes," Waite said falteringly. "Congratulations."

They rode the next minute or two in silence.

"Where are we headed now?" Waite asked finally.

"To my office," Pinky replied.

It was dark when they entered the alleyway to the rear of Pinkerton's offices, but Waite could pick out the movement of shadowy figures against the doorway. "Hold it," he whispered.

"It's all right," Pinky said. "It's only the DeLacys."

As the carriage approached, Peter DeLacy and Dottie stepped out of the shadows and greeted them. "I'm so glad you're safe," Dottie said.

"Did you get my message?" DeLacy asked. "I had to sneak away from those angry associates of mine to send it. I thought for a second they were going to tar-and-feather me."

"Yes, I received it," Waite said. "And thank you."

They were in the office. Despite the grim situation, it was rather like a going-away party for him, Waite realized. Everything was there: a bottle of champagne from Pinky; a train ticket from DeLacy; a basket of food and some wrapped presents from Dottie—just as if he were going on vacation. "You'd hardly think I was being run out of town,'' Waite smiled. "Everything looks so good. Thank you, all of you."

"Don't look upon it as being run out of town," DeLacy said. "Think of it more as an opportunity, a promotion, if you will." Then raising his glass in a toast, he added: "Not so much the sad departure, but ever the happy arrival!"

"Here, here!" cried the others, as glasses were raised.

Waite solemnly nodded to the others, raised his own glass, drank, and then laughed.

"By the way," DeLacy said. "I would like you to take charge of some holdings of mine in Chicago. I need a bright young man out there to protect my interests."

"After the way I ruined things here?" Waite asked. "How could you trust me to handle anything for you?"

"Well, this disaster wasn't your fault," DeLacy smiled. "You really did a remarkable job, everything considered. And we had some pretty stiff competition."

Pinky raised his glass in acknowledgment. "You also had some bad luck. Even I'll admit that."

Waite grinned quickly, a bit nervously. "Well, look, Mr. DeLacy," he said. "There are a few things I should explain about how this whole mess got started . . ."

"Don't bother. It's water over the dam."

"But I want to," Waite protested.

"And he should," Mary interrupted. "After all, you two have dined together, so to speak."

Waite winced.

"Waite," DeLacy said, putting a hand on his shoulder. "Let me tell you something. Confession may be good for the soul, but it's bad for business. Look, I knew what you were up to in the beginning, but I was enjoying it too much to stop you. So you made a mistake or two. But that was because you're young. The important thing is you've learned from your mistakes. Most of us don't. Maybe you just pushed too hard, and relied on your charm too much.''

''I've got so much charm, they want to hang me,'' Waite smiled. ''But I'll be happy to work for you, in Chicago or any place else, if you can get me out of this town in one piece.''

''Good,'' DeLacy said. ''I'll wire my Chicago people tonight. Meanwhile, you'll find everything you need in this envelope, including some money.'' Thrusting the envelope in Waite's hands, he turned to Pinky and said: ''Now let's get this boy back in his whiskers and on the train or they're liable to hang all of us.''

As the train rattled across central New York state, Waite finally began to relax. Smiling, he thought of Dottie's brief conversation with him on the station platform before he had left. ''If I do go to work for the Pinkerton Agency,'' she said, ''Pinky has agreed to arrange for me to be in Chicago next spring. They have a large office there.''

''That would be nice,'' Waite said. ''If that's what you want, I hope your work allows it.''

''Even if it doesn't,'' she replied, ''I have an aunt there whom I haven't visited in quite a while.''

''Do you think you can forgive me for the way I've used you and everyone else?''

''Of course,'' she said. Then, with a slightly defiant tilt of her chin, she added: ''Maybe we DeLacys allow ourselves to be used sometimes because that's the way we want it.''

''Oh.''

''What I'm trying to say is, I'd like to see you again.''

''You would? Well, I'd certainly like to see you again. In the spring. Darn it all, that seems a long way off now.''

"It does to me, too," Dottie laughed. "So we'll both have to keep very busy to make time fly."

She reached up to kiss him then, not quite the brushing type Mary gave him moments before. Certainly it was more intimate, but not extravagantly so. Perhaps it merely contained the subtle promise of future closeness.

Pinky came forward a moment later, his hand outstretched. "Don't try to ride any more fifty-foot horses, young fellow," he said. "The fall's too painful."

"Thank you for all—" Waite began.

But Pinky cut him off. "Listen, partner, it's me who should be thanking you for bringing this concrete waterhole to life for a few weeks. Give my love to Chicago."

With waves to all, Waite hopped on the train.

Now, hours later, he suddenly remembered that Dottie had given him a small going-away present. He reached under the seat to pull it from the handbag and unwrap it. The weight and feel indicated immediately that it was a book. Letting the paper drop to the floor of the car, he laughed aloud as he read the title: *The Adventures of Pinky Pinkerton.* And on the inside, written in Dottie's hand: "To Waite. Looking forward to the day when we're on the same side. Dottie. Sept. 22, 1891."

As he read the inscription, Waite became aware of a figure standing next to him. He looked up to see the conductor, his knees slightly bent, shoulders dipped so as to give him a better view of the book title. As his eyes caught Waite's, he chuckled and said, "Pinky Pinkerton. Thought that book looked familiar. Sorry for looking over your shoulder, young fellow, but I always been a real follower of them Pinkerton boys, especially Pinky."

"Is that so?"

"Yep. About four, maybe five months ago, his pappy rode this same train, except going the other way."

DATE DUE

FEB 6 1978		
AUG 2 1 1979		
OCT 1 8 1982		
NOV 1 9 1982		

GAYLORD   PRINTED IN U.S.A.